THE MULE TAMER

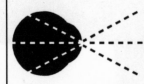

THE MULE TAMER

JOHN C. HORST

WHEELER PUBLISHING
A part of Gale, Cengage Learning

GALE
CENGAGE Learning·

Farmington Hills, Mich • San Francisco • New York • Waterville, Maine
Meriden, Conn • Mason, Ohio • Chicago

GALE
CENGAGE Learning®

LIBRARY OF CONGRESS CATALOGING-IN-PUBLICATION DATA

Names: Horst, John C. author.
Title: The mule tamer / John C. Horst.
Description: Waterville, Maine : Wheeler Publishing Large Print, 2016. | Series: Wheeler Publishing Large Print hardcover
Identifiers: LCCN 2016039866| ISBN 9781410494023 (paperback) | ISBN 1410494020 (softcover)
Subjects: LCSH: Frontier and pioneer life—Arizona—Fiction. | Large type books. | BISAC: FICTION / Action & Adventure. | FICTION / Westerns. | GSAFD: Western stories. | Historical fiction.
Classification: LCC PS3608.O7724 M85 2016b | DDC 813/.6—dc23
LC record available at https://lccn.loc.gov/2016039866

Published in 2016 by arrangement with John Horst

Printed in the United States of America
1 2 3 4 5 6 7 20 19 18 17 16

For Peggy and Kate

Be kind, for everyone you meet is fighting
a hard battle

TABLE OF CONTENTS

Chapter I: Jezebel 11

Chapter II: The Proposition 46

Chapter III: Chica 63

Chapter IV: Alliance 76

Chapter V: Col. Charles Gibbs,
Esq. 92

Chapter VI: The Limping Deputy . . 111

Chapter VII: Rangering 129

Chapter VIII: Anarchy 160

Chapter IX: Ashtoreth 167

Chapter X: Alejandro Del Toro . . . 189

Chapter XI: A Deal with the
Devil 238

Chapter XII: Waiting 244

Chapter XIII: Muses 253

Chapter XIV: Joaquin 269

Chapter XV: Indios 293

Chapter XVI: Subterfuge 307

Chapter XVII: Interloper 325

9

Chapter XVIII: Portent 333
Chapter XIX: Blind Charity 340
Chapter XX: Artemis 355

CHAPTER I:
JEZEBEL

Arvel Walsh had gone down early to meet the posse. He could not sleep and decided to head to town instead of lying in bed, staring at the ceiling. The story told to him by the chattering young hand about the slaughter kept him awake. By midnight he was dozing in a small room at the end of town. He leaned against some rope hanging on the wall of the cramped quarters, the air dense and still, rank with the odor of horsehair and rawhide and hemp.

He regretted his decision, now, as he recalled that old Will Panks had removed the bed just recently. Arvel had to try to get a little rest sitting on the dirty floor.

Will was a good man and a good friend whom Arvel had discovered living under the floorboards of the dry goods store's porch in the middle of town. He was an utter wreck when Arvel first came upon him.

Most of the folks who'd come upon Will

were afraid of him and thought him either an old drunk or addle-brained. Arvel learned that he was neither and had a mind sharper than most. He was a prospector trained in geology and civil engineering. One day, due to a slight error in calculation, he made a misstep and ended his career by breaking his back in the desert. He crawled miles and ended up, penniless and without means, in Arvel's little town.

Arvel set him up in the shack which was not, at the time, more than a lean-to at the very edge of town. Will was a proud man and would accept minimal help from Arvel and no financial aid, whatsoever. Slowly, with constant hard work, Will was able to regain control of his legs and now walked stooped over in a permanent crouch.

He earned his living making rope. As he got money he'd add a wall here and a window there. At some point he'd found an old rolltop desk in the desert, the discarded flotsam from a prairie schooner, let go by an overzealous traveler. He found a chair on a burning heap and rescued it and, until recently, had an old featherbed in the cramped quarters. It eventually became quite homey and kept Will out of the elements. As his health improved, his fortunes did as well and he now was able to live rather comfortably in the only boarding house in town.

Arvel was just drifting off when the barrage of gunfire jolted him to his senses. He peered through the cracks in the door. A rider, Mexican, judging from the saddle and sombrero, was racing up the street, firing in every direction. The miscreant stopped to reload, just feet from the shack's porch. Arvel grabbed one of the ropes hanging on the wall and slowly opened the door. When the rider holstered the first gun, Arvel stepped out onto the porch, threw his loop and jerked. The rider was pulled free from his saddle and landed on the ground, neck first. The horse galloped off and Arvel walked up to his prisoner.

The offender was a woman. Arvel picked her up and quickly threw her over his shoulder, grabbed her hat and rushed inside the shack. A Mexican would not be popular now. He eased her down onto the floor of the shed, tossed her hat aside, and began looking her over to see what damage he had done. She did not appear to be more than twenty. Her loose fitting outfit, despite its manly style, could not betray a well-proportioned frame. She wore a print cotton shirt, bright red scarf and striped brown vaquero pants. Her black boots were stitched ornately. Her gun belt carried a pair of silver-colored Schofields with fancy ivory handles. A matching vaquero dagger hung in a sheath in front of the holster on the right. The rig bore an abundance of polished conchos. Her tanned skin contrasted with the many bangles running up each arm.

Arvel smiled as a memory of his wife teasing him suddenly returned. When they made their forays into Mexico, the dark beauties never failed to turn his head and she loved to give him a hard time about it.

He suddenly regretted harming the girl. She was lovely and reeked of tobacco and spirits and human and horse sweat and earth. Like the whores in Tombstone, she was alluring and off-putting at the same time. He nearly forgot her transgressions as he watched her. He was right to stop her from shooting up the town. At least he did not put a ball in her.

Her face bore a peaceful expression as she lay there on the dusty floorboards among the bits of hair and hemp. It was a face formed by the centuries mingling Spanish and Indian blood. A small scar under her bottom lip added to her beauty and imparted a not insignificant suggestion of danger. She sighed as he removed her gun belt. The little viper would be more difficult

14

to defang after she had awakened.

He removed her scarf, wetted it from his canteen and began cleaning the dust from her face and arms and decided it better to leave the rest. He turned his attention to her rig. He fumbled with the latch on one of the six shooters; they were a type he had seen only a few times. He never had much use for six shooters. The gun sprang open, ejecting cartridge cases into the air and clattering on the floor. The girl awoke at the commotion. "Ay, chingao!" She felt her head and sat up slowly. She looked around the room, and then at her captor. "Pendejo, what are you doing?"

"Waiting for you to wake up." He placed the gun back in its holster, and set the rig down, out of her reach.

"Ay, look at my clothes." She took the damp scarf and began brushing herself off. "Did you wipe me down, Pendejo?" She looked at him suspiciously.

"I did. But not where I shouldn't."

"What?"

"Not on your private parts." He smiled at her. She amused him. "Are you trying to be hanged, or are you just stupid?"

She rubbed a knot on her head with her scarf, then looked at it for blood.

"Ay, my head is sore." She looked at him

again. "What are you talking about, gringo?"

"Do you not know of the troubles?"

"No." She was trying to focus. "Are you some kind of law, mister?"

"No." He pulled out a cigarette and lit it, offered her one. She refused it and pulled out a cigar, leaning forward so that he could light it. "So you don't know about the murder of the family outside of town?" He had not given it any thought, but was now wondering if she might have been part of it. She was unfazed.

"No, I know nothing of any murder. Ay, you really hurt me, Pendejo." Rubbing the back of her neck, she looked around the room. "So, I am not arrested?"

"No."

"Where is my horse?"

"Beats me. Tombstone by now, shot dead, not certain. It ran off like its hind parts were on fire, heading south. Heard lots of shooting, so the towns' folk were probably shooting at it. What kind of stupid stunt was that anyway, shooting up the town?"

She rubbed her head then picked up her hat. "I don' know, Pendejo, when I drink some mescal, I do some things." She stood up and stretched her back, blew smoke at the ceiling of the shack. "I really gotta go, Pendejo, will you let me go?"

"Not without a horse." He looked at his watch. The posse would be meeting up just before sunrise. "I tell you what, let me go find your horse and you stay here. Don't leave, understand?"

"Sí, I understand." She reached for her gun belt and looked for his reaction. He let her.

He walked out of the shed, onto the porch, and looked around for activity. Further down the street people were milling about. He untied Sally and mounted up; he rode south in the direction the horse had galloped. He passed several townspeople and no one seemed to pay him any mind. They had been through a lot, with the murder of the family nearby and now some crazy pistolero galloping up and down the street, shooting up the place.

They were all on edge and most were armed. Many had been drinking all day and into the evening and Arvel was certain if they found the young woman, they'd all be regretting their actions in the morning. He rode a quarter mile out of town and soon spotted the fancy saddle reflecting moonlight.

The girl's pony was an equine version of her mistress, beautiful and dangerous. She looked up from browsing as Arvel approached. He spoke to her calmly and she went back to feeding. He grabbed the reins and the filly willingly followed. Sally had a maternal influence on horses; they liked to follow the mule.

Back at the shed, the outlaw girl was prying on a locked drawer of Will Panks' rolltop with her big knife. Other drawers were upended, papers scattered on the floor and desktop.

"Hey, stop that!" He pushed her away and began straightening up. "So, you're a thief as well as a drunkard?"

"I need money, Pendejo."

"Has working or getting married or doing something honest ever crossed your mind?" Arvel continued to put the place back in order.

She spit on the floor. "I don' need to work and I don' need a man. I take what I want, Pendejo, like you gringos take and take from the people who have been here for hundreds of years. You are just as much as thief as me."

He laughed. "Well, you have a point there."

She looked him up and down. "You are a strange gringo, Pendejo. You don' look very much like, like . . ."

"Not very tough?" He smiled. "I know, I know. I've heard that before."

"Why are you not so mean to me, Pendejo? Most gringo white men don' want nothin' to do with me. They avoid even to look at me."

"I think you're funny." He smiled. He looked at his watch again. "You'd better beat it out of here."

"Why so secret, Pendejo?"

"What's this Pendejo?"

"Oh, I don' know, it just seem to fit."

"It wouldn't be good if the people around here caught you. They'd likely string you up, just for good measure. A bandit gang of Mexicans and Indians killed a whole family just outside of town. It was pretty bad. The leader wears a gold sombrero. Maybe you know him?"

"Ay, chingao, sí, I know him, Pendejo. He is mal puro. One day, I will meet up with him and kill him, but he is like smoke, he is hard to catch."

"We're meeting in a couple of hours to go after that gang."

"You, Pendejo?" She chuckled. "You better not go after bandits, or they will be digging a grave for *you,* especially Sombrero Del Oro."

He was growing tired of her impudence

19

and took her by the arm. "I appreciate your concern, Chiquita, but I'll be just fine. How old are you, anyway?"

"Guess, Pendejo." She eyed him devilishly. She liked the attention he was giving her.

"Sixteen?"

"*Hah!* I have twenty-six years, Pendejo."

"Well, you won't have twenty-seven years if you keep this up. Now, get on your horse and ride. Don't stop." He tossed a half-eagle at her. He didn't know why. "And I don't want to hear from or see you in these parts again."

She turned to leave, then grabbed him and kissed him hard on the mouth. She thought for a moment, and kissed him again, harder this time. It was the first good kiss he'd had in five years. "You kiss good, Pendejo." She was gone.

Olaf Knudsen had come to the states twenty-two years ago. He was not married when he arrived and had only the clothes on his back and twenty one dollars. He worked in New York City for five years; seven days a week in a textile factory. After work, he went home and worked another three hours every night assembling ladies garters. His diet was salted fish and cabbage, not because he could not afford anything else, but because, by so eating, he could save more than sixty percent of his wages. He shared a bed with five other men. Two men shared one bed every eight hours. He dreamed of owning a dairy farm, and after five years, had enough money to purchase everything necessary to move west and pursue his dream. He picked up a nice wife along the way, and soon had a burgeoning family. They all had one purpose, and that was to make a successful farm. What took a lifetime of sweat and dreaming and toil was destroyed in less than an hour.

Arvel sat Sally and smoked. In the past twenty four hours his life and the life of everyone else in the region had been turned upside down. They had lived peacefully and uneventfully for years. No Indians, no miners, no gamblers, no Mexican bandits. The community had slipped into a quiet complacency, and that suited Arvel Walsh just fine.

He was working on five mules nearly simultaneously when the young man came riding up to his ranch, out of breath, flush with excitement, to tell him the news of the Knudsen family. He was amused by the boy, who was young and hungry for adventure. Arvel thought that he was not unlike himself thirty years ago, but now, well into his forties, hearing of this kind of excitement only

21

made him sad. He was sad for the Knudsens, of course, but he was also sad that his mundane, complacent, normal life had been disrupted. He was getting used to the sameness of the days, and the only excitement that he now experienced was when a hand got kicked by an overexcited donkey, or horse, or mule. Everything was humming along nicely for Arvel Walsh, until now.

POSSE COMITATUS

The men Arvel had been waiting for gathered just before sunrise. Since no one had been taken captive during the previous day's slaughter, it had been pointless to give chase after sunset. Twelve men responded to the request by the deputy sheriff. The fellow in charge was a small man, no more than twenty five years old. He had been one of the deputy sheriffs for around six months and had proven himself in words only.

He had a fine Stetson and a fancy gun rig. His six shooter was bright nickel and the grip had a naked woman carved garishly on the outside panel. Many cartridges, more than fifty, were snugly fixed into loops across the front of his belt as he wore his rig with the buckle in the back. He had a giant knife, like an overgrown Bowie, with an ornate handle which stuck, menacingly, in front of the six shooter's holster. He looked uncomfortable and out of place in these clothes, as if he'd put them on to have his portrait taken. His scarf was a bit puffy and too tightly tied around his neck and tended to creep up over his chin as he moved. He continuously pulled it back into place.

His past deeds were difficult to verify. He had spent some time, by his own account, as a lawman in Tombstone and, supposedly, working for the Texas Rangers. Judging by his blustery ways and fondness for hearing himself talk, everyone could pretty much agree that he likely hailed from Texas.

Dick Welles was there and Arvel was glad for it. He had known Dick since he arrived in Arizona. He was a good man, and a fellow veteran of the GAR, a rare thing in this part of the country as the land was populated mostly by former members of the confederacy.

Dick was a severe looking man with sharp features and blue eyes the color of a glacier. He sat, perched on his horse like a predatory bird, a dangerous hawk, ready to swoop down on his prey, looking on at the collection of volunteers. He looked terse, always; never cruel, but never friendly or smiling. He was the kind of man whom other men obeyed unless they were too stupid to know better.

His hair went white by the time he was forty. Once, his wife convinced him to dye it. So mortified was he at the outcome that he shaved his head, preferring temporary baldness to the hubris of such self-indulgence. He wore only brown or gray colored clothing of wool, as blue seemed too gaudy to him, silk was out of the question. He never wore black as he felt that this was the color reserved for undertakers and the clergy and he fit neither of those criteria. He was never without a cravat and waistcoat. He would wear a sack coat except in the worst heat. Today he was dressed in his hunting clothes, which consisted of his older regular clothes that were deemed worn enough to get dirty. He was not a vain man, but proud enough to always be dressed properly. His hat was the only exception. He'd gotten it just after arriving in Arizona and it was once the color of honey. Now it was about as dirty as a hat could get and the grosgrain band was colored with a hundred different sweat stains. It was an exceedingly ugly hat and was incongruous with the rest of his outfit, looking as if perhaps he'd mistakenly picked up the property of a proper derelict, leaving a well-cared-for one behind.

"Bad business, Dick." Arvel extended his hand.

"Indeed. The girl said they tortured Olaf for better than an hour. She just escaped after they walloped her good on the head and left her for dead. They were in a state, whoopin' and hollarin', so busy with the blood orgy that she jumped up when they were occupied and ran like hell all the way to town."

"How many do you reckon there are?"

"She thought ten or twelve. Half Indians and half Mexicans, except for one white fellow, looked to be just running with them, and not all that connected with the gang. He didn't seem to take much part in the really bad business."

"It is all the same, lie down with dogs and get up with fleas."

The rest of the posse was made up of young ranch hands from the area, and a fellow from the Tombstone newspaper. Word traveled fast about this incident. Decapitation always makes for exciting news.

The young deputy was animated. He barked orders, strutted amongst the posse, commenting on what was lacking in each man's outfit. He was particularly concerned about the two elderly gents joining his

25

expedition. He believed that fear was the best motivator. He eyed Arvel's kit doubtfully. "Sir, that mule is not going to slow our progress. We will be forced to leave you behind if you cannot keep up."

"Understood, Captain!" Arvel smiled.

"I am not a captain, Mister, and I'll thank you to take this a bit more serious. We're after some dangerous fellows." He looked on with contempt at Arvel's guns, consisting of his Colt thirty-six from his days in the war, and a Henry rifle, ancient by the standards of the well-equipped Texas lawman. Arvel wore his old garrison belt with the GAR buckle. It was so worn by now, that *Grand Army of the Republic* was nearly indiscernible. His big knife looked as if it had come from the kitchen. In fact, it had come from the kitchen and Dick Welles could swear it had retained the odor of onions.

"You have a cap-n-ball six shooter?" The young deputy sneered.

Arvel looked down at his revolver and smiled. He was enjoying this thoroughly now. The young man did not wait for his reply and began casting glances about in every direction, looking for evidence of even more incompetence among this group of volunteers.

The little fellow eventually wandered off, muttering something about having to nurse-maid old-timers and kids. He lambasted a few other members of the posse, poking and prodding their equipment and generally making a fool of himself.

"Well, old-timer," Arvel winked at Dick Welles, "Let's do our best at not being a nuisance on this expedition."

They rode off, last in line, Sally with her younger brother, Donny, in tow. Arvel always took two mules on an expedition, as he had an abundant supply of the beasts, and thus was well provisioned in the event that things would go wrong. With the little general in charge, he was certain things would, indeed, go wrong.

They reached the homestead quickly; it was not far from town. As they approached, they were struck with the sweet pungency of burning human flesh. Tim Brown, nephew to the slain homesteaders, broke and galloped hard to the site, rifle in hand. What he hoped to discover or achieve by doing so, no one could tell. He was inconsolable when the rest of the posse caught up with him. The scene was disturbing, even to the most hardened war veteran, and most of these boys had little experience in such matters.

Except for the one girl who had escaped, every member of the family was lying about the yard. The house had been burned, only the scorched adobe fireplace and chimney remained. Dead livestock mixed with the corpses. Olaf's body smoldered in the dying embers of the fire-ring a distance from the home. The fingers of his left hand had been torn, rather than cut away, and they protruded from his gaping mouth. He had been scalped, evidently while still alive. His throat had been cut so deeply that the head was nearly off. The wife's body remained relatively intact. They looked everywhere for her head, but it could not be found. Two small children lay on top of her; from the amount of gore soaked up by their mother's dress, it was likely they died last, bearing witness to the terrible execution of their parents. The little girl, who was approaching her ninth birthday, had been defiled.

Tim Brown was of no good use to the posse. Arvel knew this would happen, and would not have permitted him to come along, if he had any say in it. He decided the best thing to do was to talk to the deputy as the young man was going to get himself and, perhaps, several others in a bit of trouble if he was allowed to go on. Arvel looked over at Dick who understood what he was thinking, and nodded in agreement.

"Deputy." He waited to get the man's attention and knew, from his countenance, that they were in for a bad time. He had lost color in his face and had trouble forming his words. He looked at Arvel, bewildered.

"Yeah, what is it?"

"I think we should send Tim Brown back to town."

The three of them watched the young man run from one body to the next, his actions defying logic. He tried to straighten the corpses' clothing, waving flies from open wounds. "That poor fellow won't be anything but a liability going forward."

The deputy pondered Arvel's words, then stood, stupefied. He began pulling at pieces of debris, and uprighted a bucket that lay on the ground at his feet. He removed his hat and began running his fingers through his hair repeatedly. He was trembling. "Well, I guess we'd better bury these folks and get that fire put out. I guess we'd better . . ." he began muttering incomprehensively.

Dick Welles intervened: "Deputy, why don't we get these boys mounted up and follow up on the bandits? The fire will cause no further damage, and the undertaker's already been alerted. He'll be along shortly to take care of these poor souls. There's nothing more we can do for them. But we really must take up the trail and get those black devils before they go and do any more harm."

"The trail is cold." The deputy spoke automatically, without emotion. "They could be anywhere by now." He rocked from foot to foot, fingering the brim of his hat.

"No, sir!" Dick replied. He'd seen men act like this in the war. They'd lose composure and direction. Giving them a task is the only way to get them out of it. "They went off due west," he motioned with a sweeping gesture of his hand, "and the only place for them to go is Potts Springs. They must take water there before heading into the desert. That's where we'll find them. It's not more than fifteen miles away. If they've moved on already, we can track 'em down and take them in the desert."

This brought the young deputy to his senses, more or less. He soon came around, more assertive and annoying than before.

"All right, you men, mount up." He looked down at Tim Brown, still fiddling with the headless woman. In a flash of clarity he instructed the man to stay at the homestead until the undertaker arrived. The young man did not hear him.

and raised the alarm. Mexican and Indian bandits slowly roused from their drunken sleep but most were too hung over to move as quickly as they should. The bandit with the wedding dress cut it off himself with his big knife; he stood in his underwear, looking about for his gun belt and rifle.

Arvel saw the man on the rock. "Well, there'll be no surprising them now." He pointed, "There's one of them, right there, and he's raised the alarm." Arvel pulled out his Henry rifle and fired at the man, who dropped down instinctively, rat-like. The bullet parted his hair and started a stream of blood into his eyes, but he was otherwise unharmed.

The young deputy screamed at the posse. "No goddamned shooting until I give the command. We'll never catch the sons-of-bitches unawares now!" He glared at Arvel, then at Dick.

He stopped the troop momentarily and looked through his field glasses. Everyone waited for him to tell them what to do. The deputy looked bewildered. "Damn, I knew we shouldn't have stopped." He looked accusingly at Dick. "Come on, you men, let's ride." The deputy did take the lead, which impressed Dick Welles, even though he knew well enough that it was more likely due to the heat of the moment than pluck and courage.

The posse bolted forward to within a hundred yards of the gang and the shooting began. Arvel stood up in the saddle, placing the butt of his rifle on his right foot, and pulled the magazine spring up, working on replacing the cartridge he had fired as Sally galloped ahead, Donny in tow.

Dick looked over at him and laughed. "Jesus, Arvel, you look like a one-armed paperhanger trying to load that damned old rifle."

Arvel grinned. "You don't worry about me; just keep an eye on that deputy. You might learn a thing or two from him before this day is over." He got the cartridge replaced as Sally galloped on. He did not need to coax her. Sally knew what Arvel wanted, often before he knew himself.

The bandits' shots were high and wide and had no effect on the posse. They continued forward until they found themselves in an arroyo. They stopped there and dismounted. Bullets flew over their heads, buzzing past them. It was a sound Arvel remembered too well and one he had hoped he would not have to hear again in his lifetime. The deputy stood, fidgeting with his reins as the men took up shooting positions. The reporter curled into a ball, yanking his derby down over his eyes. He was acting more out of prudence than fear.

"Well, this is a fine spot." Arvel smiled at Dick as the man uncased his Winchester. "What do you say you flank left and I'll go right, and we'll see what can be done about this mess?"

"No, I think I'll stay with you, Arvel. Those old timey guns of yours might get you in trouble. You might need me to take care of you."

They moved along the depression to the left, placing themselves between the sun and the bandits. There was an outcropping large enough to afford a good vantage point into the bandit camp. The posse began to return ineffectual fire which at least served to keep the bandits occupied. Dick and Arvel made it to the high place. "There's room for just one shooter. Go on up there, Arvel. I'll keep the rifles loaded." He handed Arvel his Winchester and held out his hands, fingers laced together, to give Arvel a leg up. "Hold on, Cowboy, give me your cartridges, that relic of yours takes rimfires."

Arvel leaned Dick's rifle against the rock wall, pulled out a handful and pushed them into Dick's palm.

"What the hell are they covered in?"

Arvel looked down, "Sugar. Pilar gave me some pan de muerto," he smiled at the irony of his cook's food selection, "I guess they got covered in sugar. I had 'em in the same pocket."

"My God, Arvel, you are something. They're going to gum up your Henry." He stuffed the coated cartridges into his coat pocket.

Arvel grinned, "Come on, I've got ruffians to shoot. Lick 'em clean before you load 'em." He stepped up into the stirrup made by Dick's sugary hands.

Arvel slid forward on his belly, took up a steady position where he could look directly down onto the bandit camp. He placed Dick's Winchester beside him and proceeded to pour deadly fire into the group, first with his Henry, then with Dick's Winchester. Dick reached up and grabbed the Henry and worked on reloading it. The bandits, panicked, began to break from cover, allowing the rest of the posse to hit their marks. One bandit saw Arvel on the perch overhead. He turned, dropped his rifle and put his hands up, screaming to Arvel that he would give up. Arvel shot him in the forehead with Dick's Winchester, noting in his mind that it shot an inch high at that range. The man dropped as if he had fallen through a trapdoor.

When the shooting finally stopped all the bandits were dead except for Hedor. He lay, moaning and holding a loop of gut forcing its way through the gash made by Arvel's rifle.

"I am sorry for the low shot, son. You jumped up just as I was firing, otherwise I'd have killed you clean."

The man looked up at Arvel. He did not know what to say. He looked back down at his blood soaked hands and the gray loop of gut, like uncooked sausage, uncoiling from his abdomen. "Oh, that's all right."

He winced, cried out. He could not catch his breath. He watched as the blood flowed out onto the ground beneath him. "I ain't never been shot before." He curled his body. "I want to tell you boys, I didn't have no part in all that yesterday." He gritted his teeth. "I ain't tellin' you I don't deserve to be shot. I'm glad you killed me. I can't keep livin', seein' those folks go the way they did and ever time I close my eyes, that's all I see." He bent forward again, and let out a groan. "I didn't do anything for 'em, and shame on me. I will go to hell for it, sure enough."

"You a praying man?" the reporter spoke

up. He looked at Arvel and Dick for approval.

"I, I guess."

"Well, you may atone for your sins and see where it gets you." He regretted, as a man who used words for a living, the inarticulate way he was stating it, but he was not certain what fate awaited the dying man. He felt better when Hedor seemed to take comfort at the thought.

The deputy pushed past them. "Get him on a horse; we'll take him back for trial."

Incredulous, Arvel replied: "He won't live another hour." The dying man begged for water, he looked down at the ribbon of gut, squeezing between his fingers. His eyes darted back and forth, first at Arvel and then to Dick.

"He's been gut shot, don't give him water, it'll only make his situation worse," said the deputy, with authority.

Arvel pulled out his canteen and gave the man a drink. He glared at the deputy. Hedor drank, but just barely, the color fading from his face. He cried out again.

"Get him on a horse."

Arvel faced the deputy again: "He will not be moved."

"And I say he will," the deputy put his hand on the grip of his six shooter. He hoped for some live prisoners. At least he would have one. He stared back at Arvel, who was no longer smiling. Arvel knew the man's game. He was driven by greed for recognition and any potential bounty. Arvel had no great compassion for the miscreant, he knew he would soon be dead, but there was no call to add to his suffering.

"I say . . ." Arvel was interrupted by a shot from Dick's Winchester. The bullet pierced the desperado's heart. The deputy looked at the two old-timers. He swore, and marched off.

"Well, there's an end to it," said the reporter from under his derby.

The deputy should have been pleased. All the bandits were dead. None of his posse suffered so much as a scratch. It was true that they did not get Gold Hat but, with his reputation, it was unlikely that he would have waited around for any posse to catch up to him. He was simply too slippery. The deputy was angry, nonetheless. More likely, it was because he was disappointed in himself. He'd lost his nerve. He knew the score, and he didn't like it much. The reporter did not help as he chattered incessantly about the two real heroes of the day.

As the deputy sauntered back to his horse, the little man encountered Sally, quietly resting among the horses. He pushed her on the flank, and when she did not move, thumped her smartly across the neck with his quirt. She hee-hawed and jumped aside.

"Whoa, there, cowboy," Arvel stiffened at his mule's cry. "You don't touch my mule, son."

The deputy's face reddened. He kicked the ground and jerked the hat from his head. He swatted Sally with it, then pushed her all the harder. "Then get this god-damned beast out of my way."

"Partner," Arvel softly said, "you molest that animal one more time, and I swear I'll put a ball in you."

The young deputy scoffed and continued to attack the mule. "I *hate* mules! They are worthless beasts!" raising his quirt. Before he could hit Sally again, Arvel pulled out his Navy Colt and shot the deputy in the toe. Falling over, the deputy let loose a stream of obscenities. He held his foot, rolling about on the ground. "You son-of-a-bitch, you shot me!" He looked up at Arvel, fury and pain welling inside, and reached for his revolver. Before he could clear leather, Dick buffaloed him senseless, blood now pouring from the gash on his head as well as the hole in his boot.

Arvel attended to Sally, holding her face

and speaking softly to her. He kissed her on the muzzle. He did not look at the deputy again.

By now the others had had enough of the young upstart, and they looked at him with disdain. No one blamed Arvel. They would not blame him if he'd shot the man dead. They admired his restraint. Arvel was a legend for his love of his mules. He'd even been known to buy mules back from people whom he thought did not deserve them, or who had misused them in any way. He often balked at selling them to the Army, as there was no guarantee they'd be treated properly.

"Well, I guess we can't just leave him here," the reporter finally said. A couple of the men threw water on the young deputy, who regained his senses. They bandaged his foot, now absent one toe, and put him on his horse. One of the young men rolled up the toe in the deputy's big scarf, stuffed it in his bloody boot and tied the whole affair with a piggin string onto their former leader's saddle horn. Half of the detail escorted him back to town. The other half stayed to arrange the corpses and collect their traps. They would later inform the undertaker who would bring out a wagon and retrieve the bodies.

Arvel and Dick stayed with this group,

deciding it best to avoid any further dealings with the new amputee. Arvel thought of the Mexican girl as he looked amongst the dead men's belongings. He felt a little cocky. The evil Sombrero del Oro did not seem so difficult to beat. He was ultimately disappointed when he realized the leader was not among the corpses. The bandit leader had once again slipped away.

Dick talked the whole way back to town. It was how he unwound from battle. He liked to talk to people he liked and this was incongruous with his otherwise stoic demeanor. He laughed about Arvel's shot. He spoke of the good shooting, and teased Arvel about his Henry rifle, his old fashioned gun. "Guess those old-timey shootin' irons still work."

They rode a little farther, Dick continued: "Did you smell that white boy's breath? My God."

"I thought that was from his intestines, you did notice they were mostly in his hands."

"Nope, nope, that was definitely his breath. I definitely discerned breath."

Arvel was preparing to drink from his canteen and remembered giving a last drink to the dying man. He upended the container, draining it onto the ground, lifted the opening to his nose and sniffed doubt-fully. He recorked it and put it back on his saddle horn. "I'll boil that later." He took it back off his saddle horn, "On second thought," he flung it into the desert. "I'll just get another one."

The posse met up at the saloon later that day. They convinced the two old-timers to join them in celebration. Most of the town folks and all of the inhabitants of the nearby ranches seemed to be jammed in the saloon and overflowing onto the streets. Even Miss Edna, the church organist, made an appear-ance, pounding out some happy tunes on the establishment's upright. They all were celebrating the end of the bandit gang. It would not bring the Knudsens back, but at least some solace could be gained from the fact that the bad men were all dead.

This was a quiet town which never at-tracted the rough company such as what was seen in Tombstone and Bisbee. No gamblers found it worth their time, no cowboys had business there. Most of the men were married, or well enough settled that whore houses could not be sustained. But today, the townsfolk were giving the saloon good commerce and the beer and whiskey flowed freely.

The younger men talked and joked and

backslapped their comrades. It was only in such a life and death struggle that one could form this kind of bond. Many of these men were tough, tough from living on the land, living rough, but few had experienced the sting of battle, as they were born after the war. Certainly they had been in the occasional bar fight or disagreement at the branding fire, but none had yet experienced mortal combat.

They all spoke excitedly of the two old-timers. They had never seen shooting like this. They each took up Arvel's old Henry rifle, which most of them had never seen before. The men began pressing the veterans about their time in the war. They wanted to know where they had fought and how many men they had killed. Arvel just smiled and told them that it was too long ago to remember and that Dick was the man with the most battle experience.

Finally, when everyone was sufficiently drunk, the reporter stood up and offered a toast: "To the great toe-shooter of the East. Boot makers fear him, chiropodists revere him!"

The younger men looked on silently. Most did not understand the joke and wondered if it was not an insult. Finally, Arvel began to laugh, and everyone cheered. He patted the reporter on the back. "Anyone who can weave a chiropodist into a toast has my undying respect, son."

As the drinking continued, and the conversation inevitably deteriorated, Arvel seized the opportunity to slip out. He headed home. He rode alone and began to feel a little melancholy. He regretted shooting the boy in the foot. He always regretted doing things out of anger. He did not mind killing the bandits.

Soon, he would be back to the mule ranch. He preferred the company of mules to people. He hoped that there would now be an end to the little excitement, and that he could go back to his simple uneventful existence.

CHAPTER II:
THE PROPOSITION

Uncle Bob dropped the *Tombstone Epitaph* on the table in front of Arvel, nearly dipping the paper into his plate of eggs and sausage. "That's quite an article, son."

Arvel read it quickly. Nodded, and pushed the paper aside.

"Looks like they'll be making you a senator next."

"Or at least name a street after me." He grinned. "Let's wait for the *Nugget's* version, Uncle."

"Did you really shoot all those hombres?"

"Don't know, Uncle. It got so smoky from all the firing, I didn't get a good view." He enjoyed his uncle's ribbing.

Uncle Bob was a tough old bird. He had moved to Arizona in 1870. By 1880, he had the ranch working so well that he felt comfortable enough to convince his niece, Rebecca, to bring her husband, Arvel, out to expand the family ranch. Uncle Bob had no family other than his brother and Rebecca, and he took to Arvel immediately. The dashing young officer from Maryland had the looks, temperament, breeding and education to capture the heart of Uncle Bob's dearest possession.

The young couple was a perfect match, and both had enough wanderlust in them to find the move to Arizona appealing. Rebecca was an independent woman and soon discovered that she had nothing in common with the circles her mother and grandmother and great-grandmother moved amongst. She found them all fairly boring and pedantic. None would ever dare talk about much more than the weather, or entertainment or the latest fashions from Europe and New York. These society folk were continuously shocked and dismayed that a woman from such a fine and old family would be running about, riding and breaking mules. She never looked back, and even during the harshest summers and loneliest winters on the ranch, never missed her comfortable life in Kentucky.

Arvel and Uncle Bob were a couple of bachelors now. Uncle Bob rarely left the ranch. He, like Arvel, had received a fine education. Their families lived comfortably and had for many generations, going back to well before the Revolutionary War. Uncle Bob loved mules and had a sense for business and, as the family ranch was doing well in Kentucky, yearned to branch out, to seek his *manifest destiny,* as he liked to joke about it. A fearless man, he was a natural for the movement west. Just how far west was a source of consternation for his family. Arizona might just as well have been on the moon in the 1870s.

His instincts were right and mules became indispensable to the taming of Arizona, with their great resilience and ability to thrive in the desert. Uncle Bob brought the methods handed down by three generations of his family. He had also brought the best breeding stock of donkeys and horses to the region. He was a welcome addition to the territory.

By 1880, Arvel was a capable mule breeder, as Rebecca and her father had taught him everything they knew. He and Rebecca were ready for their own adventure. They loved Uncle Bob and the three of them formed an alliance that increased the family wealth significantly. They would never want for anything and this made them a curiosity among people of the territory. The family was neither greedy, nor ambitious. They were comfortable and loved breeding and breaking mules more than wealth or station. They were Republicans, but quietly and respectfully stayed out of politics and the inner circles of Arizona's polite and largely Democratic society. Sometimes this caused a bit of a stir, particularly their old abolitionist ways, as well as their kindly treatment of Mexicans and Indians, whom the family employed on the ranch to the exclusion of all others.

Arvel later read the article more carefully in private. He secretly enjoyed the little excitement. He did like battle. He liked it in the war, and he liked it now, more so now that he no longer had a wife and child to worry about leaving in the event that he would be killed. He was cool under fire, and the fact that he did not brag, and that he did not look the part of the stalwart hero, made the whole business that much more remarkable. He felt good about doing those bad men in. He did not like to kill. He did not even enjoy killing wild game. He was not a violent man; he demanded civility always on the ranch. But, to have a hand in removing the kind of evil capable of doing those horrible things was gratifying. Some people just needed killing and he did not mind obliging.

Governor Murphy had learned of the incident and was pleased with the outcome. The governor was so impressed with the actions carried out by Arvel and Dick that he wanted to confer with them about a more permanent role in the process of running this kind of trash out of Arizona. This amused Arvel and he thought about it a lot.

He would likely work with Dick on raising a force, but was not keen on spending a lot of time on the open frontier in search of bad men. He was not an old man, but he was no youngster, either. A comfortable bed on the ranch was more to his liking. He knew he had a God-given talent, knew he was different than most men, as he'd seen well enough how men handled the strain of battle in the war. He often wondered why he handled it so well. He was never really prepared for it as a young man. He was actually more studious than active. He had, of course, learned to ride and shoot, but he was not much for sports. He learned fencing and boxing at school, but was never remarkable in those endeavors, either.

But when it came to real battle, he knew how to anticipate the enemy's actions, seemed always to know the right thing to do. His commanders used to give him the toughest assignments and he'd often carry them out alone. At one battle he spent more time on the enemy's side of the lines than on his own, reconnoitering. He did not like to lead large groups of men into battle. He did not like to lose men, so he avoided that responsibility as much as possible. He could be careless with his own life, but not so with the lives of others. He would definitely help Murphy in raising a force, but once it got under way, he would do his best to distance himself from it.

Arvel's ranch sprawled over a dozen square miles on a large mesa at the foot of a low mountain range. It had streams running through it at the base of the mountains, and they had several good wells. The house was a low adobe building, designed by Rebecca. She built it next to a mature Palo Verde tree, so that the tree became the focal point at the front of the structure and afforded excellent shade. Most folks in the area, when they became wealthy enough, built their houses of milled lumber and copied the style of the fine homes found back East, but Rebecca loved the land and built with stone and adobe. The house blended with the terrain, and the low sloping roof with its long covered porches made the building cool during the hot months. In winter they used fireplaces in each room.

Just out front was the main corral and next to it, the barn. There were other outbuildings, ranch houses, and a smoke house. Twelve families lived on the ranch, a mix of Mexicans and Indians. They worked hard and lived well, as the ranch owners spread the wealth among everyone who contributed. The workers loved Uncle Bob, as he was not only their employer, but took care of them in many other affairs. He was a good boss.

In mid-June the delegation arrived, including Governor Murphy, Dick Welles, a rancher named Hennessy, and the young reporter who had ridden with the posse during the Knudsen affair. It was all very pleasant and Uncle Bob put on a fine spread. The hands at the ranch worked diligently for several days sprucing up the place. Both men gave a tour of the ranch, proudly showing their finest mules, horses and donkeys.

Hennessy was a dour man, and Arvel knew of him. He was stingy and obsessed with the cost of things. He could have no conversation that did not evaluate the value of everything in the discussion. He came straight from Ireland with not a penny to his name and Arvel did respect that he had made something of himself but, sadly, the man was a bore and a bigot. Arvel decided he would have some fun with him.

He stayed with Hennessy during the tour of the ranch and Dick stuck close by. He knew Arvel did not like the Irishman and wanted to be available in the event that Arvel got out of hand. Hennessy eyed the corral fence. "It seems that method of fence construction causes a lot of unnecessary expense."

"A dollar a foot." Arvel spoke automatically. He actually had no idea what the fence cost and was making numbers up to confound the man. Dick winced and tried to change the subject.

"You were going to start raising bulls, weren't you, Arvel? That's why the corral fence was made that way." He glared at Arvel.

"Yes, but they cost a thousand dollars a head, so we abandoned the idea." Hennessy was calculating feverishly.

"A thousand dollars? By Jasus and Begorrah, what kind of bulls were they, Mr. Welles?"

"Andelusian Greybacks, Mr. Hennessy. They come from Spain." Arvel made this up as well. He knew nothing of bulls.

Dick suppressed a laugh. He could not be angry at Arvel. Hennessy was an ass but very important to the success of the Ranger project. He found he did enjoy seeing Arvel tease the clueless man.

"They eat so much, Mr. Hennessy. It is estimated that you have to feed them only grain. They will not graze."

"My God." Hennessy was calculating again. "How much do they eat?"

"Oh, well, about three times what you'd feed a horse. These greybacks get up to twenty five hundred pounds."

"That is astounding, sir!" Hennessy was trying to figure the amount of meat produced by such a beast and what its offspring would likely bear.

Arvel put his arm around Hennessy's shoulder; he presented him with his packet of cigarettes. "Try one, Mr. Hennessy. They cost a penny a piece, but I think they're worth it. They're pretwisted."

Hennessy took two. He did not smoke cigarettes but could not resist the offer.

The young reporter was pleasant enough. He was an Easterner, from Maryland, like Arvel, and they had some pleasant chats about Baltimore. He had become taken with his new home, but had never made the transition to the Western garb. He wore sack suits of dark grays or black and a derby that afforded no shade. He constantly wiped the dust from his Congress gaiters and, as he seemed always to be writing, his hands and sleeves perpetually bore ink stains. He lived in Tombstone and this was the first place he had ever lived away from his family. It was a wild place and the young man was simultaneously intrigued and revolted by it. He enjoyed seeing Arizona become tamed, but not too quickly. There was something in its wildness that held a promise of adventure. It was irresistibly exotic.

Despite his profession, Governor Murphy was a fine fellow. He measured every word and was a gracious guest. He was surprisingly quiet for a politician, which impressed Arvel. The man seemed to listen more than he spoke. Murphy knew Arvel's and Uncle Bob's mules well and had respect for their craft. It was folks like the Walshes who would make Arizona a respectable, productive part of the union, and he hoped to bring it into statehood during his lifetime.

The Irishman looked with disdain at the Mexican and Indian girls serving the dinner. He huffed, "You have a lot of darkies on this ranch, Mr. Walsh."

Arvel took a bite of his meal, sensed Uncle Bob's cautionary shuffle in the chair next to him. Uncle Bob was fair-minded, but knew Arvel's abolitionist zeal could be overbearing. Arvel chewed slowly, as he collected his thoughts and prepared his words, "Well, Mr. Hennessy," he took a drink. "We find the local folks are the most reliable and handle the climate so well. In fact, these locals, Mexicans and Indians, call this place their home. They didn't come to Arizona chasing their dreams and fortune." The Irishman was quick enough to sense the barb. He sat up a little straighter in his chair. He stared down at his food.

"In fact, it seems that every young white fellow coming out from back east expects to be tripping over nuggets of gold or plans to make a fortune at the faro table. None seem to be interested in a good, honest day's work." Arvel was exaggerating, he knew plenty of white lads who worked hard every day, but he was making a point. "Or, if you do have the good fortune of getting one to stick around, he wants to be gone for days at a time once he gets a little money in his pocket, running down to Tombstone for the whores or to get drunk. At least, that's been my experience. My *darkies,* as you call them, like to work, love our mules, and are more concerned about the welfare of their families than fame or fortune."

Governor Murphy interjected, "And that is why we are here, Mr. Walsh. To discuss the welfare of the families," he leaned forward in his chair, and glanced around the room at the servants and guests, "*all* the families of Arizona. We want to make this a safe place and, unfortunately, as the last real wild place, Arizona has become a haven for outlaws. Texas pushed them out of their state with their Rangers, and we believe it is time we do the same here."

"The Arizona Rangers," said Dick.

"Exactly, Mr. Welles. And we believe you and Mr. Welles are the men to do it, Mr. Walsh."

"And there are too many cattle interests any more in Arizona to ignore the rustlers." Mr. Hennessy interjected.

"I appreciate your candor, Mr. Hennessy," Arvel began handing out cigars. He looked over at Hennessy and whispered to him, "Fifty cents apiece." Dick Welles kicked him under the table.

Arvel blew a strong cloud of smoke. "I am less interested in working on behalf of the railroad, or the cattle barons, or Wells Fargo than I am getting rid of the kind of savages who killed the poor Knudsens."

"It's all the same to me," said Hennessy. "The kind of brigands who steal are the same kind who will kill and butcher. They all need to be run out of Arizona, or forced to pay the piper."

Dick Welles had difficulty keeping his seat. He leaned forward, elbows on the table. He had the most at stake in this discussion. He was the least well off of any of the men in the room, and he could benefit from the work. Arvel knew this and spoke up. "Gentleman, all my talk is academic and irrelevant. We know well that we cannot rely on the US military, by law, to help us. Town police forces and county sheriffs have their hands full and are doing the best they can do. We know the Ranger concept works, as evidenced by our neighbors to the east. And," he patted his friend Dick on the back, "we have just the man for the job."

Governor Murphy smiled, "It is interesting, Mr. Walsh, that you say that. On the way here, Mr. Welles suggested the same thing, except that he named you."

Arvel pushed himself away from the table and laughed, "Oh no, no sir, not me. I am getting too soft and too old for a life on the trail. Dick is your man. He's a good man, and a fair man, and he knows how to fight. He's your man."

Uncle Bob intervened. In his zeal to build Dick up, he brought age into question and Dick was nearly ten years older than Arvel. "Well, you men are both fit, Arvel. You can both outwork men twenty years your junior, and with age comes experience and maturity. Both you and Dick have been around, particularly in the arena of battle. I believe you'd both be well suited for the job."

Dick leaned forward and nodded at Uncle Bob, "Thank you both, but we, that is, Governor Murphy and I, believe that the enterprise could benefit from your skill as a negotiator and manager, Arvel. You're a genius at organization. And, there's the politics of having a balanced representation. Everyone knows I'm an old Democrat, and that'll go far in recruiting men of every stripe to do the hard work of Rangering, but you being a Republican will put us in with the money folks." He glanced at Hennessy and Murphy. They nodded their approval. "In order to sustain the Rangers, we're going to need funding, and we'll get it sure enough from the territory, but also from the ranchers, railroad and Wells Fargo. They all have an interest in this concept succeeding, but they are a suspicious bunch, and want to make certain both sides of the bread is buttered."

Uncle Bob sat back, amused at the spectacle before him. None of the family had ever stooped to the lowly realm of politics. It would be interesting to see what his nephew would do. He knew this kind of thing was not to Arvel's liking.

Arvel leaned back in his chair, took a long draw on his cigar, and looked the men over. "Well, gentlemen, it seems the Arizona Rangers will be facing danger from every corner."

He looked over at the young reporter, "Getting this all down, son?"

"Yes sir, every word."

Uncle Bob was already working with a mule when Arvel awoke the next morning. Taking a cup of coffee for each of them, he stood at the corral watching the old man work. "What do you make of all this politics?"

Uncle Bob watched the young mule as he considered the question. "Well, Arvel, you know we've always avoided the politics, both your family and mine. It is a low business." He deftly coaxed the mule, "But it might not be so bad to get involved in this thing. It would certainly help Dick. He's a good man and could use a leg up. It's dangerous work, for certain, both for you and Dick, as you'll have as many potential assassins as Caesar, I'm sure of that. Once you enter the public life, your own life's not your own."

"Yes, Uncle. I appreciate what you're saying, and we've always valued our privacy."

Uncle Bob handed the mule over to Manuele, the top hand. He walked out of the corral and sat in the shade. He put a hand on Arvel's shoulder. "You're up to the task, Arvel. I'm damned proud of you, son. You're the son I never had and I'm grateful for you." He knocked the dust from his chaps and looked at the ground. "I'd never want any harm to come to you, Arvel, you know that. This is a great land, and the people who live in it deserve to live clean, decent lives. We've come a long way, but we have a long way to go yet. Any time something terrible can come to some homesteaders, like what happened to those poor souls last month, then there's work to be done."

He leaned back against the cool adobe wall behind him. "I know your concern about working for bastards like that Hennessy, and the railroad and the banks and all the other parasites who suck the blood of the hard working folk, but lawlessness is endemic, and one kind of lawlessness begets all others. I'm convinced of that. There's the old notion of noblesse oblige, Arvel, and we are the fortunate ones. I don't mean we are the idle rich. We've earned our money, no doubt, but we've been lucky and we've done well. I've always felt, at least on the ranch here, that we're responsible for the folks who work for us. You've got a gift, son, and you should probably use it for the benefit of our good land, be it this ranch or the whole territory. I just hope," he looked at his hands, "that you don't end up the sacrificial lamb."

"So, we are resolved to the fact that I'll become an Arizona Ranger and a politician, Uncle." He smiled. "I just wanted to make certain you wouldn't disown me."

CHAPTER III:
CHICA

The wild Mexican girl was having a good summer. The money and watch she had gotten from the gringo kept her well provisioned. She did a lot of traveling and visiting with many of her friends and associates on both sides of the border. She'd spent most of the summer in Mexico and was now heading north, maybe to Flagstaff to see what adventures she could have up there. When her money began to run out, she decided to take a detour and stop at a small settlement with no name, where there was a saloon and gambling house. The place was simply known as the Hump, just west of the New Mexico and Arizona border. Chica was told that a new gringo bouncer and faro dealer there was very stupid and it was easy to win money. She figured if she could double what she had, it would carry her well into fall.

The Hump had one advantage in that it

sat over the top of an aquifer that provided ample water. Over time a few people built structures around it and it became a small settlement. One man had the notion that, if he held out long enough, something would happen to turn the place into a real town; perhaps Wells Fargo would make a stage route along its road, or a rail line might come by, or someone might discover gold like what Schieffelin did for Tombstone a few miles north. There were too few people in the region to merit much, but the one building of any consequence was a saloon, boarding house, brothel, gambling hall and dry goods and hardware store all under one roof. The proprietor was a drunkard who had tried his luck in just about every endeavor the West had to offer and was finally making enough money to live in meager comfort. He was forced to cater to Mexicans, but he drew the line on Indians except in the most limited capacity. He would sell them items when it suited him, other times they would be subjected to screaming tirades and threatened with being shot on the spot. He was, essentially, the law in the area as the county sheriff was too far away and the Hump too inconsequential to merit much attention.

Chica knew the place. She had visited it a

few times. Once she nearly killed a pimp for trying to recruit her as a sporting girl. After that, no one bothered much with her. They gave the girl a wide berth. They knew it was a bad idea to offend her in any way, and the problem with Chica was that you never knew exactly what she might find offensive.

She rode into the settlement in the late morning, and already the sun was nearly intolerable. She found a shady spot for Alanza and tied her to a hitching post nearby. She found the pony some water.

Chica stood at the bar near the entrance where a light breeze afforded some relief. The door was always left open which allowed thousands of flies to accumulate on the ceiling and around the beer taps. Every surface wore a fine coating of dust. The place stunk of stale beer, tobacco spit, sweat and coal oil. The air bore a permanent haze from the poorly trimmed wicks of the lamps hanging from the ceiling and the incessant tobacco smoke. Everyone was constantly either smoking or spitting tobacco.

She quickly downed two beers and eyed the man at the faro table. No one addressed her except for the man tending bar, and he only barely. He took her money then mumbled something about the new rule they had enacted, pointing to a sign near the door, instructing all patrons to check their fire-arms with the bartender. Chica complied. She pulled her pistols out of their holsters and handed them over, the muzzles of the guns pointing menacingly at the man's chest. She smiled at the bartender and said, "Now we are all equals, no?" The bartender looked at her, stupidly. He did not remember her from her last visit.

Chica watched the dealer for a while. He was playing against another man, obviously even more stupid, as Chica observed some basic blunders that both men seemed not to notice. It was simple dumb luck on the part of the dealer that he continued to win. All the while, the dealer kept up a constant tirade about various things. Simply talk, to make himself out to be a lot tougher than he was. He nursed one foot, as if he had been recovering from having a horse step on it, and Chica thought that perhaps he was not just a gringo, but a greenhorn gringo, at that. Maybe he did not even know horses. She waited patiently until the man lost his last hand, then approached the dealer.

When dealing with men, Chica usually decided right away how she would likely appear to them solely on their body language and expression. She was always dangerous, she could not help that, and she could never appear to be helpless or vulnerable. But she could easily work somewhere between having men lust for her and fear her. In some instances, they were simply revolted by the fact that she was Mexicana. Some men were so blinded by prejudice against Mexicans or against women who did not fit the Victorian ideal, that they were immediately repulsed by the girl, even in places where women were few and far between. They'd sooner fornicate with an old worn out white hag than with a pretty señorita. These men were wise to hide their revulsion, for to show it might well be the last thing they did.

Lila, the madam, saw Chica approach the dealer and quickly moved in. She caught the girl's eye, and nodded to her. "Ma'am." Lila remembered Chica all too well. It was her pimp who was nearly snuffed out.

Chica responded in kind. She could just make out that the old prostitute was warning the faro dealer about something. She could not make out exactly what, but she had a good idea. The man sat up a little straighter in his chair. He looked at the cards and simply mumbled, "What will it be?"

Chica liked faro, but knew poker well, and

thought that she might extract more money from the stupid young man more quickly. She decided at the last moment to just go with faro, as he had won recently and would likely be overly confident.

Lila sauntered over to a piano and began playing. She had a good view of the game and wanted to keep an eye on the two. This bouncer was her latest flame and she didn't want him snuffed out. He was an idiot and a bit of a show-off, but it was the best she could do at present.

"Faro." She lit a cigar and sat back in the chair. She eyed the young man as he set up the game. He was not bad looking, but she could tell that he was one of the kind of gringos who did not see any beauty in Mexican women. He would have also not extended a game to her had Lila not intervened. Lila did this, of course, not out of courtesy to Chica; she did not care one way or another about the Mexican woman. She knew that if the little man ran his mouth, that Chica would likely shut it for him.

Chica won quickly and often, in fact, nearly every hand. She watched the dealer, reading his reaction. He was beginning to lose his temper. Chica could see that; she did not want to have to kill the young gringo. She simply needed to increase her bankroll. She suggested they switch to poker and he obliged. He quickly lamented that decision as Chica began beating him just as badly. In less than two hours, she was ready to call it quits and decided, by the demeanor of the dealer, that it would be healthier for everyone if she did. She was just about to tell the dealer that she would be playing her last hand when a commotion caught her attention at the bar.

Two Indians eased into the saloon. One was about thirty and the other no more than twenty. They were a pathetic sight. They wore essentially rags and old straw sombreros riddled with holes. The older one wore a wool vest and no shirt, the younger one peon clothes. The proprietor had a good drunk on by now and looked at the two men through bleary eyes. He immediately started screaming at them. They were only doing what he had told them to do: to come back in a month to see if he had any of the shells they needed. The proprietor, of course, did not remember.

"I told you two before, I don't have pinfire shells. And we don't sell *anything* to Indians. Goddamnit, how many times do I haveta say it!"

The Indians stood, looking at one another. They were confused. They began speaking to each other in hushed tones. This caused the proprietor even more anxiety. He let loose with a stream of profanities, so quickly that the words ran together until he was voicing nothing much more than gibberish, with a couple of good, clear swear words coming through now and again.

Chica lit another cigar and turned her attention to the yelling man. "Hey, you don' need a yell, gringo, we can all hear you, all the way over here." She nodded in the direction of the whore. "We can' even hear the piano." Lila stopped playing.

The man looked at Chica, then at the dealer. He was watching his bankrolled dealer lose his hide, and the Indians added to his frustration at how the afternoon was deteriorating for him.

"Thas nona yer business, squaw. Not sure why you were even 'lowed in 'ear."

Chica pulled the money before her into a pile; she folded it, and tucked it between her breasts. She walked over to the Indians and looked at their shotgun. It was a rusted relic, but still worked at getting game when they could find shells for it.

Chica looked behind the proprietor who stood, mesmerized by the girl.

"How much is that one behind you, gringo?"

He looked around and saw a shotgun. "Ten dollars."

"We will take it, gringo, and give you eight dollars and this shotgun in trade."

The proprietor threw his head back, remembering that he had the girl's pistols. "Hah," he slurred, "what the hell kinda trade is that? Tha' piece a shit id'nt worth ten cents, much less two dollars. I'll give ya *nothin'* for it, and you can all get the hell outta my saloon, *now*! I said it before," he wiped some spittle with the back of his hand, "I don' trade with goddamned Indians, squaw." He leaned forward, into Chica's face, squinting hard to focus. "Now, whatta hell ya think 'bout that?"

Chica closed the distance between them and from under her vest, pulled a smaller version of the silver plated pistols she carried in her holsters. She always kept this ace in the hole and her dagger hidden when visiting saloons. They came in handy with establishments that had rules against patrons carrying guns.

She pressed the revolver's muzzle against the proprietor's forehead and cocked the piece. "I think it is not good, gringo."

She anticipated the dealer's actions and waited for him to approach, which he did with trepidation. He reached out, without enthusiasm, in a halfhearted attempt to stop the girl. She pushed him off balance, and put her foot behind his heel. He pitched backward. She placed her boot on his neck and pointed her dagger in the direction of his eye. She felt the energy, through her leather sole, drain from his body. She had full control of him now. The old madam jumped into action.

"Come on, now, everybody. Let's just settle down. We can solve this civilized, like." Chica looked over at the fat woman and smiled. "Come on, Bill, go ahead an' make a trade. You've had that old shotgun back there for two years. Miss, why not sit down and we can have a nice friendly drink."

Lila was working hard. She knew how dangerous Chica was. The two men who kept Lila in business were about to meet their maker. "Ma'am, you've got beautiful hair, why don't you let me braid it for ya. I've got some nice tortoise shell combs, all the way from Paris, France. What a ya say?"

Chica ignored the woman's pleas. She smiled at the two men, and said, "You gringos ever hear of a Mexicano standoff, eh?" She looked at each of them calmly. "Well, this is not a Mexicano standoff, boys. I will kill you both if we cannot make a trade. What shall it be, gringos? Do you want to die for a ten dollar shotgun?"

The bartender stood, sweat running into his eyes. He was shaking. "I'll trade, I'll trade . . . Miss." He suddenly felt sober.

"Well, okay, then. Firs', hand me my pistols, gringo. Then hand the Indios the shotgun." The Indians stood, awestruck. They did not move to either escape or help the young woman. They were in the precarious spot of being both victims and conspirators at the same time.

Chica holstered her pistols and placed the hide-out gun back in its holster. She held the dagger and lit a cigar. She continued to stand on the dealer's neck. "An we need some bullets for the shotgun as well. We need a box of bird shot, some buckshot and some heavier shots, for rabbit. She looked at the Indians, "Anything else?"

They nodded energetically.

"How much is all of that, gringo?"

"Don't, don't worry 'bout it. Take 'em . . . as a gift."

"No, gringo, we are not robbing you, just making a good trade, we will pay for the bullets." She peeled off a few bills and put the rest in her pocket.

She sent the Indians on their way and stepped away from the dealer, who got up slowly and sat back down at the card table.

Chica looked at them and smiled. "Oh, by the way, gringo, I am no' a squaw, I am Mexicana. You might wanna change your sign," she pulled the handwritten placard from the doorway, and threw it at the bar. It read, *"No Indians allowed."*

Outside, she untied Alanza and climbed onto her saddle. She kept an eye on the entrance to the saloon, but did not need to. No one inside was interested in following her. She cantered Alanza over into better shade. It was so hot that she regretted not getting one more beer before leaving the gringo saloon. She counted her money and was pleased. She would be good through November. She glanced down the street at the Indians. They were standing under a lean-to, ogling the new shotgun. It was not a good one, but it was new and double-barreled and it handled shells that could be easily obtained. They were very pleased.

One of the Indians approached her. As if paying tribute to some pagan goddess, he offered her a silver crucifix. Chica could see its value and refused. She pointed to a brass bangle around the man's arm and said that she would have that as a gift if he would part with it. He gladly complied. The other, younger Indian summoned his courage and ran up to Chica. He grabbed her hand and kissed it, and just as quickly ran away. Chica touched Alanza's sides with her spurs, let her jog a few steps, then urged her into a gallop. They flew down the dirt road, kicking up dust which blew through the open door of the saloon. She pulled Alanza up and wheeled her around. They raced back past the saloon and sent half a dozen shots through its window, just to keep the gringos excited a little longer. She rode out of sight and was gone.

Chapter IV:
Alliance

Dick Welles sat in the lounge of the Alhambra Hotel in Tombstone, waiting anxiously for Arvel Walsh to arrive. This was their first get-together since the meeting of the delegation at Arvel's ranch. Dick was fairly giddy with excitement. He smoked the finest cigar offered by the hotel and was finishing his second scotch. He kept looking at his watch; he couldn't wait to talk with Arvel about the dozen or so ideas he had about the new Rangers.

He fiddled with the silver stars he had brought along. He had ordered them made by a jeweler in Bisbee. Each had Captain, then Arizona Ranger, engraved around the center. The other stars for the Ranger Privates would be numbered, but he purposefully did not do this with these stars. There would be no number one or number two Captain in this outfit. The whole thing was a simple five pointed star. He hoped

Arvel would approve.

Dick labored under the delusion that hard work and perseverance would guarantee success in life. Unfortunately, he was hurtling through his fifties and still had not achieved the level he had hoped for since he was a child. More than money, he wanted to be recognized as a gentleman. He worked toward this, but as the saying goes, it takes two generations to make a gentleman, and Dick's father had not made strides toward such a goal. His father was a good man, but he was a laborer and utterly uneducated. He had no aspirations other than to keep his family fed and a dry roof over their heads. He was hopeful that his children would do well, but to him, doing well meant learning a trade or perhaps becoming a farmer.

Dick had very specific ideas about what it meant to be a success, most of which were not only unrealistic but also unattainable. Society in America, by this time, was more tolerant, particularly when it came to the upper strata. So long as one was white, a gentile and not Catholic, he would be welcomed with open arms, provided he had enough cash on hand. Dick did not seem to fully grasp this concept. Try as he might, he always seemed to be on the outside.

His first experience with this was during the war. He was a supreme soldier, starting as a private. He was an enlisted man who was later commissioned for outstanding leadership on the field of battle and made a Brevet Officer. But this only made him alien in both worlds. He no longer fit in with the enlisted men, and he did not fit in with the likes of Arvel Walsh, the well-educated and well-heeled officer of the upper level of society.

And he continued to struggle with this all his life. He was not educated, and he did not like to read, although he could read well. He was not intellectual in any way. He seemed constantly to be a day late and a dollar short. He never was a failure at anything he had tried. He was always a good employee for whomever he worked. But he could never achieve any significant financial success, no matter how hard he worked.

But now, things appeared to be going his way, and he was anxious to get started.

By the time Arvel and the reporter arrived for dinner, Dick was on his way to a good drunk. Arvel was amused, as he rarely saw Dick so relaxed and animated. He was in a talkative mood. Eventually, they made it from the hotel lounge to the dinner table.

They chatted as they looked over the bill of fare.

Dick smiled. "Look at this, gentlemen. Even in this dying town of Tombstone, we have cold beer, oysters from South Carolina, salmon from the Pacific, and fresh vegetables from, from . . ." he could not remember where the fresh vegetable had come from . . . "back East. My God, when I first came out to Arizona . . ."

Arvel grinned. "Oh, God, don't tell us you drank water from a muddy hoofprint."

"No. No!" He took another drink of beer. "That's disgusting, Arvel. No, I never drank muddy water from anything. I was going to say you'd be lucky to get canned beans. Now look." He waved his hand across the table laid before them.

"Well, you've been here the longest of the three of us, Dick." He smiled at the young reporter. "You should know."

Dick laughed. "Well, I'm not boasting, I'm just saying how far we've come. It is a great thing to see, and I'm hoping we'll help to move it on even further." He finished his beer and after dinner insisted that they have one last drink for the night. They went to the hotel bar and Dick had trouble walking. He began laughing at everything. Arvel got them a table in the corner and propped him in a chair. He would not stop smiling.

Their pleasant, albeit unproductive evening, was disrupted by some loud talking at the end of the bar. Two men became engaged in a heated discussion about the war.

In short order, the hotel manager approached Arvel and his group. They had already become celebrities in the region, and everyone seemed to know the new Rangers. The manager was naturally a nervous man, and was embarrassed to approach them.

"I am sorry to disturb you, gentleman, but as you can hear, we have a rather drunk and belligerent young man at the bar." The manager wiped his brow, "We don't typically have such ruffians here. A very unpleasant business."

"Where is your hired man?" Arvel was a little put out by the request. He had forgotten that he was no longer just a private citizen. Dick was in no condition to do or say anything. He sat back in his chair and gazed vacuously at Arvel and the manager.

"He is down with a bad bout of lumbago, Captain Walsh. I am very sorry for this imposition, and your bill will be accordingly adjusted as a token of our appreciation."

Arvel sat up; he waved the man off. "No worries. I'll take care of it for you." He leaned over, close to Dick. "Give me your shootin' iron, Dick. I'm not heeled."

Dick looked at him and smiled. He pulled back the lapel of his coat and the butt of the revolver could be seen jutting from his vest pocket. Arvel grabbed it discreetly and put it in his pocket. A dozen notions ran through his mind as he considered his plan. Before he left his party, he leaned over to the reporter and asked him to put Dick to bed, then rejoin him at the bar. The young man dutifully complied, yet he was disappointed in not witnessing Arvel's first act as a lawman. He knew, based upon the look on Arvel's face, that he should not object.

Arvel walked up to the arguing men. The Alhambra was a civilized hotel and the bar was similarly populated. Sound rarely exceeded a murmur and often, well-dressed ladies could be seen seated at the tables in the nearby lounge.

Arvel sized the men up as he approached. One, the younger of the two, a man no more than thirty, was definitely armed, the other he could not be certain of. The older man was clearly working on agitating the younger, provoking a fight, and he looked as though he could make short work of the younger, drunker man. He also would be the most easily diffused, as it appeared to

Arvel that he would likely not want to get mixed up with the law. Both men were traveling through.

Arvel walked up between them, casually, and ordered a drink. He opened his coat long enough to display his star and Dick's revolver. He downed the drink and then took advantage of the temporary pause in the fracas.

"Gentlemen, I could not help to overhear your conversation about the war."

The young man huffed, "This Yankee was disparaging the honor of the fighting men of the South."

The older man snorted. "Hell, son, you weren't even born 'til after the war, I bet."

"I was five years old in sixty-five, you mudsill, and my daddy and two brothers died with honor." The young man's face was turning a deeper red. He was going to unravel at any moment. *Such anger,* Arvel thought, *and we were nearly thirty years out of the war.*

"All right, all right. Gents, the war was a long time ago. It was a bad time, but it is over now and we need to just let it go." He looked at the older man and motioned for him to leave. "I'll be happy to drink a toast to both sides." He looked at the men, "Tomorrow, when we've all had a good night's sleep and we're in a properly respect-ful state."

The older man bowed. He was not nearly as drunk as the younger one. He could tell Arvel was a GAR man and that some insults by a youngster were not worth getting into hot water over. He was moving on next day anyway. "That's a fine idea, sir. And with that, I will bid you all a good night."

He had gotten rid of one, now he had to deal with the other. He thought better of buying the man a drink, and looked over to see that the reporter had returned from his task of getting Dick to bed. The young man was muttering something about Yankees having tails when Arvel suggested they move to the lounge. He offered the man a cigar and ordered coffee. The young man was confused. He did not understand why the Yankee Captain was being so nice to him. The reporter was cordial as well.

"Mister, I am sorry, what is your name, sir?"

"Collins."

"Mr. Collins." Arvel extended his hand. "Name's Walsh, Captain of Arizona Rang-ers." Arvel suppressed a laugh. He had not introduced himself as such until now. It sounded ridiculous to him. He looked at the reporter. "Mr. Collins lost his whole family in the war."

The reporter looked at him, confused. He realized then what Arvel was doing. "Oh, oh, I am sorry to hear that, Mr. Collins. I lost quite a few family members in that terrible conflict as well, but it was before my time. Family still talks about it like it was yesterday."

"North or South?" The young man demanded.

"The Army of Northern Virginia." The reporter stood a little straighter. He spoke in a tone to suggest it was a ridiculous question. Of course he was a Southerner.

"Yes." Arvel sat back in the leather chair and crossed his ankles; he blew a long plume of smoke at the ceiling. "Yep, I believe just about every person in the country lost something in that war." He stretched. "But, it was a long time ago, and we really just need to move on." He sat up and looked at the young man. "Looks like you are putting the affairs of your family back in order, Mr. Collins."

The young man blushed. "How do you mean, sir?" He liked this Yankee. He never thought he would like any Yankee, but he did this one.

"You are well enough dressed, staying at Tombstone's finest hotel, you have money;

looks like you take care of your old mother well enough."

The young man nodded.

"Let me just give you some unsolicited advice, if you will indulge me, my friend." He touched the man's forearm. "Let it go, son. To honor your family, let it go. There is no good that can come from hating. Your father and brothers made the supreme sacrifice for something they believed in; the best you can do is let 'em rest in peace. Remember them that way and move forward. You are going to encounter more and more men of the Yankee persuasion as you move west. Some of them will kill you sooner than look at you, and then your old mother will have no one left. It ain't worth it, son."

The man sat quietly for a few moments, pondering what Arvel had said. He worked on his cigar and looked at the floor. He stood up and shook both men by the hand. "Thank you for the cigar and coffee, Captain. I have to leave early tomorrow, so I will be bidding you a good evening." It was the best he could do for an apology and thank you, and Arvel responded in kind.

The reporter was amused by Arvel's method. Most of the lawmen he had seen in Tombstone would have been rolling around on the floor by now, and someone would be missing a few teeth after such an altercation. Arvel Walsh bought the man coffee and a cigar. He likely had the man thinking about things that might well change his life. This was an unusual and remarkable lawman, indeed.

Arvel let Dick sleep until noon. He opened the door slowly and was assaulted by the pungency of a sick-room. Dick squinted up at him through one bleary eye, too weak and sick to lift his head from the cool pillow. "Do you still have my gun?"

"Sure."

"Do me a favor and shoot me with it." He slowly sat up, rubbed his eyes and the back of his head. He looked for his watch.

"It is noon."

"You didn't have to kill anyone last night, I presume?"

"No, no, everyone slept soundly in their overpriced Alhambra beds, no problem. I changed their diapers and put them both to bed without incident." He tossed the borrowed revolver on the bed.

"God damn, what is that stench?" said Dick.

"Vomit."

"Where?"

Arvel looked around the room. A chamber pot was full, and he looked further on.

"Oh, my."

"What?"

"You didn't pay a lot for those new boots, did you?"

"No, four dollars. Why?"

"They are full of used oysters."

"Damn!" Dick slowly eased his legs over and sat on the edge of the bed. He tried to twist a cigarette. His hands were cold and clammy, his fingers would not work.

Arvel handed him one from his pack. Dick lay back again. They both smoked as Arvel opened a window to let the rank air circulate. Dick breathed deeply then sat up abruptly, grabbed the least full vessel at his feet and belched into it. He waited for the next round of retching to commence. "Hey," he peered into the bowl. "I don't remember eating noodles." He looked up at Arvel, the nausea had passed for now.

"Let me see." Arvel peered into the chamber pot. "That's an onion."

Dick pushed the bowl away and sat back on the bed.

"I am sorry, Arvel. I shouldn't have been in that condition last night."

"Oh, there is nothing in it. Don't give it another thought. You're not a sot, I know that, you were just celebrating, and it got the best of you. At least you were armed. I didn't have a gun."

"A real pair are we." He grinned, embarrassed. "I'm a drunk and you with nothing more than harsh words for the outlaws."

Arvel blew smoke rings at the window. The town was bustling below and he was shocked at all the activity on a Sunday. Dick's words weighed heavily on him. Their lives were going to change, and at his age he suddenly thought it was a stupid plan. He never carried a six shooter. He never needed it. He was nearly always anonymous in Tombstone and always anonymous in Tucson and, really, any other place he would go. Now he would have to deal with drunken angry young men, had to get into their business, had to learn what sort of nonsense made them hate the world. He'd have to protect the interests of businesses, whose owners and managers didn't give a hang about him. They just needed to keep the flow of commerce going; they needed a garbage man to pick up the refuse, or diffuse it before it negatively affected the bottom line.

Dick seemed to be having the same thoughts. In the glow of a nice drunk, when you feel invincible, like you could take on the entire world, fantasizing about the greatness of your exploits, it all seems a grand adventure. You feel like a young buck again. Now, in the cold clarity of morning, with the added pain of a roaring hangover, being a Ranger Captain did not seem to have the same appeal. He thought about his vulnerability. What if they had been hosting a reporter from the Democrat *Nugget,* rather than the Republican *Epitaph?* My God, the papers would be filled with the shameful actions of the new Rangers; one drunk, the other killing a man over a Southern insult. He knew Arvel, and he knew the man didn't mind pulling a trigger on a fellow. He felt like he was going to vomit again.

"You don't look so good, Dick."

"I don't feel so good, Arvel."

"Come on, pull your ass out of that bed. What you need is some coffee and a bit of grub. We'll both feel better when you're up and moving about. You go ahead and wash up, and I'll get you some new boots. You can't wear those vomited in ones until, well," he looked at them doubtfully . . . "maybe you should just throw'em away."

They did feel better after a meal. The men who had had the argument were long gone; the young reporter observed them getting into a coach together, heading further west.

89

It would likely be an unusual ride for both of them. The manager approached the men's table and thanked Arvel profusely. He had saved the hotel from any embarrassment and kept the patrons happy. The Alhambra worked hard at overcoming the Wild West image. Their motto was, "a bit of civility in an uncivilized land." The manager chatted on for a while and, eventually, the reporter showed up and sat with the two men. He looked at Dick Welles a little doubtfully.

"Mr. Welles, you have no color in your face, sir."

Dick smiled at him. "I'll live."

The reporter was in a good mood. He liked these men. They were the kind of men he had heard about all his life, the real men who fought in the war, had seen real hardship, had been tested and showed their courage. They were, simply, men, and everything they did was always right, as far as he was concerned. Dick Welles' drunkenness did not change his perspective of him at all. He had gotten drunk a time or two himself. Dick was obviously not a drunkard. He was drinking coffee the next morning. A drunk would be drinking, at least, a beer.

Arvel received his final bill. The manager had graciously discounted it by the cost of

Arvel's sum for his Ranger services to the establishment. It amounted to eighty-three cents. There was a request for a receipt from Arvel for the payment rendered. Arvel laughed and added the amount back on his bill; he tore up the request and threw it in the trash. His actions did not seem to merit an eighty-three cent discount.

Chapter V:
Col. Charles Gibbs, Esq.

"Pendejo . . . Pendejo." He had not dreamed of the Mexican girl. "Pendejo." He felt a shove and sat up in bed. She stood over him with mescal on her breath.

"Oh, hello." He rubbed his eyes. "Why are you in my room, standing over my bed?"

"I missed you, Pendejo."

"Oh, that's nice." He looked outside. It was dark. "Most folks come calling during the day."

She began walking slowly around the room, looking at things, picking up pictures. "You have a nice place, Pendejo."

He was pleased to see her, and smiled at the absurdity of having a young señorita in his bedroom.

"Who are these people, Pendejo?"

"That is my wife, and the little one, my daughter."

"They are dead, Pendejo?"

"Yes."

"That is sad." She put the photos back. "So . . . what are you doing, Pendejo?" She began fidgeting with the lampshade tassels by his bed.

"Well," he yawned. "I can tell you what I am *not* doing." He threw his legs over the side of the bed and sat at the edge. "I am *not* sleeping."

She grinned, "You are funny, Pendejo."

"What is your name, Chica?"

"Oh, I go by many names, Pendejo, why don' you guess, and I will tell you what is right?"

"Jezebel?"

"No."

"Lorelei?"

"No."

"Ophelia?"

"No."

"Lucretia?"

"No. But I like that name."

"Chiquita."

"No." She grinned. "You called me that last time." She ran her thumbnail across her teeth.

"Diablo?"

"Now, you are being silly, Pendejo. And I would be Diabla."

"I give up, Chica."

"That is it! I am Chica."

"I doubt it."

"What is your name, Pendejo?"

"Arvel."

She laughed. "That is a funny name."

"I am a funny man."

She yawned. "You *are* a funny man, Pendejo. Why don' you get angry with me?"

"I don't know. I think you are funny, too."

"I am tired, Pendejo."

"Then you should go home and go to bed, wherever that might be."

"I am thirsty, Pendejo. Would you get me some water?"

"Oh, you are a lot of trouble." He stood up, and reached for a robe.

"Ay, chingao! Wha' happened to your back, Pendejo?'

"I got blown up, in the war."

"Ay, you are a mess, Pendejo." She stretched, catlike, "I am tired, Pendejo."

"Yes, I know."

He returned with a glass of water and she was asleep in his bed.

"You are a lot of trouble," he muttered under his breath and curled up on the divan at the foot of the bed. He dozed off and began to dream.

"Pendejo."

"What?"

"What are you doing, Pendejo?"

"Not sleeping."

"Come to bed, Pendejo, I am cold."

"It is sweltering, Chica."

"I am cold."

His mind raced.

"I am afraid, Pendejo."

He laughed. "*You,* afraid? I think not."

"You do not like me, Pendejo? No?"

"No . . . Yes, I like you Chica. Like I like a pit of rattlers." He sat up, then stood to face her. "It is not appropriate, Chica."

"What is this, appropriate? What does this mean?"

"Proper."

"Ay, you are a fool, Pendejo," She looked into his eyes and pouted her lips, like someone who had not gotten her way. She lifted the covers and scooted away from him, making room for him in the bed. She tilted her head, beckoning him.

"My God." She did not look sixteen now.

She awoke at dawn, her brown skin contrasting against the white sheets. She stretched again, enjoying the comfortable bed. She looked up at him, her head resting on his arm, "Pendejo, why are you looking at me?"

He was fiddling with the earring dangling nearest to him, and then the bangles on her wrist. He laughed. "I was thinking of something funny."

"What, Pendejo?"

" 'And I will visit upon her the days of Baalim, in which she burned incense to them, and she decked herself with her ear-rings and her jewels, and she went after her lovers, and forgot me, saith the Lord.' "

She wriggled more deeply into the bed, turned on her side facing away and pressed herself against him. "You are funny," and fell asleep.

She appeared at noon, freshly washed and wearing one of Rebecca's white cotton dresses. Uncle Bob, sitting in the deep shade of the porch, was occupied with Arvel's work in the corral and did not notice her until she was standing next to him. He jumped out of his chair and removed his hat. "Ma'am." He bowed.

Arvel saw her and stopped what he was doing. "Hello."

"Good morning."

"Uncle Bob, this is . . . Chica."

"Good morning, Uncle Bob."

"Well, good morning, Miss Chica." Uncle Bob held out his hand, took Chica's and kissed it as he bowed lower, his hat across his breast.

"It is a beautiful morning," Chica looked

96

up at the sky.

"It is now," Uncle Bob grinned. He walked over to the corral and hopped up on the rail fence.

Arvel went back to working the young mule. Chica grabbed Uncle Bob's hand and climbed up on the rail next to him. Arvel worked the jenny hard and the animal did not like it much.

"Watch him, Miss Chica." Uncle Bob leaned closer to the girl, as if to impart a secret. "This is a particularly willful one."

Arvel moved around the corral like a boxer in the prize ring. He led the animal with a long rope and spoke words to her calmly and constantly. Chica could not make out the words. He did not strike the animal, but never let her take control. In short order, both man and beast were fairly running around the ring.

Arvel would push the animal and then force her to stop, change directions, commanding the animal to do what he wanted until she complied. He did not let up for a moment and soon they were sweating, nearly exhausted, and the young mule began, as if by magic, to heed the man's every order.

"He is good, Uncle Bob." She smiled and looked at the man sitting next to her. "He does not look like a mule trainer."

Bob smiled. "Arvel's a deceptive fellow, Miss Chica."

"He looks like a mild boy." She struggled for the word, "un sacatón . . . but not really."

In the old days, they'd refer to a fellow like him as a bully trap."

"Qué?"

"A bully trap. A fellow that would appear to be a pushover, a weakling, a coward, and thus easy pickings for a bully, until the bully gets hold of him, then he wonders what fell on him. That is Arvel."

Chica watched him work. She grinned, "Sí, Uncle Bob. Bully trap."

Pilar called them for the midday meal and Chica grabbed Arvel's arm as he closed the gate. "You are pretty good, Pendejo, you know mules."

"Oh, it is easy, Chica." He smiled at her. "You just have to be more stubborn than them. Sooner or later, you wear them down, until they start thinking it's their idea to do what you want 'em to do."

They sat around the table at the veranda. A good breeze made it comfortable. Pilar poured drinks and leaned next to Chica and whispered something in her ear. Chica grinned. She nodded.

They had a fine meal. Uncle Bob treated

Chica as if she had been an expected guest. They talked of mules, mostly. Chica ate heartily, with little concern for table manners. The normal hour-long meal turned into an entire afternoon with Chica holding court. Uncle Bob immediately loved her. He always had a weakness for pretty young women and Chica was like early Christmas for him.

As the sun moved across the sky, it shone on Chica's face and Bob stood up to move a panel down from the ceiling to block it. He interrupted the midday molt of a bark scorpion causing it to drop down onto Chica's dinner plate. It got its bearings and turned, facing Chica with its claws outstretched, telson poised to strike. Arvel leapt into action, looking about for something to contain the creature as Chica pounded her small brown fist down soundly on the arthropod's head, smashing it into a white, wet goo. "Is okay, Pendejo," she wiped the mess from her hand with her unused napkin. "I got him."

"Hah!" Uncle Bob laughed out loud. "I've been trying to get Arvel to do that to scorpions for years, Miss Chica. He always wants to brush 'em up and put 'em out in the desert."

If he were not so old and if Arvel was not

already somehow caught up with this young beauty, Uncle Bob would have proposed marriage to her on the spot. He was smitten. "You should take Chica up and show her Rebecca's place."

Arvel looked dumbfounded by his uncle's suggestion. Not that it was a bad idea, but he just had not given thought about what he was to do with the girl, or how long she would be *visiting,* or what even the next hour would hold, let alone considered taking the girl to his old family retreat.

Chica was amused. She had never been treated so well by gringos. These were strange men. "What is this Rebecca place, Pendejo?"

Oh, it's a little camp my wife and I used to visit. Haven't been there for years. It isn't much, but it's cooler up there. There's a stream and an old cave dwelling that we fixed up a bit. The snakes are likely bad up there now.

"I like this, Pendejo."

"I sent Romero and a few of the boys on up to prepare it for you."

Arvel looked at the old fellow. "Well, you are full of surprises today, Uncle."

Pilar put some things together for you. If you leave now, you'll have time for supper up there."

They saddled Alanza and Sally. Arvel began looking over Chica's traps. He pulled a queer looking rifle from a tooled leather scabbard. "Where did you steal this?"

She slapped his hand. "I did not steal it, Pendejo."

"You certainly didn't buy it."

"I did."

"From where?" It was a new kind of rifle, with an action that opened the breech by pulling on a bolt handle. It was mounted with a long telescopic sight.

"I ordered it, from the Montgomery Ward catalog, Pendejo."

The stock had a silver plate inlayed which read, *Col. Charles Gibbs, Esq.*

"Oh, I know your name now, Chica. Colonel Charles Gibbs. Nice to know you, Colonel Gibbs." He reached out to shake her hand, which she pushed away. She put the rifle back in the Concho covered case. She climbed onto Alanza and they began to ride.

"What did Pilar say to you at dinner?"

"Nothing, Pendejo. Let it go."

"I want to know."

She smiled coyly. "She said I was taco-nera."

Arvel thought on it, trying to remember if he had ever heard the word before. "Qué?"

"I am, eh, how do you say, ah, traveling whore." She grinned proudly.

She liked that Pilar had given her so much consideration.

"Oh."

Uncle Bob watched them ride off. Pilar stood beside him, drying a dish. The housekeeper was never *not* doing something. She looked on at the Mexican girl. She leaned over and spat on the ground. Uncle Bob laughed at her.

"She is no good, that one."

Pilar was not an attractive woman. She was forty-five and looked sixty. She had buried three husbands. One had been killed by Apaches, one by a drunken gringo, and one of heat stroke while working on the railroad. She had seven children of which only one lived. She began working for Uncle Bob when he first arrived in Arizona. She was a pious Catholic and she did not like women to act differently than what was expected. She did not like Chica's sensuality or her crass behavior, the fact that she dressed like a man, or her general foolishness. Pilar was all business and she felt, as the matriarch of the household, that she had some obligation to protect the two men in her life.

Uncle Bob looked around, and when the

coast was clear, he reached over and kissed her on the forehead. He was not ashamed to show Pilar affection but she would not have it. No outward display of affection was permitted.

"Aw, you don't like her, old girl, because she reminds you too much of you."

Pilar did her best to look terse. She pushed him away. "You are a silly old man."

"Will you come to see this silly old man tonight?"

She put down the dish and picked up another. "Did the girl put ideas into your head?"

He sat down, grabbed her and pulled her onto his lap. "No. *You* put some ideas in my head." He kissed her neck. She pretended to push away.

Rebecca's place was on the northeast corner of the ranch, around an hour's slow ride from the hacienda. She found it one day while exploring and it became a regular retreat at the height of the summer. A deep pool was fed by a stream that cut through the rocks, carrying water collected from the mountain above. The water was cold, even in summer. An Indian family also thought it a good place a thousand years ago, and the remnants of their cave dwelling remained.

The two rode slowly and chatted along the way.

"Pendejo, why do you like mules so much?"

He reached over and patted Sally on the neck. "I never used to know anything about mules until I was courting Rebecca. Then I learned to love them and realized how wonderful they were. Better than any stupid horse."

"Now, Pendejo, you cannot say that Alanza is not pretty." She patted her pony. "She is a fine animal and muy intelligente."

"No, no, she is that, Chica. She is a lovely pony, and she suits you." It was true. The pony was beautiful and feminine, like Chica. There was no mistaking that woman and horse were perfectly matched. Sally's great ears moved back, as if she was waiting for him to defend her honor. "But look at my Sally. She is absolutely perfect, with her great, beautiful . . ."

"Jug head." Chica laughed at the Pendejo.

"No, I was going to say beautiful ears."

"Face it, Pendejo, she is an, an, how do you say it . . . aberración. Mules are an insult to God. They were not made by God, they were made by man."

He leaned over and whispered into Sally's ear, "Don't listen to her, she's just jealous.

104

Because I love you so much." He kissed her on the neck.

Sally snorted.

Chica smiled. "You are such a Pendejo."

They rode on a bit.

"Did you know that mules were prized by the Pharaohs? They were considered too good for anyone but royalty."

"Who are Pharaohs?" She leaned over and spit on the ground, wiping her face with the back of her hand. She had been riding with her left ankle propped on the big Mexican saddle horn, her skirt hiked up to the waist and thighs splayed to keep cool. She had not bothered with undergarments. Her ignorance and vulgarity were irresistible. She did her best to outrage Arvel and Arvel did his best to ignore her. She leaned back in her saddle and unbuttoned the dress to her waist. "Ay, it is hot, Pendejo."

Arvel looked on at her exhibitionism, then onto the trail. "You are going to get sunburned, Colonel."

"I like riding this way, Pendejo. What do you think?"

"Rebecca used to ride side saddle."

Chica laughed. "I like to ride this a way." She sat up straight in the saddle, scooting toward the big saddle horn. "Sometimes, Pendejo, I just ride and ride, for no good reason than it feel good." She looked at Arvel. "You know, Pendejo, it is said that a woman who rides like this is difficult to please." She threw her head back and laughed when he blushed.

When they finally reached their destination, everything had been readied for them by some of the hands. They had cleared out in time so that Arvel and Colonel Gibbs were now alone. The fellows had stocked a pile of firewood near the deep pool and fixed up the old fire ring.

"Ay, this is pretty, Pendejo." She leaned down next to her pony and shared a drink. Arvel surveyed the site, reacquainting himself with it. He had not been here since his girls had died.

"It is a pretty place, Colonel."

"I am Chica, Pendejo."

"Yes, you are."

They put bedrolls inside the cave dwelling and Arvel stepped back with a start; a rattler had been coiled, waiting for a late-day meal. He picked the serpent up with a mesquite branch and carried it some distance away.

Chica looked on.

"One day, your kindness will be your end, Pendejo."

He smiled. "Yes, I've heard that before."

He gathered more wood to keep the fire going through the night as Chica smoked a cigarette in front of the pool at the base of the cave. She pulled her boots off and dangled her feet in the water.

Arvel sat next to her and began looking through the picnic basket. "Let's see what Pilar packed for us."

"I hope it is not poison, Pendejo." She laughed and swished her feet in the pool.

Arvel looked up at her, a bit worried. "You aren't going to kill Pilar, are you, Chica?"

She laughed out loud. "No, Pendejo. I do not kill women. Why would I?"

"Because of what she called you. I don't think she likes you very much, Chica."

"Well, she would not be a good woman if she did. I would not like me if I was her." She flicked her cigarette butt into the water and watched it float away, downstream. He handed her a drumstick and a tin cup of wine.

"This is good, Pendejo. I am surprised you are not fat." She ate ravenously. "I like Pilar. She take good care of you, Pendejo. She will like me after a while, I think."

She ate quietly for a while. Arvel worked on the fire next to the pool.

"How did your wife and daughter die, Pendejo?"

"Typhoid fever, Chica." He got up and moved over to sit next to her. He took his boots off and dipped his legs into the pool. "They went to San Francisco for a few weeks and stayed at the finest hotel there. They got some bad water and both died there."

"That is sad, Pendejo." She reached over and kissed his cheek. "I am sorry to make you remember sad things."

"It is okay, Chica. They are in a better place."

"Do you think so, Pendejo? Do you believe in heaven and hell?"

"I guess." He lay on his back and looked up at the sky, "I don't know, Chica. Maybe when you die, you're just dead."

"No, Pendejo. That is not right. There is a heaven and a hell. Your wife and daughter are in heaven."

"That's good, Chica. I am glad."

Chica scooped up water and dribbled it on his head. It felt good.

"We used to swim up here."

Chica looked at him and smiled. "Why don' we swim now?"

"I didn't bring a bathing suit; don't know where Rebecca's is anymore."

Chica stood up and peeled the dress off. She jumped into the pool. "You are such a

Pendejo." She splashed water at him. He had never seen anyone so uninhibited. Even married, in the middle of the wild, he and Rebecca would never have dreamed of swimming naked. He felt himself blush, absurdly looking around for any onlookers. Chica lay on her back and spit water into the air, like an Italian sculpture he'd seen in Tivoli. When he was satisfied no one was around, Arvel removed his shirt, then trousers. He slid into the water. It was one of the single most provocative and exciting experiences of his life.

Chica wrapped herself around him. Told him to take a deep breath and pulled him to the bottom.

Later, they lay on the rocks, drying in the late day sun. Dozed, talked, loved and played until evening. They stayed there, under the stars all night, leaving the bedrolls in the cave. They talked some more, loved and slept and every couple of hours awoke and started again. She was lovely. He noticed a small depression just above her left breast. "What's that?"

"Oh, a little hole." She pressed on it.

"Looks to be about a thirty-one."

"Sí." She laughed at the Pendejo. "It was a little gift from a gambler in Flagstaff. He thought that if he bought me some drinks that it meant something else, Pendejo."

"And he didn't use enough gun." Arvel looked her over for other wounds. "Where is the gambler now?"

Chica stretched, arching her back again, like a cat. She yawned. "He is in hell, where I sent him, Pendejo."

Colonel Chica Gibbs was gone when he awakened the next day. His watch and twenty-five dollars, along with a silver money clip given to him by Rebecca on their tenth anniversary, were gone, too, as was Rebecca's cotton dress. As he carried his bedroll out of the cave, he slipped on a loose rock and fell backward. The snake he had encountered the day before struck at him and caught its fangs on the top of his boot. It hung there, coiling, attempting to disengage itself from the tough hide. Arvel severed its head with his big knife.

Chapter VI:
The Limping Deputy

The young deputy did not wait around for the inevitable. He wandered back to Texas, doing odd jobs and working some of the gambling parlors in the small towns bordering Texas and New Mexico. He even spent a few days south of the Rio Grande, in Mexico. His wound had healed but left him with a slight limp, which was the continuous reminder of his humiliation and the shame he felt over the way the bastard mule rancher had mistreated him. He was angry and grew angrier every time he heard a comment or snicker from the patrons of the establishments where he tried employment.

He featured himself a tough and wanted to be a lawman or, at least, a bouncer, but he was ineffective in these endeavors. He was convinced that the man who shot him in the toe was responsible for his misfortunes and knew one day that he would get

111

his revenge. His cowardice kept him in check.

Through the summer he scratched out a living as a faro dealer, but he did not have a good mind for cards, and consistently lost money for the house. He was developing a reputation as a rather dull-witted and ineffective enforcer. And it was not due to the debacle in Arizona, as he was relatively anonymous, and no one really cared one way or another about him.

The main problem was his inability to control men effectively. He walked the walk, more or less, as well as a man can with nine toes, but he could not deliver the goods when it came down to a real showdown with some loudmouthed drunken cowboy who, like a mean dog or horse, must sense the toughness and know that the wrath of God is about to descend upon him if he does not comply. The young deputy simply did not have that in him.

He happened on one of the Tucson papers one day and saw the ad for the new Arizona Rangers. He did not make the connection with the names of Capt. Welles and Capt. Walsh, that these were the two old-timers who had made a fool of him. He seemed cheered by the prospect of becoming a Ranger, as the only time that he'd been happy was the all-too-brief career as a Texas Ranger, until he had disgraced himself there and had been run out of that state.

It did not take him long to pack. He'd been living with the old whore named Lila who had become a third-rate madam in a small settlement known as The Hump. She had decorated the room in which they shared a bed completely in pink and he looked more the fool in it than in any other setting.

She had no respect for him, but he was companionable in a biblical sense, and young, and not terrible on the eyes. She had gotten him a job as a bill collector for a Shylock who was part owner in the saloon out of which she operated. This was a good job for a pretend tough, as his victims consisted of young widows, scrawny Indians and consumptives. He could push them around pretty handily and feel like a man.

He was so cowardly that he tried to leave before Lila returned from her night's work, but he managed to make a mess of that. She looked him over as he moved around the room, collecting his traps among the sea of pink. "What's this?" She sucked on the end of a carved ivory cigar holder and glared at him through the smoke.

"I already told you. I'm going up to

Tucson to find work."

"At what?"

"Law work."

She began coughing through her laugh. "You? A lawman?" She was a cruel woman, especially when she was not getting her way. "What kind of law can you enforce? You think the territory up there is populated with scrawny Chinks and women? You're going to get yourself killed."

He flushed with anger, but would not raise a hand to Lila as she was a big woman and he'd seen her kill men tougher than him. "You don't think much of me, do you, Lila?" He put the last of his clothes in a carpet bag.

"No, it ain't that." She decided that ridiculing him would not make him stay. She sat up straighter and leaned forward. "Sugar, you've got a good thing here. You've got a place to stay, nice companionship, you're making good money. Why would you want to give all this up for living rough and running down some silly cow thieves?"

"I'm leavin', Lila."

"Go ahead, you yellow son-of-a-bitch. You'll be dead by winter. Remember what the half breed Mexican did to you, and that was a girl!"

He looked up at her in disbelief: "You said

114

you'd never bring that up again." He looked back at his packing. "You know that if I'd a killed that girl we'd have every Mexican within ten miles of here breathing down our necks."

"Oh, Paleeze! You didn't know that when you were cowering under the heel of her boot. If you did, why'd you go after her?"

"Cause Bill's a halfwit drunk and needed my help."

"Hah!" She blew smoke at him, like spittle. "You didn't know any such thing about her, and you just walked up on her, like a lost puppy, and she took you down like she was John L. Sullivan."

He crouched over, covering his ears. Like a child in the throes of a tantrum, he turned a deep red. "Shut up! Shut up, Lila. I am sick of you. I am leaving and that's it. I'm going to be an Arizona Ranger, so just shut your stupid fat mouth." He began to cry.

She was furious now. "Go ahead, you dumbass, and don't even think of comin' back here. We're finished if you walk out that door. Hear me?"

He rode north, stopping on his way out of town to collect interest from three pathetic souls. He beat one young Chinese man until his eyes were shut. He kept the money, as there is no honor amongst cowardly thieves, madams, or Shylocks.

At one time, stealing had been repugnant to him, but as he haphazardly progressed through his twenties, and opportunities presented themselves, he learned that stealing and cheating people was much easier than earning an honest living. As he made his way up to Tucson during the dog days of summer, he found several opportunities, and by the time he reported to the application board he was in possession of over two hundred dollars and a fine horse with a Mexican saddle.

Recruiting day was big news in the territory. Many men came out just to see what it was all about. Arvel was especially cheerful, and he was pleased with the turnout. Dick bristled a little at the nonwhites, but knew Arvel too well to protest. He let Arvel deal with them. One was a middle-aged Mexican vaquero. He was once a handsome man but the sun and the hard living and stark terrain had weathered him. He was tall and wore his well-seasoned outfit with pride. He was not so ornately dressed as Chica, but also could not ever be taken for anything but a vaquero. Arvel liked him immediately and signed him up. He smiled at the man as he completed the enlistment papers. "I have a question for you."

The man looked up from his writing. He'd put on brass framed eyeglasses to read his contract and suddenly appeared more like an old grandfather than a Ranger. "Sí?"

"What is the meaning of Pendejo?" Dick looked up at Arvel, confused by the question. The vaquero smiled.

"It literally means pelo púbico, ey, a pubic hair, but it is really an insult word." He wondered at the strange captain's even stranger question.

"An insult term?" Arvel smiled.

"Sí, it means dumb-ass."

Arvel laughed out loud.

One particular man who came to see the recruiting was remarkable in that he was a wholly unpleasant being. He looked unpleasant: greasy, oily. He acted unpleasant. He was just plain unpleasant. He was remarkable in this respect. He dressed properly, but in a garish ditto suit of loud plaid in a mustard brown color, the kind much younger men wore to make a statement. He wore a brown derby a little too big for him. It rested on protruding, hairy ears. The man possessed the singular distinction of not having worked an honest day his entire life.

His family had been in the slave trade. They did not apologize for or rationalize their actions. They knew they were trading in human beings and simply did not care. This was the family legacy. They did things for simply selfish reasons, as they were devoid of any sense of morality. They would wring the profit out of every opportunity and leave nothing behind. During the war, the man was a profiteer and worked both sides. He was also an agent for the English government, and worked that angle as well, in the event that any success on the part of the South would allow a strengthening of England's position and power in the states.

After the war, he worked both sides of the growing labor disputes in the country, often finding himself on the side of the business owners and organized labor at the same time. And despite all the intrigue and his ability to make up the most elaborate and complicated schemes possible, these never amounted to any kind of significant success. He never amassed any kind of fortune. He most always had no money. He had no station, no property, and no real assets, and this was not a good position to be in for a man approaching his seventieth year.

He ultimately found his way to Arizona,

as it seemed one of the last frontiers on which to suck out some matter of wealth. Like a good parasite, he took advantage of the vulnerability caused by the lawlessness of the land. He had been here for two years and, despite the elaborateness of his plans, nothing had, up until now, panned out.

He had attached himself to a new organization, the American Anarchists, and hoped to finagle a way into some real money. He adopted a false zealotry, which got him noticed by a few of the minor officials in the organization. They gave him a stipend to make inroads into the Arizona territory in the hopes that they would be able to obtain an early foothold. The fact that it bordered Mexico and the Central/South America region was encouraging as well. Organized labor had promised to increase interest in their cause and, subsequently, increase their power at the polls, and it helped swell their coffers in the form of membership dues and contributions.

So it was in the best interest of this fellow, and the organization, to keep tabs on the new Rangers. Law and order were not ideal conditions in which such an organization could flourish. In fact, it was the antithesis of the Anarchists' creed. The man with no principles did like the Anarchist concept of

The Propaganda by the Deed, as he was a violent man and hated humanity.

He was cruel and he liked to hurt others, particularly those who were unaware of the danger they might be in, and any person unable to fight back. He was the quintessential bully. He liked to play this concept up, as he thought it would endear him to the leadership of the organization and keep the money flowing to him. It would also make them appreciate that he was quite willing to carry out acts of terror. He had knowledge of dynamite and was expert in its use. Additionally, he was given free rein to carry out robberies and burglaries in the name of the cause, with the understanding that the proceeds, after a hefty commission, would be forwarded on to the organization. After each successful caper, of which there were few, there seemed to be very little money left over. His expenses always exceeded expectations.

He observed the two Ranger captains. He featured himself a great judge of character and had overconfidence in his intellectual and observational skill. He was immediately put off by Arvel Walsh. He thought the man effeminate and priggish. He dismissed his easy-going nature and pleasant demeanor. This one would not be a significant threat or worthy adversary.

He sat and worked on a cigar, blew great clouds of smoke through his remaining yellow teeth. He watched Arvel Walsh laugh and glad-hand the darkies. The man always had a stupid grin on his face. He'd like to shove a blade into his liver and watch that stupid grin fade away. He hated wealthy Yankee carpetbaggers like Walsh.

He thought of his old father and remembered the look on his face. He'd spit on the ground, hissing; *the devil always shits on the biggest pile.* He hated them and taught his son to hate them even more. Men like Walsh, they destroyed the South, and now they were destroying the rest of the country with their do-gooder, miscegenation, their meddlesome ideas about integration and having inferior people do work that was beyond their station and comprehension. But Walsh would not be the problem. He did not worry about him nearly as much as he did the captain's partner.

Dick Welles impressed the man. He looked tough. He looked like most of the lawmen he had encountered. He would be the one to worry about, and the man made a mental note to collect intelligence on him as soon as possible. Every man had an Achilles heel, and he would find the one for Dick Welles.

He sat in the corner and eavesdropped on the clerk taking down the names and as much vital information as possible about all the new Rangers. It amused him that there was such a variety of men being appointed Rangers. He attributed this ridiculous embrace of such a diverse force to Arvel Walsh. He knew that he was a nigger-loving abolitionist. He figured it as another weakness and another opportunity to beat the new Rangers. He figured that Dick Welles, despite his Yankee past, was not, could not, subscribe to such a philosophy. He thought this might well be the wedge that could be used to push them and the organization apart. As he engaged his mind in these fanciful exercises, he saw a peculiar looking man limp into the room.

The young deputy sauntered into the courthouse, following signs to the room where the applications were being accepted. The room was hot, the air still and thick with a billowing cloud of cigarette and cigar smoke. There were many men milling around. The reporter from Tombstone was there. He had attached himself to the Arizona Rangers and was resolved to chronicle their every move. The other applicants stood around talking, sizing each other up, moving off into their preferential groups.

An officious clerk with a pen sat in the corner. He was responsible for recording each new Ranger's information.

Dick and Arvel recognized the young deputy at once, but the young man had gotten into the habit of not looking people in the eye. He would cast his gaze downward and avoid any unnecessary conversation. Dick spoke up first.

"How's the toe, partner?" Arvel looked at Dick with incredulity and then at the young man.

He sneered. "I didn't know you two were the captains." He looked around the room at the new Rangers milling about. There were Indians, Mexicans, Texas cowpunchers, a buffalo soldier, and a lanky man from New York dressed in a sack suit and wearing a derby.

Arvel tried to warm up to the fellow: "So you are interested in joining us?"

"I was. Didn't know there'd be so many darkies." He looked again at the strange collection of men, some of whom had heard him. They stopped what they were doing and looked at the little fellow. The young deputy regretted speaking so loudly.

Arvel began to speak, and Dick cut to the chase. "We don't need you, son." He glared at the young man, who by now was turning red.

"Suits me fine, didn't know this was a nigger-lovin' outfit run by two old women."

"That is a lot of swagger for a gimp in a room full of armed darkies," Arvel said with a smile. "We appoint Rangers based on their character, not the color of their skin or the flash of their outfit, boy."

The young deputy puffed up his chest; he hoped they would not see him shaking. "I won't forget you two. I'll be keepin' my eye out for you, and hope to return your hospitality some day. I'll take my talents elsewhere."

"You do that, son. You go on and do that. There's a fine place down the street needs a spittoon polisher. And if that is above your station, you can go dig the shit out of privies."

The young man wheeled and hobbled away, he looked back and told Dick to go to hell.

Dick sat up in his seat, "I'll go there before you and be waiting for you, you little bastard." The other Rangers looked on, wondering what had gotten the captain riled.

Arvel smiled at him. "Don't be getting on your high horse wearing that star, Mr.

124

Ranger Captain." He poked Dick in the arm.

"Oh, he didn't get at me." Dick smiled and tried to calm himself. "That little whelp should know better than to try to sign up here."

"I still pity him. I shouldn't have shot his toe."

"One day, your kindness'll be your undoing, Arvel."

"I know. I've heard that before."

The young deputy limped into the nearest saloon and began drinking. He tried his luck at the faro table. He was angrier than he had been since he was buffaloed and shot by the two men who had just humiliated him again. He vowed to himself that he'd get back at them some day. He would make a point of it; he'd only have to make certain that their paths crossed again.

He played badly and got drunk. He began running his mouth about the new Arizona Rangers and how they would be dead by winter.

Wade Tully followed him from the courthouse. He had seen the exchange between the young man and the captains and it intrigued him. He took a seat at a table at the end of the saloon. He watched the young man for the better part of two hours. He waited for the deputy to grow weary of losing and waved him to his table and bought him a drink.

The young deputy gazed through bleary eyes at the dirty-looking old man. He always looked dirty, even when clean. He sat with his head tucked into his collar, like a turtle hiding his neck. His flash ditto suit of broad mustard plaid stood out among the patrons like a gaudily painted sign, and he kept his brown derby on even while drinking. He was always too friendly when he first met a mark. The young deputy was definitely a mark. He would likely be of use to the greasy man.

He extended his hand and then retracted it when the young deputy ignored it. "Name's Tully."

The young deputy kept drinking, staring at the bar.

"I heard you mention the new Rangers." He waited for a response. The young man might be too drunk to have this conversation.

After a time he replied: "So what?"

"So, it's just that I wanted to say, well, that you're not necessarily whistling in the wind, if you get my meaning."

The young man looked confused, then

thought on it for a moment. Tully began to think the boy too stupid to consider.

"What do you mean?" He poured again and Tully grabbed his arm, much harder than one would expect. "You might want to stop drinking, lad, until you have heard what I have to say."

He looked at the man's hand around his wrist, then into his face. "What's this about?"

"There are others who are not keen to have another police force meddling in their affairs."

"You're talking to a member of the *police force,* Pop." He pulled his hand away and poured again.

"Hah, in a pig's eye."

The young deputy looked him in the eye again, "You'd better be careful, Pop. I've had about enough needling today. I've killed men for less," he lied.

The old man sat back and put his hands up, "Now, lad, take it easy. I meant no harm. It just seems you are too smart and big for any lawman job, that's all, no harm done."

The young deputy snorted.

"So, do you have a place to stay in Tucson? I have a strange feeling that you might be out of money and looking for a job."

He unsteadily pulled what he had from his pockets. He was quite drunk now, "I have, les' see, I don't know," he handed the bills to the old man. "You count it."

Let's see, ten, fifteen, thirty, forty, eighty . . . you have sixty dollars, chum."

The young deputy belched. And swallowed hard. "Had two hundred."

"Not enough. You come with me. I'll take care of you."

CHAPTER VII:
RANGERING

By late summer they had nineteen privates who had effected forty-three arrests. The newspapers, particularly from Tucson and, of course, the *Tombstone Epitaph* kept up a steady stream of news about the new lawmen. No one quite knew how to take them, this bipartisan, long arm-of-the-law, consisting of both Democrats and Republicans alike.

The majority of the arrests were for theft, and that pleased the cattlemen, but the general populace had something to be pleased about as well as the lawmen apprehended three rapists and seven men involved in a string of stagecoach robberies. It seemed that these new Rangers were not simply a tool of the big money interests.

Arvel and Dick exemplified good lawmen. They chose their men wisely and every one, except one, had lived up to the high standard set from the beginning. The bad one was let go early on, as he was caught stealing from a prisoner. He was a Texan. Arvel teased Dick, as he had chosen the man. "You know what they say, Dick; the fish rots from the head down."

Governor Murphy's office was a most organized administration and provided a constant stream of intelligence for the Ranger captains. Dick spent most of his time riding the rails, constantly spanning the territory, keeping open communication with his men. They became expert at using the telegraph and embraced any new technology available to them.

Arvel was pleased because, once the system was put into place, he, as planned, took a less active role and returned to his ranching life. He split his salary with Dick, who now received an income that assured his family's comfort.

Dick set up an office in Bisbee next to the courthouse. He spent his time there when he wasn't traveling. He was assisted by a young law clerk he hired as his secretary. Dan George became indispensable to the operation. Arvel enjoyed watching his partner sitting uncomfortably at his desk, pen in hand. Dick was more at home in the saddle with a six shooter. He did not like the administrative part of his job. He would look about, confused and agitated. By midday his desk would be heaped up with papers and by morning, Dan George would have it all back in order. All through the day, Dick could be heard, calling out, "Dan, Dan, where is that warrant?" "Dan, Dan, where do I sign this thing?" "Dan, Dan, where is that writ?" And every time, Dan would calmly come to the rescue. Dick was never terse or mean to Dan George.

Arvel liked Dan and was pleased and surprised at Dick's choice, as Dick seldom surrounded himself with anyone but whites. He was one of the finest and most educated young men Arvel had known in the territory. He was a Sioux and had been taken from his family at a young age and raised as a white. They forced him to go to the Indian School where he discovered a love for book learning. He read constantly and he and Arvel would often chat at length about subjects ranging from politics to history, art and literature.

Arvel and Dick had one challenge at this time which helped pull the Rangers together as a cohesive team. The Dunstable brothers had made their way into the territory after robbing a Kansas City bank and killing four people, two employees of the bank and two customers. They had also wounded a deputy who was expected to survive.

These boys were unlike the typical desperadoes who turned up in Arizona. They were Englishmen, both well-educated and well bred. They were evil to the foundation, and had run from England two years earlier when Michael, the younger of the two, had been arrested for the murder and mutilation of a young prostitute in Holywell Street, famous for its merchants who dealt in pornographic materials. Michael was obsessed with pornography and learned the craft of photography to satisfy this proclivity.

James, the older, had a penchant for prostitutes and gambling and had also been in several scrapes with the law. Colonel Eli Dunstable, father of the ne're-do-wells and hero of the Crimea, could not keep them out of trouble and the scandal which inevitably ensued. The young men escaped to America where their crime spree began in the high end gambling houses of New York City.

They were well dressed always and never looked the part of violent criminals. They were intelligent and crafty. They left a trail of dead men wherever they went, as lawmen and citizens alike mistook their foppish manner for a sign of refinement and civility.

They had made off with fourteen thousand dollars of the bank's money, and stopped periodically to steal new mounts and harass or kill whichever unwitting citizen got in their way. Their most recent and, by far, most horrific antic, occurred just twenty miles northeast of Tombstone, practically in Arvel's back yard.

The family of settlers had no reason to fear the two young adventurers from England. They were apparently kind to the children, as the oldest girl in the family, a child of fourteen, wrote of the two dashing gentlemen in her journal. She wrote that one had camera equipment and promised to photograph the entire family the next day. Her journal contained no further entries.

The crime scene was more gruesome than that of the settlers killed earlier in the year by the gang of Mexicans and Indians. It was difficult to fathom that such a blood orgy could be carried out by only two men. Every corpse, man, woman, boy and girl had been defiled. Organs had been removed and flung about the inside of the home. Intestines had been draped along the rafters, loops of gut hanging down like a macabre smokehouse of horrors. The liver and heart of each victim were gone. The oldest girl, who had written in her journal, was nowhere to be found. The trail was nearly a week old, as no one had known of the incident until a neighbor had made his monthly visit to the family. He lived twelve miles away.

Arvel and Dick received information from the bank in Kansas City, and a wire from the British Consulate in Washington. There was a considerable reward for the live capture of the two, and the communiqué stressed that unlimited funds were available to the Ranger captains to ensure the request was carried out. Apparently, Colonel Dunstable knew something of frontier justice, and was exercising all the influence in his power to protect his sons. Arvel requested twenty thousand dollars in funds to be wired to the Rangers' account. The thing was done in twenty four hours. Dick was surprised. "You aren't going to do their bidding?"

"Hell no," Arvel smiled. "But the Rangers sure can do with the extra money." He winked at Dick. "Don't ever turn down funds when they are so willingly waved before our noses, Dick."

They pulled half of their men in on this detail. The best trackers were out in front, and these men directed the scouts, of which there were two, to move forward on the trail based upon their best guesses. They followed this process for three days, and picked up corpses along the way. The Dunstable brothers stole two horses the second day out and killed the prospectors who owned them. These men were gutted, their entrails wrapped around their necks.

They next killed an Indian family, robbing them of their food stocks. They only murdered them. There was no sign of any molestation or mutilation. There was one curious similarity, however, in that the bodies were all posed, lined up next to each other, as if they were having their portraits taken.

The Rangers were on the trail, and it was getting warmer, as they had finally come upon a camp on a high mesa that had been occupied by the Englishmen that day. The murderers and their captive had spent two days here. They apparently had success hunting, as there were remnants of an elk and two deer. The animal carcasses were mutilated, much in the way as the human victims of the homestead. The girl had left her initials scratched in a boulder nearby. She put a ribbon under a rock beneath the scratches. It held a strand of her golden hair.

Arvel and Dick resolved to rest the horses at the murderers' camp, and the Rangers settled in for the night. Arvel took this time to get to know the men a little better and, as he had done in the war, made the rounds to each group. It tickled him how men liked to find their own kind. The men from back East, which included the young New Yorker, stayed in their small group, the Mexicans in theirs, the Texans in theirs.

Arvel overheard one of the Texans comment quietly to his companions that the Captain had once shot a man for molesting a mule.

A buffalo soldier kept away from them all. He worked constantly, not as a servant, but scouted and guarded the camp. He was a man of forty and had been in the army, first as an orderly then as a buffalo soldier since the time he became free in 'sixty fo', as he stated it. He had seen a lot of action, and fought a lot of Indians. He knew violence, but was shocked at the brutality of the Englishmen. He had expected such behavior from Indians, but was always surprised and disgusted when he had seen it from white men.

Some of the soldiers in the army would mutilate victims. One trooper he knew made a canteen from an Indian's uterus. He could never understand why people acted in such a way. He did not have a problem killing an

Indian but even when he saw his fellow troopers mutilated, was never compelled to retaliate by doing the same. He was a devout Christian and prayed a lot. He found himself praying more so while on the trail of these men. He thought for certain that some otherworldly evil had taken hold of them and the sooner they were taken the better off everyone would be.

Dick was running this show, and he informed Arvel of his plan. He knew they would catch up to the two around mid-day next. His thoughts were to go ahead with two of his best marksmen and shoot the horses with buffalo rifles. Once the men were afoot, they would be easy enough to apprehend, and the chances would be better that they would not kill the girl, thinking more likely that they were under attack by bandits.

They rode on for a few hours, Arvel removing his big hat and wiping his brow often. "Only a few more weeks 'til the end of summer."

Dick groaned. "Don't be wishing the summer away." He hated winter, especially the long nights, and Arvel knew this.

He grinned. "Before you know it, it'll be Christmas time. Nice crisp days and even colder nights. My God, it's hot."

"What do you have against a little heat?" Dick looked at his partner. "Where did you get that ridiculous pepper belly hat? You should be cool in that. Hell, half the troop could stand in the shade it makes."

"Got it from a pepper belly. I just hate the heat, Dick, always have."

"And you came to Arizona? For what?"

"The waters." Arvel grinned.

"In the desert?"

"I was misinformed. Can't wait 'til Christmas. Maybe it'll snow."

He thought about Dick's plan a while.

"Do you think our boys might hit the girl, Dick?"

Dick smoked his cigarette and looked up at Arvel. "No. No, I don't, Arvel. The boys are good, and they'll only shoot the horses ridden by the brothers. If they hit either of the men by accident, no real harm done. We'll wait until we get them in the right spot, that area they're heading in opens up onto a big mesa surrounded by hills. We'll get them in a spot where they'll be stuck in the open, then we can move in on them from cover."

"I don't want the girl killed, and I don't want to lose any of the men," Dick nodded in agreement.

They rode on another hour and off in the distance saw two wagons, heavily laden with a large family. They rode up to see where they were headed and what business they had out in the middle of nowhere.

"What do you make of this bunch?" Dick squinted.

"They ain't Mormons."

Arvel stood up in his saddle, removing his big Mexican hat. "Shalom Aleichem."

"Aleichem shalom." The man driving the lead wagon tipped his hat. The woman next to him smiled. Dick looked at Arvel, confused.

"What brings you folks out to the middle of nowhere?"

"I am Ariel Tuckman," he turned on the seat and looked at the people in his party, "this is my family. We are going out to my brother's place, a little west of Bisbee."

They needed two wagons for their belongings and family. There were eight children of various ages, an old woman, an old man, and Ariel's wife, who was driving the first wagon. They wore black suits of European cut. The women wore dark dresses, finely made but modestly styled.

"We are Arizona Rangers and on the trail of some bad fellows. How far is it to your brother's ranch, Mr. Tuckman?"

"We are hoping to arrive by nightfall."

Dick assigned two men to the caravan. He gave them instructions to get the family to their destination, then go on to their normal assignments. There was no point in trying to regroup with the posse as their work would likely be done and they'd waste time trying to find them.

Dick and Arvel watched them ride off. "They are a prolific bunch." Arvel smiled at Dick, "almost as busy as the Irish."

As planned, the first scout came riding back to report that he had seen the brothers; they were just a quarter of a mile ahead. They were coming off the downward slope, onto the mesa that was devoid of cover. They would be in the open and vulnerable, just as Dick had predicted. Better yet, the sun would be at the marksmen's backs, and the murderers would likely not be able to see from where they were being attacked.

Dick moved the riflemen up in a hurry. In no time, two shots were fired, and the rest of the group moved up to watch the bad men scurry about, looking for cover. They pulled the girl from her horse and crouched in a huddle. One of the Rangers dispatched her horse with a shot to the head. Arvel's job came next, as he refused to let any of the Rangers go. He tied a white flag to the muzzle of his Henry rifle and rode slowly toward the men. He got to within fifty yards and announced his intentions.

The younger brother called out, "Sod off, you Yankee bastards, we'll never be taken alive." He grabbed the girl by the neck and pointed his six shooter at her head.

Arvel dipped his flag, and the miscreant's head came apart. The other brother jumped into the air exclaiming, *"Bloody hell."* He put his hands up, "I surrender, I surrender!"

Arvel covered him with his rifle until he was surrounded by the Rangers. The young girl stood by her dead horse. She looked vacantly at the dead man who had been the source of her torture the past days. The youngest and most handsome Texan approached her. She was shaking, despite the heat. He handed her a canteen and she drank. He put his hand out to her and she pulled away. He looked too much like her tormentors.

The buffalo soldier came forward. He had comforted young women in this state many times. He spoke to her soothingly. He smiled and offered her a hard candy. She briefly looked him in the eye and then stared blankly at the sweets in his hand. He slowly opened up a bandanna he kept in his pocket, asking her if he could cover her head to shade it from the sun. She eventually let him help her. He led her away from the corpses and began telling her that he'd be taking her to her relations in Tombstone. She could not speak and only nodded. She walked away, looking back as Arvel addressed the remaining killer.

Arvel rode up to the man. He had had enough. The past several days of witnessing the butchery carried out by this pair had stretched him to the limit. Seeing the girl in this state nearly pushed him beyond. She was about the same age as his daughter would be, had his child lived. Arvel glared at the surviving murderer, "Which one are you?"

"Figure it out yourself, ya bloody tosser."

Arvel cantered Sally over to him, nearly bowling him over. He jumped to the ground and walked up on the man, stopping inches from his face. The man scowled down at Arvel with contempt. He was half a head taller. Arvel put his hand on the grip of his revolver, then decided better of it and backhanded the murderer, knocking him to the ground.

"You struck me!" He held his face then checked his hand for blood.

Dick pulled him to his feet by his collar. "This one's James. Come on, you. Getting your face slapped is the least of your worries."

The young man became more defiant as he watched the Rangers go through his belongings. One Ranger found a collection of photos. The brothers had been chronicling their escapades. The gruesome photos were nearly too much for the grizzled lawmen. The outlaw demanded to contact his father and be taken to the nearest town, where his lawyer would be summoned. He sneered at the men as they discovered one clue after another to the two men's depravity. They each had a journal and Dick Welles began reading passages from it aloud.

"Very impressive, the bugger can read." The young man laughed nervously, simultaneously looking menacingly at the Rangers. "None of this is mine. It all belonged to him." He pointed to the corpse nearby. "My brother made me do these things. I had nothing to do with it. He was always making me do things that I did not want to do. But I never harmed anyone. That was all him. I warn you that my lawyer will know how I've been treated, *and* the British consulate, so you'd better take care."

He became more agitated as the men milled about, ignoring him. Arvel stood near him, looked at him and smiled. "Nope, don't see one for miles."

"One what?" The man was irritated, especially with Arvel.

"A tree. Can't have a proper hanging without a tree, mate."

"Oh," he laughed. "Bleedin' dime novels. And, don't call me *mate.*" He laughed more nervously. "I've read of your so-called frontier justice. You'll not mistreat me. You're just trying to scare me. Well, I am *not* bloody-well scared. You are officers, not vigilantes. You can't touch me. You're obliged to follow the due course of law. You've got to bring me in. You've no proof I killed anyone. There's no call for this. You can't hang me for any of the things I've done."

"We aren't hanging you for what you have done, *mate.*" Dick spoke as he pulled a piggin string from his saddle. "We're snuffin' you out so that you can't do anything to anyone ever again. Some people just need killin', *mate,* and you sure are one of them."

Dick called to Arvel, pointing off to a distant spot. "That outcrop'll work, Arvel."

"Looks good to me." He smiled at the killer. "Guess we *can* have a hanging, after all. Come along, lad, we're gonna show you how to have at least an improper hangin' without a tree."

The Rangers mounted up. They made James walk ahead of them to the ledge of rocks a distance away. Arvel rode up beside the man and looked down at him. "This is what's called the final walk . . . like it?"

Dick sent half of the detail off to Tombstone to escort the victim to relatives she had waiting there. The others gathered up the evidence.

The Englishman continued his protest. When that did not work he threatened, then begged, then began to whine. Arvel looked at him and sneered. "Did all your victims beg like this?"

"Yes . . . *no.* I didn't do anything wrong. I didn't have any bleedin' victims. You've got the wrong man. I *swear.*" He began to cry. Arvel glared at him. "Shut up, *mate*! You had some high times and now you must pay. And pay you will, so shut up and take it."

They got him to the top of the outcropping and looked below. It dropped abruptly several hundred feet.

"Sorry, *mate,* we can't drop you hard enough to break your neck. Looks like you'll just hang a little while 'til you strangle." Arvel got his rope and tied a proper noose. He put the other end around Sally's saddle horn. He paid the rope out until it was taut and they bound the man's hands behind him.

"Stranglin' to death. That's gotta be the hardest way to go." Arvel shook his head from side to side as he walked back from Sally to the condemned man.

Dick put his hand on Arvel's arm. "Arvel."

"Yes, *what is it?*" He was irritated now, and resolved to send this boy to his doom. He was in no mood for interruptions. He looked up at Dick, impatiently.

"Should we offer him a hood?"

"Do you want your head covered, lad?"

The man shook his head. "No . . . yes!"

Arvel stormed over to Donny's rack, untied a potato sack and emptied the contents; his dirty laundry. He walked back to the man and put the sack over his head. He prepared to replace the noose.

"Stop, stop! Take it off, take it off, *please*! I can't breathe."

"That's the general idea." Arvel continued his task as Dick intervened.

"Come on, Arvel, let's take it off him." He got between the two men, removing the shroud.

"Blimey, that smells like a Mexican's bum!" He lifted his face toward the sky, breathing deeply.

The Rangers suddenly laughed. The young

146

Englishman laughed. He looked at Arvel, then Dick. "Come on gents. Why don't we stop all this and take me to town?" He smiled at them.

"No deal, son. You are hanging. Now." Arvel put the noose back around his neck.

Dick spoke up. "Do you have anything to say?"

"Yes, I do." He stopped smiling now. He was red-faced and angry. "You are all bastards, you Americans, and I wish I had more time to kill more of you." His mouth was dry and he had difficulty forming his words. "Bury me facing down, so that the world can kiss my bloody arse."

Arvel turned the man to face the precipice. "Who said anything about burying you, you bastard? You will be wolf shit by sun up tomorrow, and the animals'll pick your bones dry." He kicked the man to oblivion. Sally put her head down, the rope spun around the saddle horn, then whipped free. The young man dropped another two hundred feet. He screamed like a baby all the way down, bouncing three times before coming to rest. Arvel peered over the precipice and looked down at the remains. "Ay, chingao!"

They looked at each other a few moments, and Dick finally spoke: "I thought you were going to tie it off."

"I thought you were." They peered over the deep drop and looked at each other, shrugged, and mounted up.

They rode in silence for a while. Dick continued to look through the collection of photos. He had not seen violence such as this, even in the war. "This would have made good evidence, Arvel."

"Give them to me. I know what to do with them."

Dick handed them over to Arvel, then thought for a moment. "That boy bounced like a rubber ball. I have never seen a body bounce like that."

"That he did."

The report he sent to the governor was brief and subsequently passed on through the proper channels. Arvel reported burying both men, as there was a chance Colonel Dunstable would want to collect the bodies. Of course, it was difficult to tell exactly where they had been, and nearly impossible to offer direction to the location of the corpses. By some unknown method, some of the more terrible photos had made it to the editor of the *Tombstone Epitaph,* and the details of the young men's terror soon became international news. The rest of the photos were neatly packed and mailed to Colonel Dunstable. It is said that he was found with a single gunshot wound to the head shortly thereafter; the charred remains of a photograph collection found in the fireplace of his study.

The Rangers were heroes, thanks to the newspapers, both Republican and Democrat. Nothing further was said about the villains being taken alive after the newspapers accounts and the few photos leaked by Arvel. The men were becoming a legend in a very short time. There was a constant flow of glowing articles about them; some of the stories were, shockingly, embellished.

They did not have long to rest on their laurels. A messenger arrived from Hennessy, reporting that he was missing fifty head of cattle. They were tracked by one of his men, moving south, toward the border.

Nice indeed, Arvel thought, *going from avengers to errand boys, running down some scrawny Mexican rustlers.* Hennessy likely lost fifty head in the course of doing business, but, as the annoying Irishman said: "The kind of brigands who steal are the same kind who will kill and butcher." Arvel contacted Dick Welles, and they were off, living rough again.

Down Mexico Way

Dick chose Texan and Mexican Rangers for this adventure. He told Arvel that it took a Mexican to catch a Mexican. Arvel had no idea what this meant.

"Thank goodness Esquimaux didn't steal those cattle." He grinned at Dick who did not get the joke. He smiled at Dan, nodded to him and said: "Good thing Indians didn't do the rustling, Dan, or your ass would be in the saddle."

Dan blew on a tin cup of coffee, standing in the doorway to the Ranger office. "No sir, I was hired as your secretary; the only thing I ride is my desk chair, Arvel." He would no sooner ride into the wilds looking for cattle thieves than toil in a mine.

Dan never stood on formality, and Arvel especially liked this about him. He stretched, and looked on at the men preparing to ride out. "You boys have a nice adventure. I think I'll wander down and have a nice steak for lunch, then come back to the office and lie down for a while. I'll be keeping an eye on the telegraph wire, so you feel free to let me know how the investigation's progressing."

Arvel smiled, and looked over at Dick, who by now was preoccupied with some minor detail. He tipped his hat to Dan. "You are the smartest one of the bunch, Dan."

They made it out of town and already it was hot. Arvel wiped his brow.

"Well, this is a fine mess. I haven't slept in my comfortable bed now more than ten days in thirty." He patted Sally on the neck. "I'm too old for this rough living. I should be back with Dan, resting."

Dick looked at Arvel's mules. "You've got enough junk on Donny to live well, as far as I can see." And this was true. Arvel loaded Donny with many comforts, particularly an abundance of water. He did not like to run low on clean water.

Arvel looked back at Donny. "There's no feather bed and there's no bathtub."

They made it to Hennessy's ranch and purposely avoided the man. They picked up the trail and began following it. Arvel had some fun with his partner.

"Well, you see there." He pointed to some inconsequential spot on the ground. "We have four riders. One is a heavy man riding a thoroughbred. Those two," he pointed left, "are scrawny fellows, not much bigger than you. And the last fellow is likely half Indian."

One of the better trackers overheard him and looked puzzled for a moment. He scratched his head and rode on.

They followed the trail all that day and camped near some good water well before sunset. They were in no hurry. Arvel's heart was not in it. He was not fond of Hennessy and felt that a man like him, who had plenty, could ignore a little light thievery. Arvel did not fully understand the cattle business; he was used to making his money on mules.

The men rested comfortably around the fire. They were well provisioned and one of the Mexicans had killed a deer. Arvel handed out his fancy pre-twisted cigarettes. Some of the men examined them, gave them a good sniff and saved them for later. They rolled their own. They lounged on their saddles and blew smoke at the canopy of stars overhead. This rough living wasn't so bad.

"This camping reminds me of a story I heard about Kit Carson. Any of you boys ever hear about the time Kit was captured by Indians?" Arvel lounged back and waited for a reply.

Dick responded. He'd heard Arvel's Kit Carson story at least a half dozen times, "Which Indians?"

"I don't know, it doesn't matter." Arvel tried to continue.

"Was it during the first Navajo campaign or the second?"

"That doesn't matter."

"Well, it does." Dick was having some fun with him now.

"Do you want to hear the story or not?"

"Yes, please. It would just be nice to know when it happened, and with what Indians."

"Well, Kit Carson got captured, and the old chief granted him three requests before burning him at the stake."

"Which chief?"

"Dick?"

"Yes, Arvel?"

"Shut up."

"Sorry, Arvel, proceed, please."

The men were paying attention now. They liked to hear about the Old West heroes.

"So, Kit Carson says he needs to parlay with his horse, and the old chief allows it. Carson whispers in the horse's ear and the stallion runs off. In short order, he reappears with a beautiful young sportin' gal in the saddle. Carson takes the beauty into the woods and does his duty. The chief is pleased with Carson's first request and grants the next. Once again . . ."

"You mean he fornicated with that

woman?" Dick asked with rapt attention.

"Yes, Dick, he fornicated. So, the Chief grants another request, and Carson whispers in the horse's ear again. The horse runs off."

"What happened to the woman?" asked Dick.

"I don't know. She just stayed in the woods, Dick."

"This must have been the Southern Plains campaign. There are stands of woods up there. Don't know of any woods down in Navajo country."

"I'm sure of it, Dick. You are right. So, the horse comes back a second time, this time with a beautiful little Mexican girl. And once again, Carson takes her in the woods and does his duty."

"My God," said Dick. "He had stamina."

"Yes, well we are talking about Kit Carson. He's now down to his third request, and again, he speaks into his horse's ear. And, in short order . . ."

"Another whore?" One of the Rangers spoke up now.

"Yep. Another whore. And you know what Carson does?"

"Fornicates with her?"

"Nope. He looks his horse in the eye and yells, *'I said posse!'* "

Arvel sat back, satisfied at his little story. He waited for the men to react. One began to snicker, then another, and soon they were all laughing. Dick sat back and took another drink from the bottle being passed around. "You are too much, Arvel."

Arvel took the bottle and had a drink. He raised it to the men and drank. "True story. All true." He laid back on his bedroll and yawned. "I wish we had some prairie chicken." He picked his teeth with a knife.

"Really?"

He looked around at the other men. "Any of you boys have a shotgun?" Several reported that they did. "Anybody have any birdshot shells?" One man did.

"See if you can kill us a few chickens tomorrow, will you?"

Dick rolled his eyes. "Maybe one of the men can catch a goat and make some cheese for you, Arvel. Would that please you?"

"That would be nice." He pulled a blanket up to his neck. "Anybody have any wine or a bottle or two of beer?" No one responded.

"You are too much, Arvel."

Next morning, Arvel was up and shaving. Dick chuckled at him. "Going to church?"

"There is no reason to look like a savage just because we have to live like one."

"You are wasting water with that silliness."

Arvel looked on at the stream flowing freely below. He continued shaving. "All through the war we used to have some pretty tough times, but I always kept my coiffure in check." He looked into a little mirror. "I find it has a calming effect on the men."

"Well, too bad you don't have a fresh shirt and tie to put on; the bandits won't know whether to shoot at you or kiss you." Arvel got up, put his mirror away, and pulled a fresh shirt out of a saddle bag tied to Donny's rack. He rummaged around and found a cravat. He rummaged some more and found a bottle of toilet water, splashed some on his face and offered it to Dick, who took a drink of it.

"Hey, hey, not so much. We need to save some for Hennessy."

They were catching up to the thieves, and Arvel and Dick lagged behind. The Rangers were closing in on the rustlers.

"When we get back, you report to Hennessy. I can't stand that man. He's a bore. He'll probably want to be compensated because his stupid cattle have lost weight. *By Jasus and begorrah, me cattle have lost two stone . . .*"

"The dollar is dear to him, that's certain." Dick understood not having money. "It's easy to be carefree about money when you've plenty of it." Arvel smiled. He appreciated the little barb. "You're right about that, Dick, and your point's well taken. I've never wanted for money, but somewhere a balance must be struck. He probably sends all his fortune to the Fenians."

"He's Church of England."

"You're kidding me." He laughed. "Goddamned Irishman."

Dick misinterpreted Arvel's comment and got a little annoyed with him. "I was with those *Goddamned Irishmen* at Antietam, Fredericksburg, Chancellorsville and Gettysburg. I have no quarrel with the Irish."

"No, I don't either, Dick." He held up his hands in surrender. "I have known my share of them. They are a fine race of people. Prolific breeders. I knew an Irishman who had seventeen children. And hearty. They all survived into adulthood."

They caught up with the rustlers just beyond the border. Dick did not want to go on, as he did not feel that such a small herd of cattle was worth an altercation with Mexico, and they had no authority there. Arvel was not so concerned with such details. As far as he could see, there was no good delineation of the border and he wanted to satisfy Hennessy. They had completed all the hard work of tracking the herd and he was convinced that they should finish the job. Even though he did not like the man, he still wanted to do him service and maintain him as an ally.

The thieves were a sorry lot and they surrendered without a fight. Most of them were unarmed. They wore peon clothes with ragged straw sombreros. They huddled together as if awaiting execution. Some prayed, some just stood there, looking at the ground. They were so hungry that they had already killed one animal and eaten a good part of it.

Dick had the Rangers pull out three of the scrawniest cattle and sent the rest back north, toward Hennessy. He told a Mexican Ranger to tell the rustlers to get moving, that if they were ever seen in Arizona again, they'd be hanged.

Arvel had the Ranger ask the men if they worked for Del Toro. They responded that they did not. Del Toro was a rich and powerful man. He did not need to steal a few cattle. They were on their own. Bandits had attacked their village, leaving them with almost nothing to eat. Del Toro hated the bandits but could do little to stop them. The men were desperate.

Riding back, Arvel could not help ribbing

his partner. "You are much kinder than I ever gave you credit for."

Dick ignored him.

"Those boys'll eat good for a while, at least. How are you going to explain to the Irishman that he is shy four head?"

Dick shrugged. "Anything can happen on the trail, Arvel. Hell, the rustlers could've been rustled."

"Sounds like old Del Toro is in need of some Arizona Rangers himself."

Dick wiped his forehead with the brim of his hat. "Let's civilize one land at a time, Mr. Capitan of Rangers."

CHAPTER VIII:
ANARCHY

The young deputy followed the man to a place on a side street in the shadowy section of Tucson. They entered what looked like a laundry. He remembered walking past several Chinese working on all sorts of clothes. It smelled of bleach and starch, the air thick and hot and damp.

He was led into a back room where a tall Chinese woman called Madam Lee was sitting at a large oak desk, counting money. She looked up at the two white men. She had been beautiful forty years ago. Like the man in the mustard suit, she had come from a long line of slave traders. Madam Lee was sent to America many years ago to handle the steady stream of young Chinese girls sold by their families to feed the insatiable appetite of the outlaw west. She was better educated, more intelligent, and more ruthless than the old man. She tolerated him because he made her money.

160

She was a kind of idol to the old man and he could not help but find her alluring; he was seduced by her coldness and cruelty and was impressed with his own open-mindedness. The reality, to his thinking, was that she was an inferior member of the Mongoloid race yet he could not help having his mind wander over the fantasy of bedding this Amazonian paragon of evil.

The young man remembered the two talking. He was beginning to doze, to fall asleep on his feet. Someone led him into another room and two young Chinese women began to remove his clothing. They put him in a tub of warm water and the room began to spin. They bathed him for what seemed like hours, and he remembered lying on a low couch, wearing a robe. They gave him a queer pipe and he drew on it regularly. He had never felt better in his life.

The young deputy spent the better part of two weeks in the laundry. He never moved far from the bed, and he took the pipe often. Finally, some days later, the man in the mustard suit showed up. He pulled the young deputy up, out of his stupor. The man was diminutive and old, but tough and wiry.

Tully called out rudely to the young deputy. "Wake up, you sot." He slapped him several times across the face. The young deputy could not understand his own complacency at this outrage, but he only wanted to sleep and smoke and dream. The man was angry and he said something to Madam Lee, who in turn spoke something to the girls, who dumped cold water on the reclining deputy. He sputtered and sat up, his head was swimming, and the room was moving about him. He was going to vomit.

"Get up, you. Time to start working."

"I need a pipe."

"You'll get your reward when you've earned it." Tully grabbed the young deputy by the hair and pulled him to his feet. "This is the way it is going to be, lad. Get used to it."

"Take it easy, take it easy." He grabbed the man's hand, then thought better of it. He stood, looking sideways. "What do you want from me?"

"You'll find out soon enough."

There was a new man now. A German. He wore old fashioned clothes from Europe, though he was much younger than the man in the mustard suit. He looked the young deputy over, then turned to the tormentor. The deputy was seized with stomach cramps. He vomited on the German's shoes. The man in the mustard suit cursed him and backhanded him, knocking him back onto the bed. The German grunted and wiped his shoes on the deputy's hair.

"He does not seem of much use."

"He'll be okay. What news do you have from our brothers up north?"

"Nothing." The German was watching the deputy, checking his ability to comprehend.

"What do you mean, nothing?" The old man measured his response and checked his anger. He must be careful with the German.

"I mean nothing, as I said. When the time comes, we will take action. The Chicago group will be contacting us with instructions."

"The Chicago group be hanged. The Arizona Anarchists don't need them."

The German looked over his glasses, then around the room. "It would be wise not to mention our organization so freely." He spoke with a cold, emotionless precision. "I do not believe this one will be much good to us." He finished cleaning his shoes on the deputy's pillow.

"You've nothing to worry about here. They're all one step ahead of the law as it is. Madam Lee can be trusted, and she runs this place with an iron fist."

■ ■ ■ ■

Ging Wa cleaned the deputy, then his bed. She was fourteen when she was sold to Madam Lee. She had come to Arizona four years ago. She was a servant, as she suffered from eczema too badly to be used as a sporting girl, the cowboys and gamblers finding her skin condition too off-putting and possibly catching. So, for the first time in her life, Ging Wa's condition was a blessing. She learned quickly to never look up and to comply always with her tormentors. The way to survive the torment of a sadist is to never give them what they want; to resist only feeds their appetite. To never resist will result in being left alone. She had survived this way.

The young deputy watched the girl work. She had a lovely face, though he hated Chinese and thought the women had the bodies of little boys. He snapped at her when the red patches on her skin were exposed. "Cover yourself." He kicked the girl as she leaned over to straighten his bed, she fell backward. Another lesson she learned was to never cower, never utter a sound. Yelping or crying out only encouraged the tormentor.

He spent more time with Ging Wa than with anyone else during his confinement at the laundry. He took out his frustrations on her and, despite his best attempts to hurt and humiliate her, could seem to get no response from her one way or another. This infuriated him at first and he tried beating the girl until she cried out, but Madam Lee would have none of that. Any abuses meted out would be by Madam Lee, not some second rate thumper.

Sometimes, he would pretend to be asleep and watch the girl as she went about her chores. When she thought no one could hear her, she hummed and quietly sang songs in her native tongue. He saw her smiling when she did this. He wondered how anyone could be so pleasant in such a world. He himself felt despondent most of the time. He did not regard the girl on the same level as a white. Surely she lacked the intelligence of a white, but her resilience intrigued him.

One day he spoke to her. She did not respond but kept working diligently at her task. Another rule she followed was to never let anyone know you could understand them. "I know you speak English, girl. I heard someone talking to you in English and you knew what they were saying."

She mumbled, "I understand."

"What is that singing you do?"

"No, nothing." She rushed her work, trying to get out of his room.

"It is something. What is it?"

"It is a song I learned as a girl, at home."

"Well, it sounds stupid. Don't do it anymore." He rolled onto his side and faced the wall.

Later he watched her. She made no sound, yet her lips were moving. She was singing her song.

CHAPTER IX:
ASHTORETH

Ariel Tuckman was waiting for them at Dick's office in Bisbee. He was pacing about the office when the Rangers walked in. Dan George had informed them that Tuckman had been waiting for two days. He had come calling four times each day since then. Arvel shook the man's hand and beckoned for him to sit down. "How're you settling in to your new home, Mr. Tuckman?"

"Well enough, Captain Walsh, but we are having a particular crisis at the moment." He handed Arvel a page from a newspaper. It read:

Freak of Sixteen-Year-Old Girl in Arizona Territory.
Published in The Daily Nugget News, Arizona Territory — [Special] — Ashtoreth Tuckman, 16 years old, was captured at Strowbridge Saturday night after an exciting chase. She is the victim of dime novels

and says she wants to be a cowboy. Her father says Ashtoreth declared her intention to become a cowboy while en route to Arizona. Two or three times she has arisen at night, saddled a pony and with provisions, camping outfit and pistols, started for the mountains. She was, however, each time brought back by neighbors.

Saturday Ashtoreth started out again, first going to her father's barn with two pistols. She remained there several hours and when discovered fired a shot, scattering her pursuers. A parson ventured into the barn, hoping to quiet the girl but she thrust a pistol into his face and he retired. Ashtoreth soon ran out of the barn and made for the river. The crowd started after her. At length a constable fired two shots over her head which startled her and she sprang into some bushes, which stopped her progress and she was captured.

Arvel read with interest. He tried not to laugh, as Tuckman was visibly shaken by this turn of events. "How can I help, Mr. Tuckman?"

"She has done it again, Captain Walsh." He stood up and began pacing again. "Look at this, Captain Walsh. Look at it." He hit the article with the back of his hand. "This is most shameful to our family. The girl has been called a freak! A freak, Captain Walsh. It will not do."

"I understand." He offered Tuckman a cigarette and they smoked together. "When did she go?"

"Three days ago. Understandably, the constable and the parson and the rest of the neighbors have grown tired of these antics. It is not wise for Jews to become so notorious in the community, Captain Walsh, if you get my meaning."

"Understood." Arvel thought for a moment. "Perhaps your daughter needs an adventure that's not so romantic as what's found in the novels."

"I cannot just leave her in the wild, sir."

"Agreed, that'll never do. It's far too rough and dangerous for a girl of sixteen, particularly one who has not grown up in the land." He looked over at Dan and smiled. The secretary was busy at work, oblivious to the conversation.

"Where do you suppose she headed, Mr. Tuckman?"

"She continues to return to the same place in the mountains, west of our homestead. There is an abandoned mining operation there. Some of the dwellings still afford shelter. I am hoping she is still there, but when I tried to track her, I lost the trail. My wife urged me to come to look you up, as you and Captain Welles were so kind to us."

He urged Tuckman to go back to his hotel and promised he would go with him later that afternoon. He assured him that he would have his daughter back by the end of the day, and was certain she would stay home, once there.

Tuckman shook his hand. "Please, tell me your fee, Captain, and we will gladly pay it."

"You don't worry about that, just get some rest and be ready when we come to fetch you."

Arvel got clean clothes from Donny's rack and washed up in one of the vacant holding cells. He walked to the doorway to Dan's room. Dan was a careful fellow with money and had made a deal with Dick that he could set up living quarters in the office. He lived here and thus avoided paying rent. It was a small room with a desk and single bed.

Dan stood in front of the mirror and washbasin when Arvel knocked on the door. "Big plans, Dan?"

"Going to the Opera House. They're doing excerpts from *The Mikado.* Opening night. There's a sweet lass from New York there and I intend to meet her."

Arvel wandered around the man's room. He looked at the books stacked by his bed. Dan was working on *Lectures on the Early History of Institutions,* and beneath that, *Village-Communities in the East and West.* These sat precariously on a half dozen books on philosophy. The room was not decorated in any way. Everything was business, selected only for its utility.

"When you going to do some man's work and give up this damned lawyering nonsense, Dan?" He began paging through a thick textbook.

"Hah, what do you know of man's work, Arvel?"

"Breaking mules isn't?" He grinned at the back of Dan's head.

"Shit, everyone knows Uncle Bob does all the work on your ranch, Arvel. You're just there to take up space." He spoke to Arvel's reflection in the mirror. "What's on your mind, Arvel?" He could tell that the Captain was up to something. He knew Arvel too well.

"Just wondering why a man of such learning," he picked up one of the weightier tomes, "would be interested in that tripe. Rebecca dragged me off to see that in New

York back in eighty-five. Can't believe they're still playing it."

"Well, you haven't seen the principal singer or you wouldn't wonder." Dan wiped the shaving soap from his neck. He looked at his reflection, first left, then right. He was a handsome man.

"Well, I kind of need some help." Arvel waited.

Dan turned and faced him, draping his towel over a bar on his washstand.

"What kind of help?" Dan did nothing free. He knew that Arvel knew this. He would begin negotiating now.

"That fellow, Tuckman. He's got a real problem on his hands. I was just thinking, if we could give that girl a real adventure . . ."

"What kind of adventure?"

"Well, something that would kind of get her thinking that being at home on the farm is not such a bad place to be."

"You mean to scare her?" Dan smelled under the sleeves of a shirt, then pulled it over his head. He picked out a cravat. He was dressing for the theatre. "Like to help you out, Arvel, but, like I said, I've got plans."

"Not even for twenty dollars?" Arvel knew that with Dan, you started low.

"Hah." He smiled at Arvel as he got into

his best striped trousers. He pulled the braces over his shoulders. "That's funny, Arvel." He began sniffing his waist coats, looking doubtfully at the first two, then settling on the third.

"Well, what would be considered *not funny,* Dan?"

"One-fifty." He began buttoning his watch chain into his vest, then wound his watch. Arvel watched him and laughed out loud.

"What's so funny?"

Arvel waved his hand. "Nothing, sorry. Just had a funny thought. Nice watch. How about fifty?"

"How about one-fifty?"

"How about one-twenty and I'll buy you dinner?"

"What do I have to do, Arvel?" Dan was pleased with making nearly a month's pay in one evening. The little Mikado singer could keep for one day. "Nothing dangerous."

"Nope, just a little theater." He picked up one of Dan's books, *Blackstone on Law as Theatre.* "It'll surely be a cinch for a fellow like you."

"I don't like that look on your face, Arvel. I've seen that look before and it usually means some kind of foolishness. What do I have to do?"

Arvel put up his hand. "Now, now, Dan. I am paying you top wages. No questions." Arvel was not certain what he was going to do, as he was making this up as he went along. "I'll be back in an hour. You might want to change out of that pretty outfit and save it for Yum-Yum."

They collected Tuckman and rode on through the afternoon, arriving at the brothers' ranch by early evening. Mrs. Tuckman came out to greet them. She shook Arvel's hand and held it tightly, giving it a squeeze.

"I told Ariel you would come. Thank you, Captain Walsh."

"It is our duty and pleasure, Mrs. Tuckman." Remaining in the saddle, he introduced her to Dan. They continued to the old mining camp. They stopped a mile out and Arvel handed Dan an overstuffed carpet bag. Dan opened it and looked into the bag.

"You are kidding me, Arvel."

Arvel laughed. "Come on, Dan, it's for the welfare of the girl. And you agreed. As a good lawyer, I expect you to honor your contract."

"You owe me, partner. You owe me." Dan dismounted and began to change.

"There's paint in a couple of tins in there, too."

"For what?"

"Well, your face, of course."

In short order, Dan was in full Sioux regalia. He wore a buckskin beaded shirt, a headdress and breastplate. He looked up at Arvel. "Can I just wear my trousers?"

"Sure, that'll be fine. You look . . ."

"Like an idiot. Where did you get all this junk?"

"No, no, you look very authentic. And I got it from the Bisbee Opera House. And, my friend, I put in a good word about you to Yum-Yum." Dan brightened and then thought of how Arvel could possibly make matters worse for him.

"What did you do, Arvel?"

"Oh, not much." He pulled an envelope out of his vest pocket and handed it to Dan. "Here is a box-seat ticket for tomorrow's show, and a note to get you backstage at the end of the performance. You make certain to clean up nice, Dan. I built you up pretty good."

Dan was pleased but would not show it to Arvel. He thought he might be able to extract more out of this deal. "What am I to do with the paint?"

"Well, I don't know. How did your ancestors wear it?"

"I have no idea, Arvel. They all starved to

death on a reservation. I never saw or wore any of this."

By now Tuckman understood Arvel's plan. He got off his horse and took the paint. He placed lines on each side of Dan's face like he had seen on the cover of one of his daughter's dime novels. He finished and stood back, admiring his work.

"Well?" He looked at Arvel.

"Perfect, Mr. Tuckman. Are there any Indian Jews?"

"I don't know."

"Can we please get on with this? I feel like an ass."

"Not so fast." Arvel removed the saddle from Dan's horse and motioned for Tuckman to proceed with the paint. He painted a circle around the horse's right eye, then put a red hand print on the horse's rump. Arvel tied a feather to the mane, just below the animal's right ear.

"Damn it, now the horse looks the fool. This paint better come off, Arvel, or you will be finding me another mount."

"I'm almost certain it will come off, Dan. No worries!"

"Almost certain?"

"Well, pretty certain. At least I know it'll eventually wear off." Arvel thought for a moment. "No, it will wash off. I'm sure."

He wet a finger and rubbed a spot where Tuckman had just finished applying a red design. He looked back at the horse and then at his hand. He shrugged.

Arvel and Ariel got onto their saddles. Dan jumped up onto his horse's back. He complained the entire way about riding bareback. "Didn't you learn *anything* about being an Indian?"

Dan mimicked Arvel's voice: *"Didn't you learn anything about being an Indian . . .* Didn't you learn anything about sailing a ship when your ancestors came over on the Mayflower?"

Arvel laughed. "Mr. Tuckman, does your daughter know Latin?"

"No, she does not, Captain." He looked on, confused at the question.

"Good." He winked at Dan. "Very good."

They came into view of one of the more complete shacks at the abandoned mine. Smoke poured from the chimney. It was coming on dusk. Dan peeled off and rode south. Arvel and Tuckman dismounted and hobbled the horses. Arvel advised Tuckman to take up a position on a high rock, overlooking the shack. He then took out his Henry rifle and tied a white flag to the end of the barrel, and called out to the girl.

"Miss Tuckman?"

The door of the shack opened slightly. "What do you want?"

"I am a Captain of the Arizona Rangers. I have been sent by your parents."

"Go back, Captain. I have no intention of going with you. Please do not make me shoot, Captain. I am a capable shot."

"I am not here to make you go back."

"You aren't?"

Tuckman grabbed Arvel's arm. He whispered, "What are you doing?"

Arvel pulled away, "It is okay, Mr. Tuckman. Just let me play this out."

He turned his attention back to the girl, "No. I just need to talk to you. About an Indian chief in these parts. Have you seen him yet?"

"I have seen no Indians, Captain." She spoke haltingly.

"Okay, that's good. May I come up and have a parlay, Miss Tuckman? I have some important information about this Indian. You are on his burial ground. It is very important I warn you."

She was silent for several moments. Then he heard her call out. "Okay."

"I am coming up unarmed, Miss Tuckman. I need you to come out the same way."

"This better not be a trick."

Arvel smiled at Ariel Tuckman. "She's a

clever girl."

He snorted. "Lokh in kop."

"I'll take that as an insult." He called out to the shed. "No tricks." He handed Tuckman his Henry rifle. "I'm coming out now. Please meet me halfway."

The girl slowly emerged. She had put together a rather impressive cowboy outfit. She had dutifully removed her gun belt and carried no shooting irons.

Arvel approached her slowly. He held his hands in the air. He beckoned her to sit on the remnants of a trough. He sat across from her. He removed a packet of cigarettes and offered her one. She nearly refused, then thought better of it. A female cowboy should smoke, and it was time she did.

He lit the cigarette and looked off in the distance. She thought certain she heard cursing in Yiddish. She inhaled the smoke and began coughing. "Okay?" Arvel leaned forward, ready to offer assistance.

"I am fine, thank you. Just not used to this brand. I prefer a different kind of tobacco." She looked off again. "My father did not accompany you, did he?"

"No, no. I am alone. I was contacted by your father to find out if there was anything he had to do, legally, to cut the ties." Arvel smoked pensively, looking about a little

179

nervously. He pulled a flask from his pocket and took a drink. He wiped the rim and handed it to the girl. She hesitated again, then took the vessel and threw her head back. The strong drink burned her throat and she thought that she might vomit.

Suddenly, Arvel jumped up, pulling his Navy Colt. He looked around suspiciously. "Did you hear that?"

"No! Hear what?" The girl looked about nervously.

Arvel sat down. "Okay, then." He took another drink and smoked some more.

"What ties, Captain?"

"What?" Arvel was distracted. He continued to peer into the shadows which darkened as evening turned into nightfall. A strange animal sound could be heard off in the distance. Not quite a coyote, more like a human imitating the sound of a creature from the wild.

Arvel held up his hand, commanding the girl to be quiet. "He's coming."

"Who?"

"Shh!"

"What is it, Captain?" The girl's eyes widened.

Arvel froze; he turned his ear toward the sound. "It's him!" he whispered. "Dear sweet Jesus, it is him! Don't move." He pulled his revolver out of the holster again. He lunged forward, stood up and emptied the gun into the night. He dropped the hammer a couple more times on empty chambers. Then peered off into the darkness.

Suddenly, behind him appeared the great warrior. The girl screamed, "There he is."

"Where?" Arvel looked everywhere but behind him.

"There, there!"

The Indian chief jumped from his horse and pounced on Arvel, knocking the empty revolver from his hand. He held a big knife to Arvel's throat and spoke in hushed tones: "Who dares to trespass on my land?"

The girl fell backward onto her back and began crab-walking toward the shed, away from the wild Indian. The Indian commanded her to stop.

Arvel cried out. "Miss Tuckman, stop! For God's sake, don't move another inch."

The girl froze and began to cry. Panic washed over her.

The Indian picked Arvel up off the ground and sat him next to the girl.

He raised his head and screamed into the night in a tongue the young girl could not understand. "Arvel Walsh, Vos es a stolidus ass."

Arvel worked hard at suppressing a laugh. The girl grabbed Arvel, a death grip on his shirt. She tried to get inside his skin. "What did he say?"

"He said we are trespassing on his ancient burial grounds and we must pay."

Dan began to enjoy the drama. He started dancing in circles, crying out to the heavens.

She whispered, eyes fixed on the chief, "I thought this belonged to the mining company." Arvel looked at the girl for a moment, then back at the wild savage.

"It did, but they had to abandon it." He thought hard about what to say next. "This chief killed all the workers."

Dan called out again, in Latin, "Who is this girl who boldly tramples the bones of my ancestors?" He pointed the big knife at her.

"He wants to know who you are."

"Tell, tell him, that I am a woman cowboy and am just passing through. I will be gone tomorrow."

Arvel relayed the message. The Indian became furious. He kicked dirt about the ground and screamed more loudly into the night. "You will owe me one hundred dollars extra for this performance, Arvel Walsh!"

"How does he know your name?"

Arvel began to shrug then thought better of it. His mind was racing to come up with an answer. "He, he knows all the whites of this territory. He is not only a chief but a shaman. He has magical powers.

The Indian looked up into the heavens. "Magical powers to drain your bank account."

Arvel suppressed a laugh. "That's for certain."

"What? What did he say?"

Arvel looked at the girl. He wanted to end the performance before it was too dark, and before Dan thought of any other forms of compensation.

"He requires a blood sacrifice."

"No!"

"I am afraid so. He says that the people living down below, the ones with the queer dark clothes and strange religious rituals, must die."

"That's my family, Captain!" Tears welled up in her eyes and Arvel wondered if he was not overdoing it. "That can't be, Captain. Tell him I am sorry. Tell him to kill me, but please leave my family alone." She began sobbing.

Dan stopped and looked down at the girl. The sound came to him automatically: "Awe."

Arvel glared at him. Dan coughed and sputtered. "Awe, eeh ah. Some blood must be spilled."

Arvel stood up, then got down on one knee before the Indian chief. He begged for mercy. He offered his own life in place of the family.

"Arvel Walsh, I would gladly kill you now for making me do this ridiculous thing, but I would never get my money."

Arvel looked, hope in his eyes. "He said he will do a blood ritual, but you will have to lose a little blood in order for it to be accepted." He looked at the girl with pity, "But at least no one has to die."

She looked up, rubbing the tears from her eyes ineffectively. "I'll do it, I'll do whatever he wants, just tell him please do not hurt my family."

Arvel gesticulated and babbled to the Indian. The Indian nodded. He grabbed the girl by the arm, then turned her head away. Arvel grabbed her dramatically. He grabbed a lead ball from his cap pouch. "Bite down on this and hold onto my arm! Squeeze it as hard as you like and try not to cry out too loudly when the cutting starts."

She closed her eyes and sobbed, offering up her arm, which she was convinced would soon be severed at the elbow. Arvel pulled out his penknife and pricked the girl's thumb. She made no sound.

The Indian whooped a war cry and danced around them three times. As suddenly as he appeared, he was gone. The girl collapsed, exhausted. Arvel grabbed her hand and bandaged it to the wrist. He pierced his hand and applied a liberal amount of his own blood to the bandage. He helped her up.

"Miss Tuckman?" She had fainted momentarily. "Miss Tuckman?"

"Ye . . . yes?"

"It's over. He's gone. You have saved your family, Miss Tuckman."

"He is? He really is gone?" She looked around.

Off in the distance she could hear a cry in a tongue she could not comprehend, "Arvel Walsh, this paint better come off or you will owe me five hundred dollars!"

"What did he say?"

"He said, Arvel Walsh, take the fair maiden back to her family and tell her that she now is the spiritual light of her clan. She must protect and guide them for the rest of her days."

"He did?"

"This is powerful medicine, Miss Tuckman. The shaman chief has put a curse on you."

"Oh, my God!" She began to panic.

"No, no, this is a good curse. I guess really a blessing. Not a curse. That's right, it's a blessing."

"He called me a maiden?"

"He did. A fair maiden. And his curse blessing cannot be undone."

She stood up, wiping the tears away. She stopped crying. She hugged Arvel. "You saved my life."

"No, *you* saved your family's life, Miss Tuckman. You should be very proud, but we should leave this unholy ground right away."

"Yes, yes. I'll get my things."

Ariel Tuckman had ridden quickly back toward home, then turned and waited a mile out for his daughter to return.

She galloped toward him. "Father, Father! I . . . we saw an Indian chief. He made me do a sacrifice. I am sorry, Father, I will never leave home again. I cannot!"

Arvel slowed and watched them together. He saw Mr. Tuckman hold up his hands, clenched into a fist, signifying victory. His eyes were wet. Arvel tipped his hat and turned Sally, heading back toward town and Dan. He met the Indian a few miles down the trail. Dan tossed the carpet bag at Arvel and pulled up next to him.

"That was some performance for an Indian who knows nothing about Indians."

"I read it in a dime novel."

"How's the law study going?"

"Fine, but it's a fool's errand. One must be twenty-one and white to practice law, Arvel. I can meet the first, but not the second requirement." They rode along and smoked.

"That doesn't seem right, Dan. They did everything they could to make you a white man then they won't let you do the same things that a white man does?"

"It is the way of the world, Arvel. It is just the way of the world."

Arvel thought on this and Tuckman's comment about keeping out of the public eye when one is a Jew. It was a cruel world.

"That poor girl. I felt terrible for her when we scared her so badly," said Dan.

"I thought you were going to give us away with your 'awe'."

"I know. I just felt bad for the child. Those dime novels are something. Isn't it strange how we are trying our best to be like the folks back East, with taming the land, setting up law and order, civilizing and modernizing our towns, and the folks back East want to escape to the Wild West."

Arvel thought about that for a while. "You are correct, Chief. I guess we always yearn for what we don't have."

He looked over at Dan and smiled. "You should've seen Tuckman's face. He was very happy to have his girl back. We did good, Dan. She will likely have a story to tell for the rest of her life, and she won't be tempted to wander off on any fool adventures. Hell, maybe if you had been around when I was seventeen, I'd *be somebody* back in Maryland instead of running around this God-forsaken land." He laughed.

"Maybe you would be a Senator by now." Dan knew Arvel's disdain for politics.

"Or a free, white and twenty-one lawyer. God help me."

CHAPTER X:
ALEJANDRO DEL TORO

The old cattle thief had been run out of Texas by the Rangers and moved his operation to Arizona and New Mexico many years ago. He had never considered himself a thief, as most of the original stock from the cattle ranches up north had once been owned by Mexicans or had at least ranged wild on Mexican soil. The Americans had been sneaking into Mexico for years, taking the largely unguarded cattle and moving them up north to feed the insatiable appetite of the Americanos back East. Alejandro Del Toro simply did the same thing, except in reverse.

He was a tough old hombre, and it was rumored that he carried eleven bullets in various parts of his body, most of them in his lower back and buttocks, as he was good at outrunning posses. If you pushed hard on the region of his Adam's apple, you could feel the stone point of an Apache's arrow. They say he killed twenty one white men. No one bothered to keep count of Indians.

He was not an ignorant man. He could read and write fluently in Spanish and English. He liked to read English novels and collected Chinese fans. He had a Koi pond in the desert.

His letter read:

Honorable Captain Walsh:
I would be pleased to entertain you at my hacienda and am honored by your request. I, too, have grown tired of the lawlessness of our great nations and look forward to your arrival with enthusiasm.
Your humble servant,
A. Del Toro

Arvel and Uncle Bob sat smoking on the veranda as the sun set. Uncle Bob wanted to talk.

"Wonder what ever happened to that little Mexican gal?" He didn't wait for a reply. "Do you have everything you need for the trip? You sure you don't want me to go along? You think that mule is an appropriate present for that old scoundrel? I don't know that you should be giving him anything, you think . . ."

"I'm fine, Uncle. I'll be just fine, it's best if I go alone. I know the area, it's not far. Del Toro will likely have me shadowed when I cross the border." His thoughts had drifted to Chica. He had been wondering about her, too.

"I'd like you to take my new Winchester."

"That would leave you without it."

"Hell, son, we have a cabinet full of guns. You know that." He checked himself. He was anxious about this journey and didn't want to take it out on his nephew. He sat quietly for a while. "Wonder what happened to that Mexican girl?"

The trip south was uneventful. Sally led, followed by Donny and the new mule that was to be a gift to Del Toro. He had named the mare mule Dina. She was carrying provisions, as was Donny. He would travel comfortably. The trip was just over ninety miles and he decided to take his time and complete the journey in three days. It was good to be out with his mules, alone. He had time to think and enjoy the starkness of the countryside. He thought more clearly when he was riding, and he liked to ride to a destination instead of just for pleasure. It gave him some direction. He loved Mexico, even the wild lands, and there was no recent news about rogue Indians or bandits in the area. The weather was pleasant enough and he thought he would try some hunting on the way. It would be nice to eat deer or javelina rather than the salt pork Pilar had packed for him.

The trip was important as he and Dick worked out their plan to placate the ranchers while simultaneously achieving Arvel's goal of not wasting the Rangers on a lot of work just to serve the territory's business interests. He did not want to give up a Ranger's life to protect a steer.

Del Toro was just as vexed by the problem as were the Arizona ranchers. Small bands of rustlers were hitting everyone, and it was beginning to take its toll. Del Toro had not needed to break the law for some years now, as he had a thriving operation, breeding a good stock of healthy and fat beef cattle on his own. His lands were measured in miles rather than hectares. He had a staff of fifty vaqueros, and they were an industrious bunch. He was a father figure to them and he'd just lost a half dozen of them to a band of particularly ruthless bandits, comprised of Texas cowboys, Mexican vaqueros and a half dozen rogue Apaches. He wanted the bloodshed to end.

This was the kind of alliance Arvel hoped

to form. If he could get a commitment from Del Toro, and use his money and men to fight the cattle thieves, he could focus his Rangers' efforts on serving the burgeoning population of settlers, such as the ones who had lost their lives earlier in the year.

Near late afternoon he had settled on Javelina for dinner, as the deer would not cooperate, and he'd killed a young sow. While he was dressing it, Sally warned him of company, as she brayed and stiffened, her ears laid back in alarm. Arvel slowly looked up from his work to see a lanky Negro man watching him from a rock above.

"G-day."

"Hello." Arvel went back to his work. The man was queer looking. He had blue eyes and reddish hair. He stood with a straight back, and he gave Arvel a curious look.

"Care for some pig?"

"No, thank you, they give me the wind colic something fierce. I have some chicken and rattler stew going at camp, if you'd care to join me."

The man's camp was in a low valley against a steep hillside. There was a cave and deeper into it was a spring. The man more or less lived there. They ate silently. Arvel finally spoke.

"You are evidently from another land, sir."

The Aborigine worked on the campfire. He did not look up as he spoke. "I am from Australia." He sat back when he was satisfied with his work. "Came out here in fifty-nine."

"You are a long way from home." Arvel remembered reading about the place as a young man. It had always fascinated him and now he was meeting one of its people. He imagined this fellow dressed in the native garb he had seen in the photographs those many years ago. He wondered if the man had ever hunted with a spear.

The man went on to tell him that he'd been sent to Arizona by an entrepreneur who had a notion that camels would be the future for Arizona. That he was promised a great fortune in the camel trade, and that the gold would be an added bonus. Most of the camels died coming across, and the ones that survived proved no better than horses or mules and were sold off to various circuses and traveling shows as curiosities. He ended up drifting about the desert and was currently making his livelihood killing wolves for the government. The Indians and Mexicans never bothered him, as he never had anything worth stealing except for his mule, and they seemed put off by his strange features, which he attributed to a Dutch father and Aborigine mother. The natives never saw a red-haired blue-eyed Negro before.

He admired Arvel's mule and proudly talked of his own. Arvel replied that the Aborigine's mule was a hinny.

The Aborigine was intrigued by this. "How can you tell?"

"You can't, actually. Well, sometimes a hinny looks more horse-like, but I know this mule. I bred him. He's one of mine. Where'd you get him?"

The Aborigine was amused. "I got him the last time I turned in my bounty, up in Tucson. He's a fine beast, and I am pleased to meet you. You have a great gift, sir."

Arvel went on to tell him that the mule was four years old and originally sold to the Army. He was pleased to see the animal in such good shape and to have gone to such a worthy master.

They sat back and smoked. The stars were in full splendor and it was bright and cool.

"I'm glad we had the good fortune of our paths crossing, sir."

The Aborigine agreed. They chatted into the night. The Aborigine told him of his home in Australia, how the two lands were similar and also how they differed. He seemed without regret or remorse for leaving and was happy to be the only one of his kind in this land. He liked to be alone in the desert with his work and his mule; a true vagabond and hermit.

The conversation turned to Arvel's favorite subject, mules, and he told the Aborigine about the time that he'd seen President Lincoln when he was in the army, and that it had tickled him to see the president more concerned for the welfare of the mules than for the men. This was before Arvel had learned to love the creatures so much, but the experience had a considerable impact on him.

The Aborigine, Arvel learned, was named Billy Livingston. The man had never seen a mule until he came to Arizona and always thought them to be curious creatures; far superior to the camel, to his mind. His own mule had been responsible for saving his life at least three times, as far as he could remember, and likely more often when the man had fallen asleep while riding.

"That is the truth," Arvel said. "You can run a horse off a cliff and they'll go happily to their deaths, but that will never happen on a mule."

Arvel pulled a bottle of whiskey from his pack and took a long drink. He handed it to his companion. Billy Livingston drank from the bottle, then pulled out a couple of cups and poured some for each of them. Arvel drank, and emptied the bottle's contents equally in each cup. They drank until it was gone.

They smoked in silence for a while, and Arvel's thoughts had wandered to Chica. Before he could check himself, he was asking Billy Livingston if he knew her.

Billy Livingston pulled out an ancient clay jug and pulled the cork on it, handing it to Arvel after taking a swallow. Arvel liked the odd tasting liquid. "What is this?"

"Don't know. I traded a Mexican for it. He says it's made from spit."

"Seriously?" Arvel swallowed hard to keep the drink down. Then drank more. "Well, I'll be."

Billy drank again, wiping his mouth. "I don't think it's made of spit. That's Chicha and is more like a beer, it doesn't keep. You have to go far south for it."

He sat back and began rolling another cigarette. Arvel handed him a packet of pre-made ones from back East. Billy lit one and looked at the curious paper cylinder filled with tobacco and grunted in appreciation.

"Only know the girl by stories," he said between draws on his cigarette. "I have heard of a wild young Indian girl in these parts, not Mexican. She dresses in men's clothing and has two silver six shooters. She's a dangerous creature. They say she's killed a hundred men. She beds her victims, like a black widow spider, then cuts their throats. That's what I've heard. She carried one bloke's head in a bag, tied to her saddle. At least, that's what I've heard. I have never seen her." He flicked the end of his cigarette into the fire.

"Probably not all true."

Arvel flicked his cigarette into the fire and lay back on his saddle. He dozed while dreaming of heads rolling about the desert floor. The spit drink, on top of the whiskey, was strong and induced him to dream fitfully. At one point he watched shadows dancing against the fire. He saw Billy Livingston stripped naked, walking about and then gyrating in an odd fashion. He was carrying a long spear and he danced on one foot. Arvel didn't know if this was real or imagined. At some point during the night, Billy Livingston stood over him, holding an ember. He spoke in a tongue Arvel had never heard. He finally spoke some words in English, "You will suffer, Arvel Walsh, for your kindness."

Arvel heard himself mutter with great difficulty, as the spit drink made his tongue work poorly, "I have heard that before."

Chica appeared and took the torch from Billy Livingston. She held it for a moment, then dropped it at her feet. She spit on it and the flames leapt up around her, as if a jug of coal oil had been thrown on the fire. She opened the palm of her hand on which sat a black widow spider the size of her fist and she blew on it, launching it at him.

She laughed and was suddenly a serpent. She licked the air with her forked tongue, dropped to her belly and slid away toward the moon. White molting scorpions rode on her back. She turned back into her human form and was sitting on her pony; her Conchos reflected silver in the moonlight. She wore Rebecca's white dress. She rode away.

Billy Livingston applied symbols to Arvel's face with yellow paint. The paint was cool and the Aborigine's fingers tickled. He said some more words and Arvel fell into a deep sleep.

Arvel awoke the next morning. It was well daylight. He was alone except for the empty jug and his mules. On a scrap of brown paper was a cryptic handwritten note with *'Thanks for the smokes, mate, stay as long as you like.'* Billy Livingston was gone.

He did not see another person for the remainder of the journey. He thought about Chica more than he cared to and more than he had thought he ever would. His Quaker mother and Presbyterian deacon father would not know what to make of the spitting, cursing, vulgar Chica.

His mother taught him tolerance. She was an abolitionist and believed that all people must be respected, regardless of the color of their skin or the cut of their clothes. She had taught Arvel to be kind. Arvel had broken her heart twice and he always regretted it. The first time was when he ran off to war; the second when he ran off to Arizona. She, in an absurd gesture, being a pacifist, bought him his guns. She told him to use them wisely and to never take a life without reason. It was likely why he never replaced them, even when they had become obsolete.

His father was proud of his war record but thought the move to Arizona ridiculous. He believed that Rebecca's uncle was a lunatic and would lead to Arvel's ruin. It is unfathomable what he would think of Chica, which amused Arvel all the more. He rode on, trying to imagine his father's face — the grimace — or would it be revulsion? Perhaps horror, or a combination of all three if he would ever meet the girl face to face.

So he rode on the last leg of the journey pondering these things. The dream was the most remarkable thing that he had experienced in a long time, and he wondered if *any* of it had been real. The dancing by Billy Livingston seemed very real, but how could it be? What did Billy know about him? Did he say those things to him? Did he paint his face? How could he be dressed in native garb and carry a spear? He felt for any remnants of paint but discerned nothing. What did Chica's presence mean, if anything? He decided that he would never drink strange spirits from jugs again.

He arrived just after noon, and was told by some peons which road to take to get to Del Toro's. He rode another half hour and could see the ranch a mile ahead. It was a low, sprawling affair. With its adobe walls and tile roof, it rivaled the finest houses around Tucson. No one met him, no guards were present. Arvel thought it certain he would have been stopped and escorted the rest of the way. He stowed his guns to present the least threat. He had his badge in a saddle purse. He never wore it.

Alejandro Del Toro towered over all he

could see on the porch wrapped around the front of his hacienda. He wore a black sack suit with a red brocade vest of Chinese silk and a beaver felt sombrero. He smiled at Arvel and welcomed him to his home.

Arvel smiled back, then looked beyond the man to the figure sitting at the far end of the porch. "Hello, Colonel."

Del Toro looked around. He smiled back at Arvel. "So you know my niece, Capitan Walsh?"

"Please, call me Arvel," then added, under his breath, *"or Pendejo."*

The old Mexican walked out to greet him, took his hand and held it for a long time. His eyes went to the three mules.

"Ay, what fine animals, Capitan."

"The one at the back is for you, Señor."

Del Toro walked back and held his hand to the mule's muzzle. "She is a fine beast. Gracias."

They sat on the veranda for most of the afternoon, sipping mescal and drinking beer. Chica said nothing to Arvel, but sat back, out of his view and, at the least opportune times, ran her bare foot up his leg to see just how annoying she could be to the Captain. She was impressed with his ability to hide his consternation.

Del Toro's ranch was a showpiece, set at

the southeast corner of the foot of a mountain range. There were mountain springs which Del Toro used to create fountains and, more importantly, power. Each room had a grand ceiling fan, moving the air and making the adobe walled rooms cool and comfortable. The hacienda was actually made up of four buildings, joined at each corner. They formed a square, and in the middle of the square was a courtyard; a large fountain was its centerpiece. The long over-hanging roofs and open airways kept the courtyard cool and inviting.

He was eventually shown to a spacious room in the hacienda, and unpacked his carpet bag. It was as fine as the Continental Hotel in Philadelphia, where he and Rebecca spent time on their honeymoon.

Chica slid into the room, staying in the late day shadows as they advanced against the adobe walls. Arvel did not acknowledge her, but kept unpacking. He spoke into his bag, "You'd better not be in here, Colonel." He put some clothes into a wardrobe. "*Uncle* might not like it."

She laughed. She wore a sheer cotton dress off her shoulders and had collected more bangles since the last time he saw her. She grabbed him by the shoulders and spun him around, pushing him off balance and onto the bed. She straddled his hips, and kissed him hard on the mouth. "I am glad you are here, Pendejo."

"Stop that, Chica. You'll get me killed."

"You are afraid of Del Toro?" She began to laugh and caught herself. "That is good, Pendejo, you better be afraid of Uncle Alejandro."

"What are you doing here, anyway?"

With effort, he managed to push her off of him. She had a strong grip for such a small woman. She wandered around the room. She put his hat on and began pulling at his clothes.

"And where is my watch and money clip?" She kissed him again.

"Hurry, Pendejo, you will be late for dinner." He ignored her. He had several hours until dinner. The cool breeze of the fan overhead and mescal and beer made him drowsy. He planned to make good use of Del Toro's fine feather bed.

"Pendejo, are you not glad to see me?"

"I am, Chica." And he was, more than had could ever imagine.

"You never act very glad to see me."

"I am good at hiding my enthusiasm."

"Are you not jealous, Pendejo, that I share a bed with the Mexican jefe?"

"No."

She acted hurt. "Why not?"

"I don't own you, Chica."

"You are strange, Pendejo."

"I've heard that before."

"I've missed you, Pendejo."

"Really?"

"Yes."

"I doubt that. But, I have missed you, too, Chica."

"Really, Pendejo? I like to know that." She smiled. "You never are afraid to look at me, Pendejo. Gringos never look at me."

"Oh, they look at you, Chica. They most definitely look at you, but not so that you know it, and not for too long. To look at you, Chica, is like gazing at the sun. It's not possible to do so without doing permanent harm."

He ushered her out of his room and went to sleep.

Del Toro spoke slowly and carefully. He spoke English well and it impressed Arvel that he did not care to be impressive. He knew that he was successful and he knew that he was a Mexicano. He did not see this as a handicap. He never tried to act like a gringo.

They dined on roast pig, bull and chicken, lounging on the terrace overlooking the valley below. The sunset changed the earthen colored walls, first to a warm auburn, then purple. Servants lit Japanese lanterns. The lights danced and cast shadows on the walls. Arvel was overcome with a sense of calm.

Del Toro spoke plainly of the fact that he could not tolerate the bandits in his land, or for that matter in el Norte. He was proud of what he had achieved and had no apologies for his past. He was proud to say that he never stole from a poor person, or took food out of a baby's mouth. He never killed a man who did not deserve it, and he had never killed a woman or child.

His was a chivalrous kind of banditry. The cattle from which he built his empire really did not belong to anyone, just as the wild horses or elk or deer roaming the desert never actually belonged to anyone. They were there for the taking. Sometimes they had been taken from the wild by aspiring cattlemen first, but simply putting a brand on them did not make them automatically off limits, to his mind. You had to possess them once you branded them and, if you had been too greedy or ambitious and branded too many to watch, then you would have to suffer the consequences. Del Toro learned to watch many many head of steer.

"So, my friend, Capitan," he leaned forward and put his hand on Arvel's shoulder. He liked to touch and be close to his friends. "Your Rangers will be like the boys from Texas, and we will run the bandits off the land of Arizona, no?"

"That is our intention, Señor Del Toro."

"Please, it is Alejandro or, if you do not mind my little joke, Jefe."

"Absolutely, Jefe."

"You know that we are not good here in Mexico at fighting the bandits. We do not have a good force, such as the Texas Rangers and, now, the Arizona Rangers. I would like to offer what assistance I can, but it will be limited. What I can offer to you is the cooperation of my neighbor ranchers, and the eyes and ears of the peons who live on my lands. They do not like the bandits. Our region is wealthy enough, with opportunity enough to keep the young men from choosing the bandit life."

"And that is all we can ask, Jefe."

He paused, trying to find the right way to say what he felt. "I am an old man, Capitan. I was ambitious as a young man, and I wanted to be rich and powerful and, in some part, I have done these things. It is a great, how do you say, motivator, when you have little to eat and see the suffering of your friends and family. I did work hard for my fortune and now I will soon die. I am more interested these days in making life better for my people."

"Noblesse oblige."

"Qué?"

"Something I was reminded of not long ago, Jefe. Those who have privilege and wealth bear the responsibility to help those in need."

"Sí! Sí, Capitan. Thees is exactly what is in my heart."

They talked into the night, mostly of cattle and mules and bulls, as Del Toro was an aficionado of bulls and bull fighting. His dream was to someday visit Spain and see the great bullfights. He talked of the toreadors and how he had tried a little bullfighting on his own but, he grabbed his belly and said that he was too fat to get close enough to the bull. He began to grow tired and finally suggested they retire, as he had much to show Arvel the next day.

Arvel retired to his room. His bed had been freshly made and lamps had been lit throughout the room. They had prepared a big metal tub for him. The water was tepid. Del Toro was an excellent host. He soaked in the tub until midnight, smoking a cigar left on a small table and finished off the last of a bottle of wine he and Jefe had been working on after dinner.

He wondered at how nicely Chica could fit into the tub with him and it gave him some ideas. He thought about creeping about the compound looking for her. He thought better of it and went to bed.

Chica finally arrived, just as he was fully asleep. He did not mind one bit. She was gone when he awoke momentarily at three. She was like a ghost, silently wandering in and out of his life. He slept soundly to the gentle rhythm of the big fan overhead. Such sophistication compared to his humble ranch . . . and the Americanos featured themselves superior.

He awoke at sunrise to the crow of a cock that had wandered into his room pecking at centipedes and spiders. Del Toro let them roam as natural pest control. He slept well and wondered what happened to Chica. She was a busy girl. He wondered if she was with Del Toro and experienced a fleeting twinge of regret. The girl was getting to him, despite his attempts at nonchalance.

He shaved and got dressed. He wandered out to admire Del Toro's gardens and fountains. Great clay pots abounded with hibiscus, richly colored flowers adorned their branches. An elderly housekeeper beckoned him to the veranda. She had no

English but Arvel understood her all the same. She had laid a table with fresh bread, tomatoes and goat cheese. He relaxed while waiting for his host to rise.

He wished Rebecca could share this with him. She loved the desert and would have enjoyed Del Toro's place. He had not thought of her for a long time, and oddly, now that Chica had come into his life, he thought more and more of his dead wife. He missed her and his little girl. He had done a good job of forcing them to the back of his mind, filling his life with the mundane tasks of running the ranch and managing the mules. It seemed that the more leisure time he had, the more time for contemplation he had and this engendered a melancholy that was not necessarily bad, but often overwhelming.

At that moment, he felt an overpowering desire to see the girl, punctuated by a sense of doom, and wondered how much longer he'd have to wait for her.

The entire idea was preposterous, of course. Notwithstanding the difference in age, the fact that she was beyond crude, ignorant and seemingly either incapable of or completely unwilling to learn any sort of manners or propriety. It was as if he had fallen in love with some otherworldly creature; to have a love affair with a muse. What could she ever want with him?

As difficult as it was for him to admit it, he was old enough to be her father. Admittedly, he had kept himself well enough, and he wasn't a bad looking fellow, also he was quite handy between the sheets.

He thought about that a bit. Of all the people in the world, his mother was the one who opened his eyes in that arena. Just before his wedding, his mother gave him a copy of Martin Luther's writings on marriage. This was no small thing at the time.

She never spoke of it, but she taught him to reject the Victorian notion that sex was relegated strictly for the act of procreation, and that it was not just to satisfy the desires of men. It was a great lesson, and one that Rebecca always appreciated. It seemed Chica was benefitting as well. Despite this, it was certain a beauty such as Chica would have many much younger men at her disposal and he found it vexing that she would give him any consideration at all.

And then there was the fact that she constantly left him without saying good-bye — not knowing where she went, with whom she kept company, and when she would return. Could he tame her? If he did, would she cease to hold such an allure for him?

Would he destroy in her what made her so exciting and appealing? It was like living out a tragic play, and he feared that he could not withstand any more heartache or pain. Could he simply let this play unfold? Forget about judging her, controlling her, making her comply with his sense of comfort or propriety? Could he not just let go and enjoy her for what she was, live in the moment and let her come into his life, bring joy into his life on her terms and let her go off until the next time?

If only he could be left to his mules.

They rode together at a leisurely pace, Arvel on Sally and Del Toro on a giant roan stallion. The animal had to be big to handle Del Toro's weight, but the horse was so tall that Arvel had to look up whenever he spoke to the Jefe. He understood that the old bandit did this for a reason. He was wearing riding attire today, consisting of striped wool trousers, tucked into his boots, a brightly colored cotton shirt, and a short vest. He wore the sombrero he had on when he greeted Arvel the previous day. His saddle and gun belt and holster were nearly as fancy as Chica's. He was evidently fond of silver.

They headed south, across the big mesa

that held Del Toro's hacienda, to a steep decline, down to another large flat area. It was here that he had his cattle operations. He stopped at the edge and looked down. He pointed for Arvel. "Over there, Capitan, is where we get the cattle on the train."

Arvel squinted to see the rail line off in the distance. In front of it, men worked on horseback, looking like an army of ants preparing for winter. He estimated that two thousand head of cattle roamed below.

"It is astounding, Jefe."

The old man smiled. "Let's go down and see the men, shall we, Capitan?" They made it to a branding fire where several of the hands were gathered. They did not look like the rustlers he and Dick ran down for Hennessy. These men were well-to-do cowpunchers. They were older than what one would normally see up north. These men were cowboys for life. They had excellent horses and their outfits were similar to that of Del Toro's. Arvel always liked the way the Mexicans and Indians dressed. They were not timid about bright colors and patterns.

Arvel's eyes wandered to the railroad siding. Jefe responded: "We were able to lay tracks west, to the sea. From there we ship the cattle all over. It is more efficient and safer that way, and cattle do not lose so much weight."

My God, Arvel thought, if only Hennessy could see this operation. He could hear him now, "By Jasus and begorrah, how much did the track cost per foot, Mr. Del Toro?"

They were back by midday and had dinner. Chica did not show when he and Del Toro had returned from the ride through the estate. Neither he nor Del Toro had spoken once of his *niece*. Del Toro acted as if she did not exist other than in the form of one of his inanimate fixtures, as if she was nothing more than a beautiful fountain or flowering bush, something to add to the scenery.

Jefe continued to put plate after plate of food before Arvel who overindulged and wanted desperately to sleep. He finally forced himself away from the table.

He packed and waited for Chica to interrupt him. She did not come into his room.

Once he was packed and on Sally, Arvel thanked the Jefe for his hospitality. The old fellow handed him a package wrapped like a Christmas present. He looked strange; the big, tough bandit in a vaquero outfit, holding a present in his hands, like an overgrown child.

"A little token, Señor Capitan."

Arvel smiled and took it, laid it on his saddle horn and carefully opened it. It was a big Mexican daga, with an ivory inlayed handle decorated with silver. The sheath was leather, tipped in silver, all matched the engraved pattern. It was a fine piece of work and reminded him again of Chica's.

"It is fine, Jefe." He pulled the knife out of its sheath and admired it. He wondered how much teasing he would get from Dick Welles when he wore this on his old, beat up belt with the GAR buckle he had had since the war.

He tucked the knife in his waistband and headed north. He looked back and Del Toro was waving, smiling as if he had known Arvel for years instead of two days. As he rode off, he did not see Chica appear next to the Jefe out of the shadows. He was annoyed again that she did not show up or see him off.

Despite this, he left Del Toro heartened by an alliance that would help him and Dick Welles achieve their ultimate goal of taming the territory and the Mexican border along its boundaries. He liked and trusted the man.

He rode steadily the rest of the day; Sally was happy and fit, Donny plodding along behind them. His mind wandered, pondering what was happening to his nice, normal, ordered life; how and why things became so complicated in just a few months.

After Rebecca and Kate's deaths, he successfully shut off his emotions and happily plodded along, like Donny, drifting through his existence without much effort or care. Now he was having a strange affair with an unpredictable señorita, and he was a captain of Rangers, making alliances with Jefe, the cattle baron. It was all simply ridiculous.

His musings were interrupted periodically by a feeling that he was being shadowed, and every now and again he would see a bright flash off to his southeast. Whoever it was stayed a good quarter of a mile away.

Something metallic, worn by the rider, gave him away in the late-day sun. Arvel kept counsel of this stranger and was careful not to be obvious about measuring the rider's progress.

That night, Arvel slept fitfully between Sally and Donny and relied on his trusted mules to raise the alarm in the event of danger. He could not understand the rider's behavior, as he continued to shadow him the next day until late afternoon.

Arvel lost contact when he made camp. He decided to eat a cold supper of Del

Toro's goat cheese and bull jerky. He chose not to even smoke and wished for the company of the strange Aborigine man. At least he would not be alone.

The rider continued to shadow him the next day. Arvel picked up the pace and hoped to be in Tombstone by dusk. He did not enjoy this return ride nearly as much as the trip down.

The rider shadowing him shook his confidence and the thoughts of his dead wife and daughter threw him into a state of melancholy. Chica failing to see him off probably had the most to do with his mood, and he continuously chastised himself for having such thoughts about the girl. He was convinced it would lead to his ruination.

He also secretly hated the idea of her being with Del Toro, or any other man, for that matter. He felt like a hypocrite. He felt that he had been with her, no strings attached, and it would only seem natural that she bedded down with others. He was convinced that he meant nothing to her. He was just some *funny* gringo, who happened to strike her fancy at the moment. He was likely one of dozens.

He became angrier at the thought. He thought about the fat Mexican Jefe on top of her, grunting and sweating like a big bloated hog and he suddenly wanted to shoot the man through the head with his Henry rifle. God, he hated feeling this way. Why did she affect him so?

So distracted was he that he failed to sense Sally's hesitation. He continued to urge her through a narrow path between two boulders by tapping her sides with his spur. He knew this would open up to a plateau, which would help reveal the rider shadowing him more clearly. He was anxious to get through.

As he turned a corner, he surprised several Apache bandits and was equally surprised by them. He had not unpacked his six shooter and his Henry rifle was tied down. Before he could react, a rifle shot exploded, just inches away; he suddenly found himself on the ground, hot blood covering his face. He regained his senses and realized that Sally was down, a bullet through her neck.

Donny broke and ran off. Several shots were fired at him but went wide. Arvel lay next to his favorite mule and held her, speaking softly into her ear, oblivious to the danger all around him. Her eyes were wild with fear and confusion; her great, lovely ears moved about, trying to comprehend what was happening. She breathed in deeply, and brayed weakly. She was dead.

Everything went black.

Arvel woke, his hands and feet bound. He was propped against a rock. Blood had dried his eyes shut. Only with great difficulty could he open them to see what hellish situation he was in. There were seven of them, all outlaw Apaches. They were drunk and gathered around some form which Arvel eventually determined was a Mexican soldier.

He was in much worse shape than Arvel; the Apaches had captured him the day before and had been working on him, off and on, ever since. He had no ears, nose, lips or eyelids and, absent those appendages, his face put Arvel in mind of a bloody skull. He was beyond the ability to speak; his screams had so abused his vocal chords that they no longer made sound when he cried out. He had become blind as he was unable to close his eyes over the course of two days. His teeth were constantly exposed in an horrific grin.

One of the bandits noticed Arvel stir and ran over to him, whooping war cries. He kicked Arvel in the nose, opening a stream of blood which washed over his mouth and down his throat, adding an intense thirst to his pain and discomfort. He fell back again into darkness.

When he awoke next, the bandits were working on something with a saw, and he finally pried his eyes open enough to see them sever the man's remaining foot, just above the ankle. They used an old rusted saw, abandoned from some mining operation. It cut through the bone with difficulty.

Once his feet were gone, the bandits all screamed joyously. One grabbed the severed feet and made them walk around their captive. Sensing he was close to dying, the lead bandit told him to march back to his army post. They kicked and prodded him until he was up on his bleeding stumps and, walking a few yards, collapsing at Arvel's feet. He was finally dead.

Their attention now turned to Arvel and they began to giggle like school children. The leader pulled out his big knife and came at him. He loomed over Arvel, ready to begin cutting, when suddenly, as if an errant gust of wind had kicked up, the Indian's hair rose and as if by magic, a neat hole appeared just between his eyes. He gazed more stupidly than he had ever done in life.

The back of his head became an open crater, his brain splattered on three of his companions. He pitched forward on top of the Mexican soldier. Now Arvel had two corpses at his feet. The others looked on in bewilderment. The faint sound of a gunshot could be heard far off to the southeast, but it didn't seem to register with any of the miscreants that they were under attack. The two drunkest Apaches started to laugh at the plight of their leader. The others looked on dumbfounded.

The second Indian was hit a bit lower, the bullet shattering his jaw, removing a good part of it. He slowly reached up with his hands and felt the spot where he used to have a face, then pitched over. The others finally comprehended and began milling about, holding their guns at the ready.

As they were distracted, Arvel grabbed the knife at his feet and freed his hands. He jabbed the knife into the gut of the nearest Indian, raking it sideways and severing the artery in his abdomen; the bandit collapsed. Arvel just as quickly turned and slashed the neck of the next one. Another fell to a long range rifle shot and the two remaining Indians ran for their horses. Arvel grabbed a Winchester lying among the corpses and placed a shot into the back of the head of each escaping bandit.

He fell over, exhausted.

He dreamed of Chica again. "Pendejo, Pendejo, wake up."

He felt her shoving him on the shoulder.

She turned him over and assessed the damage. His nose was broken and he was having trouble focusing. He wanted only to sleep. She got him up and out of the sun. She poured water over his head and cleaned the blood from his face and eyes. He looked better, at least. "Stay awake, Pendejo. I knew a man who got kicked in the head by a horse. He went to sleep and he never woke up. Come on, Pendejo, stay awake."

She tried to get him on a horse, but he was too unstable and vomited every time he sat upright. "Let me just lie down, Chica. I'm very tired. I'll be all right in the morning."

She pushed him hard on the shoulders and became angry. "Pendejo, you must wake up. Please Pendejo."

He understood and focused. "I'm sorry, Chica. I'm not trying to cause trouble."

She found Donny and fashioned a litter similar to the kind the Indians made from their teepee poles. She coaxed Arvel into it and he lay back in the hammock formed by the bedroll Chica stretched over the long branches she had found. She formed a tent over him to keep him out of the sun, and doused him again with water. "We must get you to Tombstone, Pendejo, there will be a doctor there."

She rode hard for most of the day, impeded here and there by uneven terrain and loose rocks. By late afternoon she stopped to check on him. He had fallen in and out of consciousness. He looked up at her and smiled.

"Rebecca. Rebecca, it's awfully hot."

"I know, Pend . . . Arvel, I know it is hot. Try to rest, we are almost there."

"Will Kate be there?"

"Yes, sure, she will be there, Arvel. Now lay back and rest, we are going on."

He babbled incoherently. "Kate, Kate, my little baby-cake, Kate." He sat up again. "Rebecca, I'm awfully hot. I have a headache."

"It is okay, Arvel, I will put some wet cloths on you. Have a drink."

He smiled at her again. "Give us a kiss."

Chica leaned over and kissed his cheek and he grabbed her, trying to pull her onto the litter. She pushed him away.

"Now, now, Arvel," she pulled away, "Not while Kate is around."

He smiled again and held his head. "Not while Kate is around," he became quiet.

Billy Livingston had seen her off in the distance while checking his traps and soon arrived to render help. He approached cautiously. Chica was dangerous in the best of circumstances and in her anxiety, she was deadly. Billy looked under the tent covering the litter.

"It is the mule breeder," he blurted out, thinking at first that Chica did not know. He remembered Arvel speaking of the Mexican girl and now he was meeting her. She looked just as she had been described in all the stories he had heard. He looked at her pony to see if any heads were tied to her saddle. He now understood why Arvel had inquired about her.

Chica told him about the fight. Billy had heard the shooting earlier in the day and wondered what was going on. "You got that bunch? That is good, they were some bad hombres."

"Indios!" Chica corrected him. "Goddamned Apache bastards."

She spat on the ground between them.

Billy led her to his camp and went about making Arvel comfortable. Chica protested and insisted they get to Tombstone straight off.

"It's a bad idea, Miss." He looked Arvel over. "How long has he been in this state?"

"Since early today."

"Look at his eyes, Miss." The pupils were dilated. "Now, look at mine." He grabbed her hand and put it to Arvel's neck. "Feel his heartbeat? Feel how slow? Now feel your own."

He stood up and looked at Arvel. "His brain's swelling."

Arvel looked up at Billy Livingston. "General? General, everyone's dead, General." He sat up on his elbows. "I told him not to attack straight on, I said flank, flank, flank, but he wouldn't, he's dead, too. I'm the only one left, General. I wasn't yellow. I got hit, spun around and hit again. I got hit in the back, but I wasn't running away General, I wasn't running. I wasn't. I told him to flank, I told him, General, but he wouldn't listen." He lay back, exhausted.

"What can we do for him? He *cannot* die." For once in her life she felt vulnerable. It was the first time in her life she had felt real compassion for any man.

"I can help him, but you will not like my idea, I think." He looked at Chica. She looked back at him, helpless.

"What can you do?"

"Cut a hole in his head."

"Ay, chingao!" She began pacing, not knowing what to think. "You are a Wolfer. What do you know of these things?"

"I have done some doctoring in my time, Miss. My father was a healer."

"And you are sure of this, Wolfer? What is your name?"

He told her.

"I am sure of one thing, Miss. It is more than thirty miles to Tombstone, it's getting dark, and the Captain here's gonna die if we don't take the pressure off his brain."

She thought about what he said. Why did she get involved in this gringo? She should have let the Apaches have him, or shot him the first day she met him. She should not have begun to like this Pendejo. She paced around a bit more and looked up at the strange Negro. "Okay, Billy Livingston, but if he dies, you will follow him. I promise you."

Billy swallowed hard. He knew she would not go back on her word.

Billy did yeoman work on Arvel's skull. As he worked, Arvel looked up at Chica. He said: "Rebecca, that hurts. What is it, Rebecca, ticks?"

"Yes, Arvel, it is ticks."

"Oh." He held her hands tightly. "Got to get those ticks off. Don't want tick fever." He drifted off again.

Billy finished up.

The pressure was relieved, and Arvel slept where he lay in Chica's lap during the operation. Billy boiled a half eagle coin and

226

plugged the hole with it, neatly suturing the scalp back in place. He looked odd, bending down as if kissing Arvel on the head, in order to bite the suture off close to the skin.

Chica watched him intently. He did everything with care, and so cleanly. He boiled every instrument, and washed his hands thoroughly before and during the procedure. She looked at his stitching and decided she would not kill him, even if Arvel did not survive. The Negro had done everything he could, and his handiwork showed that he cared and wanted to help.

"Feel his heart, now, Miss." Chica felt at the spot Billy had shown her before. His heart beat more regularly and more strongly now.

"We can let him sleep now, Miss. I'll help you move him to his bedroll if you like."

"He is fine here." She held him like a newborn in her lap and they both slept until morning.

They stayed at Billy Livingston's camp all the next day. Chica rode Alanza back to the battle scene and stripped the corpses of any valuables. She rounded up the horses and took the saddle off of poor Sally and collected all the guns. She did her best to clean up the Mexican soldier's corpse, found his feet and buried them with his body in a shallow grave. She took her favorite crucifix from around her neck and placed it in his hands and covered him with rocks, then fashioned a cross from some branches. She said a prayer she learned from the old priest who taught her to be Catholic. She left the Indians to rot. She propped their corpses up for all to see, in the hopes that other Apaches would happen on them and fear their ghosts and be damned.

One of them was not dead. Arvel's shot had gone wide, gouging out a portion of his skull and severing his right ear. The Indian jumped up, startled by the young woman moving amongst his dead comrades. He managed to climb on one of the horses and rode away as fast as he could. Chica shouted at him in Chiricahua, "You run from a woman, you dog."

The Indian stopped, wheeled his horse and kicked its flanks. He began a long scream, shouldering his Winchester. Chica drew her Schofield and pointed it at him as if she were shooting bottles off a log, her left hand resting on her hip. She did not fire.

This unnerved the Indian even more and he picked up the pace, closing the distance more quickly between them. He began firing wildly at her as he closed. Rocks and dirt kicked up around her and the steadier she stood the wilder and more ineffective he became.

One shot creased her left cheek, just below her eye. The Apache was certain he hit her well, yet Chica stood like a rock, unmoving, unflinching, a stream of blood washing down her neck. She did not even put her hand up to assess the damage inflicted by the ball's impact.

He was committed now; there was no turning back. Like a moth hurtling toward a flame, he somehow knew that this would be his end. She was irresistible, like a witch who had cast a spell over him. She pressed the trigger of her silver six shooter and the Indian pitched backward. He went down hard, on his neck, blood flowing freely from the hole Arvel had given him in his head, where he once had an ear.

Chica walked up to him, pointing the revolver at his head. She lowered the gun, fired, severing his spine, just below the jaw. The Indian's body flopped, lifeless, while his eyes darted about him, trying to comprehend. She spit on his face: "Hijo de tu puta madre," is all she said. She left him to die slowly in the company of his friends.

When she returned to Billy Livingston's camp, Arvel was sleeping soundly. Billy met her as she rode up and helped her with the horses and traps. He forgot himself for a moment and grabbed Chica under the jaw, turning her face to the sunlight. Her eyes flashed, but she allowed him to look at her wound. She was still flush from battle and a little keyed up.

"I can fix that, Miss."

"It is nothing, leave it alone. I need a get Pendejo to town."

He beckoned her to the spot where he had treated Arvel and began pulling out his kit. He smeared something on her wound which made it feel as if she had slept on it funny. He began suturing her face. "Much too pretty a face to end up with an ugly scar, Miss."

She sat, uneasy, not comfortable with the man sitting so close, not liking the feeling of being out of control. She looked over at him. He was not leering at her; there was nothing bad in his eyes. He was simply caring for her.

He finished and looked back at his work. He handed her a wet rag and broken piece of mirror so that she could clean the dried blood from her neck and breast. He sat back and surveyed his work. He grunted in satisfaction.

He gave Chica an unguent and told her to

put it on her wound every day. In ten days, she could remove the stitches.

Chica looked at her reflection in the mirror. She was pleased with Billy's handiwork.

"You are good, Wolfer."

Billy looked on at Arvel, who was sleeping quietly. He looked at Chica and spoke more than he normally would to a pretty young woman.

"He's a good bloke but he's too good for his own good, Miss." He waited for her reaction and continued. "You saved his life, Miss. You need to keep sayin' it, for the rest of your time." He immediately regretted meddling into the affairs of these strangers but was compelled to say it. He knew how different these two were, how they had so many barriers between them, that their alliance balanced on a razor's edge. He got up and began busying himself with insignificant tasks.

"You see a lot, Wolfer."

She stayed the rest of that day with Billy Livingston and left early the next morning. She took Arvel into Tombstone and found a doctor who looked Arvel over and kept him in his home for a couple of days. He was impressed with Billy Livingston's work.

Arvel slept soundly for a full day and

awoke in a strange room. It smelled of antiseptic and leather. The doctor was dining in another room with his family. Arvel asked them what had happened to the girl who had brought him. He realized he no longer had any money and his new pocket watch was gone. The doctor simply shrugged. He told him that the girl had left the same day she had delivered him there. She said to tell him that Donny was in the stable and his clothes had been laundered. All bills had been paid. The doctor went back to his meal.

Arvel moved into a local boarding house where he would end up staying for a few days, still too weak to travel home. He sent word to Uncle Bob and Dick Welles to report on his whereabouts and checked on Donny at the livery stable where Chica had left him. The proprietor was a short, dirty fat man by the name of Dobbs. He was too friendly to Arvel. He assured Arvel that everything was in order and inquired into how he had come upon the horses and equipment. Arvel let his Arizona Ranger badge show for the first time on his lapel. He tended to Donny.

"Didn't the young lady tell you?" He didn't look up at the fat man.

He laughed lewdly. "That little squaw's

quite a firecracker . . . a real wildcat, I bet."
He winked at Arvel.

Arvel's eyes flashed; the man responded by cowering and averting his eyes. "She's not a squaw, you fool, and she's got a name, but you can refer to her as the lady. I see you exhibited better manners around her than you have with me."

"How . . . how's that?" the fat man stuttered his reply.

"Because you're still alive."

Arvel finished with Donny. "Let's see those traps left by the lady."

"I've figured a good price for everything, it's all here and accounted for. I'm certain you'll find it to your satisfaction. None of the horses bore brands, so they all belong to you *and* the lady. She told me to deal with you once you were feeling less poorly."

The guns and other valuables lay on a table. Arvel recognized the big knife and the Winchester he used in the battle with the Indians. The knife bore dried blood on the blade and hilt. The Winchester was in fair condition, the rest of the guns were poorly maintained and had little value. The sight of the equipment made him ill. He quickly signed the proposal and handed it to the fat man without looking at him.

"How'd you say you came across all this,

Captain?" He forgot himself, and continued to get under Arvel's skin.

He looked the fat man in the eye. "I didn't say, but I was attacked by a band of Apaches in the desert while returning from Mexico. They were torturing a Mexican soldier to death and when it came my turn, the lady killed most of them with a fancy hunting rifle she stole from a wealthy Colonel. I killed the rest with that knife there, and that Winchester.

"I'll take cash if you please. Send it to the Harper boarding house. I'm leaving for my ranch in the morning. Please have it to me by then. Good day." He turned away, wanting to leave before the stableman said anything further to annoy him, his head was spinning and when he walked out into the midday sun, he thought he would fall over. He took a deep breath and grabbed onto a nearby stair rail and slowly regained his composure.

He wandered about Tombstone for the rest of the day. He felt ill at ease, spent, washed out. He had never been affected by combat, but the killing of Sally and the brutal torture of the Mexican soldier and his wounds made him feel vulnerable and weak. It was the first time in his life that his confidence had really been shaken, and it was the first time in his life he had known fear. He did not like to feel this way. He saw a gun shop and thought about his old timey guns. He considered trading them, buying a new set. He kept walking, he was having difficulty focusing. He did not want to talk to anyone and he was in no mood for conducting such business.

Chica was on his mind constantly. He was awestruck by her courage and fortitude, and just as vexed and frustrated by her constant leaving. He hated that she always left without so much as a goodbye. He would have to wait for her to turn up, at her choosing, at her whim. It made him hate her as much as he loved her.

He thought a lot about the fat man at the livery stable. He was typical. The whore Indian and the old white man. He hated the thought of men thinking lewd things about Chica. He imagined that, despite her bravado, she must feel the sting of their gestures and sneers. The bloated cowards. They could sneer and mutter under their breath, but they would never outright ridicule her, as they knew that it would likely be the last thing they'd ever do.

He heard a woman laugh and could swear it was Chica. He quickened his pace and walked around a corner toward the sound and nearly bumped into a group of vaqueros. They were loading a wagon. A young woman was with them. It wasn't Chica. They looked at the pale gringo looking at them. The leader nodded to him.

Arvel caught himself, and greeted them, "Buenos dias." He looked at the ground. He looked up at the woman sitting in the driver's seat of the wagon. He tipped his hat to her, "Ma'am."

The vaquero leader gave him a smile and they all went about their work. Arvel wondered if any of them knew Chica. These were the kind of men she should be with, young people of her own kind, not some aging gringo.

He stopped at a shop specializing in women's clothing and stood, uncomfortable, in the doorway. A pretty young woman greeted him. He nodded and removed his hat. He looked around nervously. The young woman inquired into what he was seeking.

"I don't really know."

The young woman had been in Tombstone long enough to know not to inquire too deeply into the affairs of gentlemen customers. She did not ask for whom the purchase was intended. After watching Arvel fidget for a few minutes she finally spoke.

"We just got in some of the latest fashions

from New York. They're quite lovely." She grabbed a dress and held it up under her chin. She smiled at Arvel. Arvel stared at her for several moments. She was a lovely young girl from back East, considering her accent. She reminded him of the young ladies he knew just before the war. He wondered why she was here. He wanted to ask her, then didn't. He wanted to tell her to go back home, where there were no Apaches or Mexicans or bandits, go back East to civilization. His mind was off onto a dozen different thoughts.

"Or perhaps something else?" She brought him back from his preoccupation.

"No, no, that's fine, that would be nice." He imagined Chica's brown skin against the white fabric. "Will that fit you?" The girl seemed about Chica's size.

"We have one that will."

"Yes, that's, that'll be fine. And all the undergarments that would be appropriate to it, if you please. And shoes. I don't know the size, but something that will go well with the outfit, but the best you have. It has got to be the best you have."

He thanked the woman and left. He felt better now. He felt good when he was doing things for Chica.

Chapter XI:
A Deal with the Devil

The young deputy was visited three more times by the man in the mustard suit. He was beaten each time. He did not know why. He did nothing wrong. He did nothing really but sleep, eat a little and smoke the pipe when they let him, which was less and less often. He seemed to need more of it as time progressed and they gave him less. He could not understand.

One day the old man and the German came to visit. The deputy sat up in bed. He swung his legs to the side and straightened as much as he dared. He was always about to vomit it seemed. He received no beating this time. He sat quietly and did not look up. He responded to their questions, but volunteered nothing more.

"He's ready, I believe." The German was impressed. He did not hold much hope and did not really care. The man in the mustard suit was a minor player in his scheme, but he was a zealot for the cause and a zealot anarchist was not to be ignored. He let the man in the mustard suit proceed. They talked with their backs turned to the young deputy. He could not hear what they were saying. He had no energy and wanted to sleep. He found himself unable to hold himself upright any longer and fell back on the bed. The man in the mustard suit looked over his shoulder, then back at the German. They spoke some more.

The deputy was jarred from his sleep as he was being pulled by his hair from the bed. The old man threw him to the floor and began kicking him. He kicked him on every part of his body, then grabbed a coal shovel and beat him with that. He beat him until the old man was wheezing and too weak to swing the shovel any more. Great streams of drool ran out of the old man's mouth as he worked the young deputy over.

The young deputy could feel the saliva run onto his neck and back. It made him more nauseous. He could feel the beating and the drool but by this time he could not see. The old man left him there on the floor of the laundry. The deputy did not understand.

Ging Wa waited until the old man left. She pulled the deputy with all her might and got him back on the bed. She cleaned him and made him comfortable. She went out to get him some soup. When she returned he was staring at the ceiling. He cried great tears that rolled down his face and onto his pillow. He did not try to hide them from Ging Wa. She fed him, all the while dabbing his tears away and saying nothing. He shook and cried until his hysteria gave way to exhaustion. He lay still, breathing shallowly, trying to gain control.

Ging Wa held him, brushed his hair away and hummed her tune. He was utterly broken. He had no dignity left, he cried in front of Ging Wa, he would have cried in front of his own mother had she been there. He did not care who saw him cry. He just wanted to make the torture stop; he wanted the pipe so badly he could not stand it.

They awoke some time later, not certain how long they had been asleep, likely through until morning. The windowless room made it impossible to tell the time of day. The young deputy woke and felt the girl resting her head on his chest. He could smell her hair. She woke and looked up. He looked into Ging Wa's eyes. He held her tenderly. He felt better today. Ging Wa was given courage to speak. "You must not cry out when he beats you." The young deputy welled up again. He wanted to cry.

"I want to go home." He turned on his side, facing the wall. "I just want to go home."

She rubbed his back gently. "You must not take the pipe the next time they give it to you."

"I can't help it. All I want is the pipe."

"I will help you, but you must not take the pipe." She left him and came back with a plate of meat. They had been starving him. He had only eaten soup since he had gotten there. He picked at it and became ill. He finally kept some down.

"If you can keep away from the pipe, I can get you more meat and you will be stronger every day."

He turned toward her. "Why would you do this for me?" The meanness came through. She did not know the answer to the question. She just wanted to help him.

She stood up. "When I bring you the pipe you will smoke it, but it will contain only herbs. You must act as if it is real. You must be dreamy."

He thought about this. He wanted the pipe badly, but he wanted to end this torture more. He nodded agreement.

They played out their deception for a week. The young deputy was stronger. He could keep food down now. He still wanted the pipe, but took Ging Wa's advice and denied himself of it. The man in the mustard suit did not come around. He would have to be prepared for him when he did.

Ging Wa would sneak him newspapers and milk. He did not find her damaged skin so appalling. He began to see her as a human being. He missed her when she was not around.

He was terrified on the day the old man arrived. He greeted him more lucidly. The old man was shocked to find him in good order. The young deputy told him that he would be leaving, and would like his traps.

The old man sneered. "I thought you'd turn yellow. You might want to look at this before making any bold plans, my lad." He handed him a letter from his mother. She had responded to the anarchist's letter. She was pleased that her boy was in his employ and thanked him for paying her son such generous wages. The deputy looked on, not comprehending.

"So what?"

"I won't dance around it, lad. If you don't do what we want, we'll kill her."

He felt ill again. He looked beyond the old man and peered into Ging Wa's eyes.

The old man looked at the two of them and smiled.

Ging Wa was beaten for helping the young deputy. Madam Lee had a special treatment for the young woman and locked her in the laundry's garret without light, food, or water for four days. The temperatures reached one hundred thirty degrees. She hummed her song and never uttered a word to Madam Lee.

CHAPTER XII:
WAITING

Arvel was feeling better, less vulnerable, as he regained his strength. He still grieved over Sally. He loved her so much, as she was the best mule he had ever owned. He never had even a dog that was so good a companion. He blamed himself for her death and had difficulty getting over it. He was also annoyed with Chica. She had not come to see him; he did not know where she was or what she was doing. It was beginning to occupy his mind constantly. The waiting was unbearable; he would wander out to the edge of the ranch, looking for signs of a rider coming up the dirt road to visit. He often woke in the night, believing he had heard her sneak into his room. She was never there and a pain struck his gut at every realization. He stopped eating and lost weight.

Finally the opportunity came for him to get away from the ranch, to deliver some mules up to a customer outside of Flagstaff. He liked to travel north. There were fewer Apaches up that way. The Indians who did live around the area were fine people. He traded with them when he could. He resolved to ride by train most of the way as it was especially hot this summer and there was talk of a drought.

He left early. Donny and the sale mules were behind his new mount, Tammy, whom he had been training to handle riders. She was gentle and of the same parentage as Sally. She actually looked a lot like Sally, and this made him feel a bit less blue. He made his way to the train station and from there would ride the rails up to Flagstaff. He'd then ride Tammy for the rest of the journey.

He had avoided trains mostly because they reminded him of his little girl who used to love them so much. She would sit on his lap so that she could watch out the window. She would never take her eyes off the countryside and asked one question after the next. She wanted to know everything. She had a wonderful, curious mind.

He decided to stop over in Phoenix to let the mules exercise and recover from the ride. It would be a leisurely journey; give him some time away from the ranch and to keep from constantly looking for Chica.

He had a couple of hours to kill and made his way to Washington Street, one of Rebecca and Kate's favorite places to visit. He wanted to get something else for Chica. He'd left the dress he'd bought her at the ranch and held out some ridiculous hope that perhaps he'd bump into her during his travels. He stopped into Dorris Brothers. He missed coming here with his girls. It always smelled good at the Dorris Brothers. It smelled of new things, of opulent things: new, finely dyed wool, exquisite leather, perfume.

He could not decide what to get for Chica. None of the jewelry at Dorris Brothers looked anything like what she wore. He'd already gotten her clothes. He wandered over to the perfume counter. A lovely, mature woman was busily working behind the counter. She looked as if she'd just arrived from Paris. She looked at Arvel over her pince nez. She smiled and addressed him in a heavy French accent. She showed him some perfumes and he settled on Eau de Cologne Impériale. He was pleased. The box itself was worth the cost and he was excited about presenting it to Chica. He added some hair combs and a mirror.

He decided against having them wrapped;

the Dorris Brothers bag was ornate enough and for some reason he could not articulate, he wanted to show off the packages. He wanted to let everyone know that he'd bought some things for Chica.

The train ride was pleasant enough and he passed the time by reading the latest newspapers from back East. He found a fairly recent copy of *The Daily Record*, a newspaper from Baltimore. He was amused to read about things happening in his hometown. It seemed like a world away, and the memories it brought back made him melancholy.

A rotund man in a striped suit sat across from him. The man fidgeted, then coughed, and finally started talking. Arvel looked up from his paper. He had read the same line five times and was thinking of Chica. He smiled at the man who desired so much attention. "I see you noticed my hat, sir."

Arvel had not, but smiled politely.

"It is a dandy." Arvel looked out the window briefly. The fat man stood up and bowed briefly, he extended his hand.

"Name is Chaney." He plopped down abruptly as the train lurched. "They call it a Homburg." He pronounced it carefully, as to assure he had gotten it right. He fiddled with the brim, turning it over and over in his hands.

"Are you on business, Mr. Chaney?"

"Oh, yes. But I've been in Arizona for a month now. Lovely country, Mr. Walsh."

The big man handed him a card, National Cash Register. "I am in the theft avoidance business." He smiled and offered Arvel a twenty-five cent cigar. "These are for the customers when we close the deal."

Arvel smelled it and allowed Chaney to cut the end for him. They smoked in silence for a while.

"I hope you don't mind, but I like to play a little game."

Arvel nodded, "Be my guest." The fat man sat back and looked at Arvel for several moments.

"You lost your wife around five years ago. And your daughter, too, I am sorry to say." Arvel squirmed in his seat.

"You are some kind of law, but not in a full capacity." The fat man blew smoke at the ceiling. "You have had two watches stolen recently. You were in a battle lately, which has affected your health, and you are presently courting a younger lady, which is giving you some anxiety."

Arvel looked at the man and smiled, amused. "That's some parlor trick, sir."

"Oh, it's no trick, Mr. Walsh." He tapped

a long ash off his cigar. "Strictly observation. I am paid to observe folks, to find out what it is that will make them buy, close the deal."

"Will you share with me how you know all these things about me?"

"Well, yes, first, your wife has passed away, as you are wearing quality clothing, but nothing purchased within the past five years. That suggests to me that you will wear fine clothes, but will not bother to buy them for yourself.

"Your daughter, I am sorry to bring up sad memories, and please forgive me, made part of your watch chain of her own hair, but it is not as neat a job as if she had done it recently.

"You also have gifts, but none of them are for a child. The gifts you do have are for a lady, fine perfume by the style of the box and the scent I detect and some other baubles that a young beauty would appreciate.

"You have pin holes on your lapel from wearing a law badge, but you are not a retired detective, as I see you are well off, far beyond what could be obtained from that of a lawman's salary, and I saw you handling your mules before embarking on our trip. You handled them as one who has been doing such craft for many years. And, I see no evidence that you are armed, so, you must be some kind of law in a nonspecific capacity.

"You have been in battle, as I see the wound on your head. By the way, a very capable trepanation, if I do say so.

"You have lost weight, as your clothes are loose on you, so I surmise the young lady has put you off your grub and, I suppose, that's about it."

"And the stolen watches?"

"Ah, yes. Well, the chain does not match the current watch you wear. The watch is quite new and the chain is old."

"Would that not be the second watch, then?"

"No, because the clasp on the chain has been altered twice. Once for the second watch, and again for the third."

Arvel sat back and laughed. "You are a remarkable fellow, Mr. Chaney. "Now, let me give it a try." Arvel grabbed his chin and stroked it, observing the fat man.

"Okay, Mr. Chaney, you are a man. You like to eat . . . a lot." The fat man started grinning. "You were in the GAR. You are a mason. You like to wear Homburg hats, and you sell cash registers."

"Well done sir, well done."

"But, Mr. Chaney, one word of advice. If you're going to sell cash registers here, you might want to get rid of your GAR pin and mason fob. There are many former confederates in these parts and not a small number of Catholics and Jews. Money has no political affiliation, or religious agenda. You'll do well to not advertise these things."

"Point well taken," he began removing the items and placed them in his vest pocket. "This calls for a celebration, Mr. Walsh." Chaney was always pleased to make the acquaintance of men like Arvel Walsh. He pulled out a large flask and two small silver cups. He poured each of them a drink. "This is the finest Bourbon I could find."

They drank and Chaney looked out the window. He finished his cigar and sat back in his seat. "Mr. Walsh, I am an old, fat man and all alone in the world. I have my work, and I have my travels. So, I spend my money on indulgences of food, clothing, fine spirits and cigars."

"Sounds like a comfortable life, Mr. Chaney." He smiled at the man. "What did you do in the war?"

"You will be shocked to hear." He puffed his chest out. "I was a commissary officer." He smiled, and patted his belly. "One thing I know, Mr. Walsh, is food. It was not a glorious post, but crucial, none the less."

"Agreed. We always appreciated our grub, Mr. Chaney. It may not have been home cooking, but it kept us alive."

"And you, sir?"

"Infantry."

Chaney poured again. He raised his cup, "To the Infantry."

Arvel drank. "To the Grand Army of the Republic."

They drank and chatted and laughed through the rest of the trip.

Chapter XIII:
Muses

Arvel delivered the mules to his client without incident. It was refreshing to travel unmolested, and Arvel felt strange. The land up north was so much more civilized than down south. He did not need to touch his guns. He was feeling better now, but not quite ready to return home. He decided to take a detour and stop at a place known as Walnut Canyon.

He and Rebecca had visited this place a year before she died. Rebecca loved the history of the place; Walnut Canyon had been the home of cliff-dwelling Indians many hundreds of years ago. For reasons unknown, the place became abandoned and was a treasure trove of relics. Rebecca decorated most of their hacienda with the items they had found there. Arvel always considered it to be a rather eerie and lonely place, but his conversation with Chaney and the ride on the rails drew him to the past and memories of Rebecca and little Kate. He felt that visiting the ruins would do him good.

It was a fine day, hot, with a nice steady breeze, and he dozed as he rode along. His mind wandered with the steady rhythm of Tammy's gait. He began to dream of music, the kind that he once heard in Philadelphia with Rebecca. It was Mozart's dance music and he could swear he heard it for real, rather than in a dream.

He pulled himself out of his stupor and listened more intently. It was coming from the center of the canyon, magnified by the echoes common to the place. He began to follow it. Off in a distance he saw movement and as he approached, could see two lithe figures dressed in flowing white togas, dancing about the waters at the floor of the canyon. Off to the side, a young man's voice could be heard, calling out directions in a muffled tone. Arvel finally picked him out amongst a copse of trees, his head buried under a black cloak behind a camera. Arvel sat a little straighter in the saddle and rubbed his eyes. He knew that he was not dreaming.

Suddenly, one of the young nymphs looked up and shouted to the others. "Oh, goody, a cowboy!"

The two young women ran to him, lifting up the skirts of their togas to keep them from dragging on the ground. The young man emerged from behind his camera. He attended to the gramophone. They all smiled as they addressed Arvel.

Arvel stood up in his saddle and bowed, tipping his hat. "Ladies."

"We were dancing." One girl looked at him and giggled. They were all slightly inebriated.

"I am sorry to disturb your party."

The other young woman grabbed his hand. "Come, you must join us. I am Ellen and this is Jess. We are having our photographs taken." She beckoned him off his mule. "This is André." She pointed to the young man, who wore a loose white shirt, untucked from his trousers, and a wide leather belt, in the style of a Russian peasant. "André is an artist."

Jess leaned close to Arvel and whispered. "He is in a foul mood. He doesn't believe photography is really art, and it's put him in a terrible state of melancholy." She suddenly became distracted and flitted away to the phonograph and got it started again. The music was a strange addition to the already surreal scene.

"Oh, don't mind her," the other young

woman took his hand, leading him to their encampment. "André gets into moods all the time. He is a suffering artist."

"I am *not* in a *mood*!" André threw his head back, pushing his locks out of his eyes. He bowed to Arvel, nearly to the ground. "It is true, sir, that I love my work and am too often disappointed in myself, and it is also true that photography is a crude medium. It is *not* an artist's medium." He looked away, not a little dramatically.

"Oh, show him your work, André." Ellen, seemingly the most lucid and sensible of the two, spoke again. She pulled Arvel to a marquee tent set up in the center of a meadow by the stream. Arvel was impressed with the camp, and knew by its location and care by which it had been laid out, that these three were not alone. He stepped through the flap in the tent and observed André's collection.

"Maurice says photography is a rubbish medium." André looked on at his work.

"Maurice is an English Philistine who knows nothing of art." Ellen stroked his long tresses, attempting to comfort him.

"Well, he *is* studying this year at Cambridge."

"And learning to ape the old masters, in old, outdated and boring mediums. You, meanwhile, are pushing the very boundaries of art. You will be famous some day."

"Famous some day!" Mimicked Jess, in a babyish voice, then hiccupped. She looked at Arvel and giggled.

André had some works of the canyon and many of the young women in various poses, with the dwellings in the background. They were intriguing.

The first young woman pushed her way into the tent. "Show him the naughty ones, Ellen." She giggled again.

"Shush." Ellen pushed the silly one, admonishing her with a glare. "They are *not* naughty." She smiled and began to giggle herself. "I swear, you are silly."

"All rubbish, all rubbish." The young man looked on with a pained expression.

"If I may be so bold," Arvel continued to survey the photographs. "These bring to mind the artist Cameron. You certainly would not say she was no artist, sir."

André brightened. "Do you mean it, sir?"

"I certainly do. I saw Cameron's work back in Philadelphia, just after she died. You must know her work."

André stood, pensive for several moments. He smiled at Arvel. "You are an oasis in the desert, sir."

"Oh, show him the naughty ones." The

silly one was flitting around the inside of the tent; she brushed against Arvel several times, extending her sheer toga with outstretched arms, as if forming wings. "He is an aficionado. He will appreciate the artistic merit in them."

"You are a shameless exhibitionist, Jess." The more sober woman seemed to be having second thoughts.

"I would like to see them, if they won't embarrass Miss Ellen."

André pulled aside a large canvas to reveal the "naughty ones." They featured Jess and Ellen in various poses, in various stages of undress. They were well done. The girls were nude, certainly, but not in any way to be compared to the pornographic material he had seen in the Dunstable collection.

They insisted that he stay and camp with them for a few days. André, in addition to his art photography, had been commissioned to chronicle the West. He asked Arvel to pose for him, as he was a "real" cowboy, as Jess had put it.

Arvel settled the mules down for the evening and let the young people continue their activities in front of the camera. He spotted an older man dozing under the shade of a tree. He approached him. "I thought you fellows never sleep."

The man looked up at him under the brim of his hat and smiled. "That is just the Pinkerton hoopla." He stood up and rubbed his head, then stretched. He extended his hand.

"Name's Thoby, Henry Thoby." Arvel shook the man's hand. He was well dressed in city clothes and wore a big six shooter. He had a Winchester and shotgun close by. He offered Arvel some tobacco, and Arvel offered him a pre-twisted one from his pack. They sat down and smoked.

"I imagine you did not expect to find that out here." He pointed with the end of his cigarette toward the young troupe.

"Can't say that I did."

"You are looking at the heirs to eighty percent of the wealth in this county, Mr. Walsh. The tall one, Ellen, has a family in railroads; the other girl is in shipping, and the boy, coal." He crushed the cigarette out on the sole of his boot. "God help us."

The girls began to splash each other as they danced through the river. The young man called out for them to stop getting his equipment wet, then joined them. They began rolling around in the grass and laughed and giggled to exhaustion.

Thoby smiled at them. He didn't really mind them. They were spoiled, and useless, but not unkind to him. He had been hired as an escort through the Pinkerton agency. It was a high profile job and Arvel knew the man must be capable, despite his years and mild exterior.

They were planning to stay out West until Christmas, moving their way on to California, where they were going to get a ship for New York. Other than this rough plan, there was no real itinerary.

"How is the travel south, Mr. Walsh?" Arvel understood what he meant.

"Mr. Thoby, you have to be careful south of Tucson. There are a fair number of bandits: white, Apache, and Mexican. They will not be kind to your entourage. I would recommend train travel in these parts. I'm not certain what you can expect if you stay north and move on to California overland. I'm not familiar with that territory." They were interrupted by more commotion.

Jess had captured a frog and was chasing the others with it. Arvel and Thoby looked at each other and Thoby just shook his head.

"You will not believe this when I tell you that those girls have had the best schooling money can buy. Their parents would be mortified if they knew of this behavior."

Arvel enjoyed them. He watched them run wild. "Are they romantically involved with the young lad?"

Thoby grunted. "There is no risk of progeny from those loins, Mr. Walsh, if you get my meaning. On the contrary, I do make up two cots, but the boy does not enter into it."

Arvel felt his face flush. "Oh, I see." He smiled at the girls; running, playing, just being happy with each other.

André called him over, beckoning him to get in front of the camera. "Go ahead, Mr. Walsh, he has taken enough likenesses of me and the gals. It won't hurt a bit."

Arvel took it in stride. André photographed him with his hat, without his hat, holding his Henry rifle, holding his revolver, holding a rope. While André was fiddling with his camera, Arvel began twirling his rope, the way he used to do to entertain his daughter. He was quite handy with a rope and soon the girls were oohing and ahhing at his prowess. Soon, Jess got some creative ideas, and had Arvel rope her, pretending to be a slave girl, feigning distress. Ellen joined in. Arvel was enjoying the silly behavior. The girls reminded him a little of how he felt around Chica.

Arvel saw a man ride up, older yet than Thoby. He had a small doe carcass slung over his saddle horn.

261

"Mose is back!" Jess jumped up and down, clapping her hands. Mose was the other escort, and responsible for, essentially, everything related to the care and feeding of the trio. He nodded to Arvel, who suddenly felt a bit silly; Mose treated him indifferently.

Arvel watched the old man work. He was an interesting fellow. He had known Jess's father for many years and was a man of many talents. He quickly went to work on the deer, preparing the heart and liver, starting it in a skillet with some onions and lard while he skinned the animal and prepared the remainder of the meat for later.

Eventually, they sat around a big campfire Mose had built up. They dined on fresh meat and red wine. Everyone laughed and enjoyed the fine evening. When they were finished, Ellen stood up, a little unsteadily. She grabbed Jess's shoulder for support. "Time for performances." She nodded at Arvel. He looked at his hosts, confused.

Jess grabbed Ellen by the arm, and stood up next to her. "Everyone has to do something for their meal."

Arvel smiled, uneasily. "Such as?"

"Sing, or recite, or dance, or sing and dance and recite," said André, whose mood had improved significantly since Arvel's arrival.

Thoby smiled at Arvel through a cloud of cigarette smoke. "No getting around it, Mr. Walsh. You've had your meal, the girls must be compensated."

"Compensated," Jess hiccupped.

Arvel thought for a moment. He stood up, and put his hand in his vest. The words came slowly, but more easily as he went along:

"Love is sunshine, hate is shadow,
Life is checkered shade and sunshine,
Rule by love, O Hiawatha!"

From the sky the moon looked at them,
Filled the lodge with mystic splendors,
Whispered to them, "O my children,
Day is restless, night is quiet,
Man imperious, woman feeble;
Half is mine, although I follow;
Rule by patience, Laughing Water!"

Thus it was they journeyed homeward;
Thus it was that Hiawatha
To the lodge of old Nokomis
Brought the moonlight, starlight, firelight,
Brought the sunshine of his people,
Minnehaha, Laughing Water,

Handsomest of all the women
In the land of the Dakotas,
In the land of handsome women."

He stopped speaking, and no sound was heard for several moments. Suddenly, Jess began clapping frenetically, "c'est magnifique!"

It was the girls' turn. They looked at each other and giggled. They sashayed a little distance away, then crawled up on a high rock, using a ladder Mose fashioned to get them into some of the dwellings.

"Watch for snakes," said André, nervously. He did not like to range far from the fire after dark.

The girls faced away from the party, looking down, into the ravine. They began singing in harmony:

"She is far from the land
Where her young hero sleeps,
And lovers are round her, sighing;
But coldly she turns
From their gaze, and weeps,
For her heart in his grave is lying.

She sings the wild songs
Of her dear native plains,
Ev'ry note which she loved awakening -

Ah! little they think
Who delight in her strains,
How the heart of the Minstrel
is breaking.

He had lived for his love,
For his country he died,
They were all that to life
Had entwined him -
Nor soon shall the tears
Of his country be dried,
Nor long will his love
Stay behind him.

Oh! make her a grave
Where the sunbeams rest,
When they promise a glorious morrow;
They'll shine o'er her sleep
Like a smile from the West,
From her own loved
Island of sorrow."

The cavern echoed their plaintiff chorus
and gave the impression of several beautiful
nymphs, singing through the ages. Arvel
blushed. He quickly lit a cigarette and let
the smoke burn his eyes to hide the tears
that he could not control. He did not know
why he was so emotional.

The other men bowed their heads and

tried to look distracted, while the hair on their necks stood on end. It was a moving and sad song, befitting their surroundings. No one clapped as the girls returned, hanging on each other as if to give support for fear that the emotion had drained all the energy from their limbs.

Jess was sobbing, and kissed Ellen. "That was beautiful." She sniffed, then wiped her eyes with the back of her hands. "Mon cœur se brise."

Now André stood up, raising one leg up on a log. He stuck his thumbs in the heavy leather belt around his waist. He gazed at the moon and began his recitation:

"Ancient Person, for whom I
All the flattering youth defy,
Long be it e'er thou grow old,
Aching, shaking, crazy cold;
But still continue as thou art,
Ancient Person of my heart.

On thy withered lips and dry,
Which like barren furrows lie,
Brooding kisses I will pour,
Shall thy youthful heart restore,
Such kind show'rs in autumn fall,
And a second spring recall;
Nor from thee will ever part,

Ancient Person of my heart.

Thy nobler parts, which but to name
In our sex

(Jess giggled until she was swatted soundly
by Ellen)

would be counted shame,
By ages frozen grasp possest,
From their ice shall be released,
And, soothed by my reviving hand,
In former warmth and vigor stand.
All a lover's wish can reach,
For thy joy my love shall teach;
And for thy pleasure shall improve
All that art can add to love.
Yet still I love thee without art,
Ancient Person of my heart."

Everyone clapped. André sat down. He was
pleased.

Arvel was up early. He ate breakfast with
Mose and the Pinkerton. He felt a little silly
around the rough men with his recitation.
They did not seem to care one way or the
other. He heard André stir and took him a
cup of coffee. The girls were sprawled on
the floor of the tent, their togas heaped in a
pile near the flap of the tent. Arvel covered

them. Jess mumbled in her sleep and snuggled closer to Ellen.

"I'll be heading out, André. Tell the girls that it was a pleasure."

"The pleasure was ours, sir." André shook his hand. The boy was frail, both in spirit and physicality. Arvel felt touched by the young man's reaction to his encouragement. It felt good to do such a kindness.

"Mr. Walsh, you have renewed my passion."

"That's good, André. You keep to your work. One day, people will appreciate your art and your chronicling of this land. Don't worry about the Maurices of the world. You'll constantly be confronted by them. Pity them for their ignorance, and try to be patient with them. You may, or may not enlighten them."

André, without drinking, grabbed Arvel and hugged him, and just as quickly pulled away. Arvel patted the young man's shoulder. He climbed into the saddle and tipped his hat to the young artist. "Au revoir, André."

"Au revoir, Mr. Walsh, au revoir."

Chapter XIV:
Joaquin

Chaney was waiting for him at a table by the front window of the Flagstaff hotel. He was just buttering his toast. He stood up and shook Arvel's hand, dropping crumbs from the napkin covering his lap onto the floor. He poured coffee for Arvel and smiled. Arvel felt good. He'd been enjoying the salesman's company and the diversions of the land up north. The weather was cooler than at home and he felt a sense of accomplishment at delivering his mules to a grateful customer. The young artists had also improved his spirits. He drank coffee with Chaney and waited for his meal.

Chaney pushed his spectacles back up onto the bridge of his nose and looked at the morning paper. "This is what I love about your land, Mr. Walsh." He cleared his throat and began reading,

Cora Chiquita, Female Desperado, Runs Amok

Flagstaff. — The peace officers of this county have arrested Cora Chiquita, known as "Cora the Cowgirl," who made a sensation here on Friday night by riding up and down the main street, a revolver in each hand, yelling and shooting at everyone whose appearance did not suit her fancy.

Not until the girl, who is known far and wide as "the beautiful devil," had loped out of town did the sheriff and his posse show their heads. They later found her unconscious in an abandoned Indian hogan.

La Chiquita is one of the best shots in the Arizona territory, and is said to be in close touch with a bad gang of outlaws in the Southwest. She is 23 years old, pretty as a picture, about a quarter-blood Cherokee, wears man's attire, always carries two revolvers and is a fearless rider. Not long ago she was driven out of New Mexico for general reckless shooting. She has killed several men. She is being held in the Flagstaff jail, under triple guard, awaiting trial.

He looked up at Arvel. "Where else in the civilized world would you find such characters, eh, Mr. Walsh?" He stopped grinning when he saw Arvel's face. He'd lost color and looked as if he had just learned of the death of a loved one.

Arvel looked blankly at the salesmen. "I *am* sorry, Mr. Chaney, but I have business to attend to. He absent-mindedly took Chaney's paper, folded it up and tucked it under his arm. He quickly walked out of the hotel's dining room. He was tempted to gather up every copy of the paper he could find, and burn them.

"Pendejo! Wha' are *you* doing here?" She smiled broadly at him. She was glad to see him. "I am in jail," she spoke through the bars of her cell. She had been confined alone, as she had been *'fomenting a riot'* according to the jailer.

"I see you are in jail, Chica."

"Oh, Pendejo, I got too much whisky the other night."

He did not speak to her as they rode back to the hotel. He told her to wait for him down the street, while he gathered his belongings.

"Are you ashamed to be seen with me, Pendejo?"

271

He glared at her as they rode out of town. He felt that every eye was on him. "Not now, Chica, I don't want to talk about this now."

She sulked for a while, then tried to tease him.

"I don't want to talk right now, Chica. Please keep your mouth closed. I don't want to discuss anything; I don't want to hear your voice right now."

She had never seen him angry. She didn't like it. They finally stopped for the night at a boarding house just south of Flagstaff. He got them separate rooms. She left him alone for a while, then knocked on his door. He would not answer.

He had just begun to fall asleep when he realized she was in his bed. He sat up with a start.

"How did you do, that, Chica?"

"I come in through the window." She grinned.

"You'd better go back to your room, Chica." He turned away from her.

"Wha' is wrong, Pendejo?"

"I am just tired, Chica. I am tired of all this. I am not cut out to live the way you live. I missed you, you go off, you don't tell me where you are. Now, I have used my influence as a Ranger to get you out of jail.

272

I constantly . . ." He was too angry for the words to come.

"I am sorry, Pendejo. I should not have had so much whisky."

He looked at her. "You don't get it, girl. You just don't get it, do you?"

"I see that you are sad, Pendejo. I am sorry that you are sad. I like you a lot better when you are funny."

He put his hands over his face and rubbed his temples. "I have lost my wife, my child, my Sally, and now I am constantly thinking of you."

"Sally? Who is this Sally, Pendejo?"

"My mule."

"Pendejo, you need a get a grip on yourself. Sally was a beast of burden."

"Well, I loved her."

Chica shrugged. "I am sorry if I make you sad, Pendejo. I din' never mean to make you sad. If you like, I will go back to jail and take my medicine."

He turned and grabbed her. "I can't stand this uncertainty. You come and you go. I don't know where you are, what you are doing. I look for you to show up and you aren't there. I, I just don't know, Chica. I just don't know."

"Well, Pendejo, I don' see, how do I say, no estímulo a permanecer."

"I have no idea what you are saying, Chica."

"You never ask me to stay, Pendjeo. I have never heard you say, don' go, Chica. Not once."

She got up and lit two cigarettes. She handed him one. "Come on, Pendejo, les' stop arguing." She smoked while taking off her dress, crawled into the bed and pressed herself against him. "You are jus' tired. Maybe that Wolfer drilled too deep in your head."

She was gone the next morning. He thought, hoped, that she perhaps had gone back to her own room, but when he checked, the room was empty. He found a note, badly written, in a childlike scrawl, half English and half Spanish on a table in his room. It was her attempt at meeting him halfway; she could not stay around, be tied down in such a way. It was a promise to see him again soon, but not where or when. He was missing another watch.

Arvel turned back and rode to Flagstaff to get the train to Tucson. He felt hollow, drained. All the good that the trip had done him up until this point had been undone by Chica's arrest.

He did not know why he never asked

Chica to stay. He could not put his finger on it but something about her or the two of them together simply did not make sense. It was not necessarily the difference in age, and he was certain it was not her race. He was completely smitten, physically. He loved her mannerisms and the way she spoke. Her broken English was wonderful. It wasn't so much even the fact that she was uncontrollable and a thief.

He felt stupid for being ashamed of using his influence to get her out of jail. She had done no real harm. Truth was the sheriff and the jailer had gotten a kick out of her. Anyone with a brain, with a sense of humor, who could see without prejudice, seemed to enjoy Chica. But there was something about the strange interlude with the young debutantes at Walnut canyon, the fine conversation, the sharing of ideas that made him realize how much he missed intelligent conversation with clever and educated women. He missed that about Rebecca more than anything else. And Chica, it seemed to him there was no way the girl would ever be interested in such things. She was not incapable, she was a bright woman but she was so ignorant and uninterested, as far as he could see, in ever exploring that world, that he wondered how long they could endure. Could he try to mold her, to teach her to be another Rebecca? Would he want her to be Rebecca?

The whole business gave him a pain in his gut. It had only recently occurred to him that he had never felt this way in his life. With Rebecca, it was essentially an easy courtship. He met her and knew they would be married the moment he saw her. They were perfectly matched: the same age, the same social standing. She was physically attractive, as he was to her. They just fit and they always loved each other, but he was never really smitten with Rebecca.

She had been the first woman he had ever been with, Chica the second, but even then, when he and Rebecca enjoyed the first forays into carnal knowledge, he had not felt the way he had with Chica. And was this not the most fleeting, the shallowest of all emotions? Wasn't it the thing that was the least likely to engender a lasting marriage?

He had known men from his school days who had become smitten with the most beautiful of the society girls. They were vapid, insipid, inane girls who were stunningly attractive but, after a couple of years, the young men were ready to either open a vein, become drunkards or take on mistresses, just to escape spending time with their stupid wives.

But Chica was not in that category, either. It was not only her carnal offerings; it was something about her, something so irresistibly pure, a purity of spirit that he could not resist. Chica was the genuine article. She said what she thought. She did not care to dance around the issues or say or do things to please. But she was not a selfish monster, by any means, either.

He thought about Chica during the entire train ride to Tucson. Chaney was gone, off to some other city to sell his cash registers, so he had no lively conversation with the big man to occupy him. He stared out the window as the train pulled into the station, and something, a glint off on a high hill, caught his eye.

He looked up and Chica was sitting on her pony, watching the train pass. He was dumbfounded, as if he had conjured her by his thoughts of her. She was watching the train go by, studying each window as if she were looking for something. Arvel thought that perhaps she was looking for him, or perhaps contemplating the best way to get onto the train, to rob everyone of their pocket watches. Without thinking, he jumped up and opened the window. He called out to her as he passed, and she looked in his direction and waved. He gathered up his things. He was trembling at the thought of seeing her again so soon.

She rode up to the platform, and addressed him as if they had been traveling together all along. "Pendejo, there is a traveling show behind your train."

"Hello, Chica. It is good to see you, Chica."

She paid no mind to his sarcasm.

"We have to see this show, Pendejo."

"You go on, Chica. I have seen them. They aren't for me." Arvel hated traveling shows. He felt, once again, that nagging feeling in the pit of his gut, Chica's interest in the gaudy exhibition, just another example of the many differences between them.

"It will be open tomorrow," she seemed to not hear what he was saving. "We will go then."

They went the next day; Arvel paid the admission for both of them. Chica was quiet and seemed on a mission. She went directly to the freak show entrance and purchased entrance for two. Arvel stopped short.

"Seriously, Chica, I don't want to go in

there." He hated the freak shows in particular.

She grabbed his arm and headed in. She walked past the various exhibits until she got to the Wolf boy. She waited patiently until the crowd cleared, then approached the young man on the stage. For an extra ten cents, customers could stroke the hair on his face. Chica looked the young man in the eye and called out to him. "Joaquin!"

He looked at her, surprised. "Maria?"

"Sí!"

He jumped off the stage and embraced her. They chatted animatedly for several minutes. Joaquin looked on at Arvel and held out his hand. He was wearing a fine ditto suit of wool, white starched shirt, and silk cravat. He was covered from head to toe, as far as Arvel could discern, with long dark brown hair. They were speaking in Spanish to each other so excitedly that Arvel could make out but a few words. Arvel stepped back, to give them time alone together. They embraced again and Joaquin returned to the stage.

Chica grabbed Arvel by the arm, "Is okay, Pendejo. We can go now."

Chica fairly skipped along, she was happy and chatted constantly. Arvel walked along, amused at her new demeanor. She stopped at various stands, pointing to objects which she had Arvel purchase for her. Once she had collected an assortment of candies and toys, she was nearly ready to leave. She smiled at Arvel, whose hands were full of the collection of junk. She squeezed his arm, then kissed his cheek.

"What has put you in such a good mood and why am I buying all this junk?"

"It is not junk, Pendejo. It is for my babies." She waited for him to give her the expression she expected. "They are not really *my* babies, Pendejo. They are the Indios, who I go to visit. They are very poor, Pendejo, and they need candy and toys."

Chica strolled along. "I thought I was going to have to kill some gringos, Pendejo, but it is all right." She saw a fortune teller. "Come on, Pendejo, we need to see this lady."

They stepped into the tent and were greeted by a young gypsy woman, about the same age and build as Chica. She was beautiful. She beckoned for them to sit down and immediately requested a fee for the two of them. Once business was completed, she focused her attention on Arvel. She read his cards, then motioned for him to leave the tent. He waited outside impatiently. He had experience with spiritualists when Rebecca and his daughter died, as Rebecca's sister was thoroughly convinced that one could reach out to the beyond and interact with dead loved ones. Arvel thought it nonsense and felt the fool when he had any dealings with it.

Chica came out soon after. The fortune teller followed her. She hugged Chica and spoke to her quietly; they both looked at Arvel and laughed. Chica grabbed him by the arm and moved on.

"We can go now, Pendejo." She looked at him and kissed his cheek again. "We have to come back later, at eleven o'clock. Do you have your watch?"

"No, you do." She smiled. "Hey, what was my fortune?" He looked at her, was pleased at her delight.

"You don' have to worry, Pendejo." She squeezed his arm tighter. "You don' believe any of it anyway, do you, Pendejo?" She smiled coyly.

"Why do you say that?"

"It doesn' matter why I say it, it is true, am I not right?"

"Well, you tell me what my fortune is and I'll tell you if I believe it, Chica."

They walked back to the hotel. The clerk rushed toward the door, to open it for the young girl and her escort. "Good afternoon,

Miss Chica." The young man had recently combed his hair. Chica smiled and gave the man enough attention to keep him under her spell. She took Arvel by the arm and led him to her room. They stayed together until it was time to meet Joaquin.

They woke at nine and had dinner. He had remembered the gifts he had gotten her in Phoenix. He wished he'd brought the dress along as well. She was pleased. It made him happy to give her the gifts. She dabbed some of the perfume behind her ears then began playing about with the combs and mirror. The gifts put her into a particularly good mood. They were nearly late for the meeting with Joaquin.

This time, she wore the dress she had taken from Rebecca's wardrobe. She looked stunning and more dangerous than when she had her gun rig on, earlier in the day. They strolled onto the show grounds and were treated like royalty. Everyone seemed to know of the Mexican woman.

She talked as they made their way to the back lot of the show, the part not accessible to the customers. The place had a queer atmosphere, lighted by large torches; it put Arvel in mind of a medieval town, as if they were in King Arthur's Camelot. Everyone was happy and pleasantly talking and singing, many of the performers were practicing or simply engaging in their craft, just for the sheer joy of it.

Chica told Arvel about Joaquin. She knew him as a boy. He was a few years younger than Chica and everyone in the village where he lived was afraid of him. His mother had had a liaison with a traveler and became pregnant with Joaquin. When he was born, the villagers believed that she had been cursed for having the illicit affair. He was scorned and taunted all his life. Chica was the only one in the village to ever treat him with compassion, and one day, after she had gone off on one of her adventures, she discovered that a gringo had come to the village and bought Joaquin from his mother.

They were told that the man was evil and mistreated Joaquin and was planning to put him in a show. The man made Joaquin wear a chain and nothing else, and forced the boy to act like a wild animal and eat raw flesh of goats and pigs. He had a horrible life and Chica vowed to kill the man if she ever caught up with him. After she had left Arvel outside of Flagstaff, she wandered south, along the rail line, and saw the image of Joaquin painted on one of the rail cars carrying the contents of the show.

Arvel now understood Chica's behavior. She was planning to rescue Joaquin. He looked at her with a new appreciation. He held her arm tightly as they walked around the grounds.

"Chica, what happened to the bad man?"

"Joaquin says the bad man sold him to some Mexican bandits, but they killed the man instead of paying him. They just let Joaquin go on his own, as they were afraid of him. Then he wandered a while and met an old man selling medicine from a wagon and the man sent him to this place. He has been here ever since. The man here is good. He pays Joaquin three hundred dollars every month and Joaquin keeps any extra money he can make. He gets ten cents to let a gringo touch his beard. He has a house in Bayonne, New Jersey, and a wife, and a child who is not hairy." She thought for a moment. "Is Bayonne, New Jersey, good, Pendejo?"

"I've never been there, but I'm certain it's fine, Chica."

Chica, the avenging angel. He smiled at her and reached over to kiss her forehead. "You are full of surprises, Chica. You are full of surprises."

They wandered through the staging area of the show. A young woman walked up to them and handed them paste jewel encrusted goblets filled with wine. She told them that Joaquin would be with them shortly.

As they waited, Arvel glanced between the flaps of a tent and saw a large glass jar which contained the severed head of a dark-haired man. The man had a stupid look on his face, which was swollen from soaking in the alcohol bath for God knows how long. It reminded him of the story told by Billy Livingston. "Chica, have you ever carried heads around in a sack?"

"Wha' . . . hey!" She pushed him out of the way and walked into the tent. She examined the head in the glass. There was a plaque with an inscription on it. "What do this say, Pendejo?"

She was forming the words, but read English poorly.

"This is the head of Enrique Gomez, the famous murderer of California, who was killed by a posse in 1861. Too far out in the desert to carry the entire body, the industrious lawmen severed the brigand's head in order to prove his demise."

"Tha' is not right, Pendejo." Before he could say or do anything, Chica had the

285

head upended and removed the lid.

A young man rushed in to stop her. "Madam, please, please."

Chica continued her work. "This is a not Enrique Gomez, or whatever you say, Pendejo."

"Miss Maria?" Another man joined them. This one was wearing a Prince Albert suit and long cape. He wore a high silk topper. He had a strange accent, never heard by Chica before.

"Sí, I am Chica." She looked up from her work of removing the head from the jar.

The man in the topper bowed to Arvel and Chica. "I am Ivan Yakovlevich." He reached out and took Chica's hand, began to kiss it, then thought better of it. He pulled out a handkerchief and dabbed at her hand. "Mr. Joaquin has told me so much about you."

The young man interjected, "Mr. Yakovlevich, the lady is taking the head out of its container." He was flush with excitement.

Yakovlevich patted the man on the shoulder, "Now now, Vladimir, it is okay. Miss Chica, how may we help?"

"This is not Enrique Gomez. And none of that written there is right."

"How do you know?"

"Thees hijo de puta is just a head, because

286

I made him that way."

Yakovlevich chuckled. "Miss Chica, he died a long time ago, and you are a young lady. Perhaps you are thinking of another head?"

"This is my head, go ahead an' look at his mouth. He has a gold tooth, right here," she pointed at the upper front tooth of her mouth. "And he has a no tooth next to it."

"How so?" said Arvel. He was intrigued now. Chica never stopped surprising him.

"He had two gold teeth and I pulled one, but the other I could not pull. Go ahead and look." She began to reach into the blood tinged alcohol to retrieve the head.

Yakovlevich waved her away gently, "Madam, please, you will soil your dress." He nodded to Vladimir who unwillingly carried out the morbid task, peeling back the bloated lips to reveal the interior of the miscreant's mouth.

"See, see, I told you." She looked at the men, satisfied. "I sent this one to hell. Look, pull his hair up; you will see the bullet hole. I shot him in this side." She pointed at the left side of the skull. "A little hole, I used a little gun, two-shot I had in my sleeve. I cut his head off and carried it in a bag for three days, then sold it to a prospector. This was at leas', let's see, four years ago."

"What did he do to you?" Vladimir asked, intrigued.

"This excremento did nothing to me. He hurt a child I knew. He did not kill her but he hurt her. And that is all I will say. He is in hell now, where he belongs, but he has no head, so he cannot see where he is going. He cannot hurt little children anymore."

"Then the plaque will be changed and, Miss Chica, we shall make certain it is accurate."

He asked Arvel for permission, and took Chica by the arm. "In all my years, traveling the world, I must say, Miss Chica, that you are the most lovely and remarkable being I have yet to meet."

He patted her hand and leaned close to her ear. "But please, don't tell any of the others I have said that. I have many remarkable ladies here and some have rather fragile egos."

Chica smiled and looked back at Arvel. She gave him a wink and walked proudly with her new admirer. He led her to a bonfire, surrounded by benches. Joaquin was there, as were a man well over seven feet tall, two ladies who were identical and joined at the hip, two young men with beady eyes and sloping pointed heads, known by all as The Lads, and a middle-aged woman who looked like anyone you'd pass on the street.

Her talent was that she could swallow a sword three feet long and breathe fire. Her name was Pat.

The men stood up when Chica arrived, except for The Lads who had no more understanding than a three-year-old child. They smiled and laughed and looked on at Pat, who had become their surrogate mother.

Arvel sat down next to the sisters who had a penchant for flirtatious behavior. They loved reserved men like Arvel who were typically shy around women. They liked to make them blush. One placed her hand high up on Arvel's thigh, then pulled away abruptly and smiled at him, stating, "I am sorry! I thought you were my sister." They would then giggle together in a high pitched tone. They were really quite lovely and Arvel could not help but think what it must be like to be intimate with conjoined twins.

Joaquin sat next to Chica. He hugged her and told her how happy he was to see her. He told her how he never forgot her compassion toward him. Out of all the people he had ever known before the show, she was the only one to ever offer him any kindness.

He had put on a fresh suit and looked more dapper than he had when she had seen him earlier in the day.

He smiled at Chica admiring his suit. "I have eleven suits, Chica." He was not telling her this to impress her or to show off. He wanted her to know that she did not have to worry about him. Yakovlevich was a good man. He respected the people in his show. If it had not been for him, most would have ended up in asylums or destitute. They all felt wanted and loved. They were treated with great respect and every one of them was well compensated for their work.

They were especially festive tonight. The Tucson show was bringing in major crowds and people were in a spending mood. They laughed and drank and talked well into the night. Arvel had gotten used to the twins and began regaling them with stories of Chica, which inspired Yakovlevich to make his move.

"Miss Chica, I do not know if Joaquin mentioned anything to you, but the Wild West is big business in the East, and beyond. In Europe, the people cannot get enough of it. And, well, ma'am, I will cut to the chase, I would be honored if you would be part of our show."

Chica smiled, she had moved close to

Arvel, sitting across from the twins who had been taking turns running their fingers through his hair. She pressed her fingers into his arm. "That is a very interesting, how do we say, que es asunto?" She looked at Joaquin.

Joaquin leaned forward, "Proposition."

"Sí, Proposition. That is a very interesting proposition, Señor Yakovlevich. What would I do in your show?"

"You would be Chica."

"I don' think anyone would pay money for this, Señor."

Yakovlevich laughed and held up his hand. "Miss, Chica, you are wrong. You are . . ."

"Magnificent!" Vladimir blurted out without thinking; the moment, the wine and the allure of Chica too much for him to contain. He looked down at his hands, trying to hide in the shadows of the dancing fire.

"Bravo, Vladimir, bravo!"

He bowed to Chica. "You see, Miss Chica, just as the others around the fire have a special gift, given them by the Almighty, you have a gift, too. You are Chica. There is nothing more to be said."

She leaned next to Arvel. She pressed her cheek against his. "What do you think, Pendejo, should I get a house in Bayonne, New Jersey?"

291

■ ■ ■

Early next morning, Chica woke Arvel.
"Pendejo, I have to go."

"Why?" He looked for his watch.

"I gotta go, Pendejo. But, you see, I did
tell you. Are you not happy?"

"Yes, Chica." He wanted to tell her not to
go, but something kept him from commit-
ting to it. He looked at her and thought
about how much he loved her now. "Where
are you going? When am I to expect you
back?"

"I gotta go, I gotta get these things to my
Indios babies, Pendejo." She waited for a
moment, put on the last of her bangles and
fixed her hair. She waited a little longer,
shrugged.

She was gone.

Chapter XV:
Indios

She rode back to see the Indian family. She felt strangely sad. She was really happy to see Joaquin and very flattered at the attention paid to her by the show people so she should have been happier. The fortune teller gave her good news and she had fine presents to give the children. She even had a wonderful time with Pendejo, but she could not deny to herself that she was deeply hurt when he did not ask her to stay.

She wondered what was wrong with the Pendejo. She was trying her best to behave herself, and still be herself. This time she even woke him, and she stole nothing from him. She wondered if the Pendejo really cared very much for her. He seemed to be much happier with her. She could not help but see that he was proud of her before the show people. She could see that the head did put him off a little, especially when she pulled it from the bottle, and that confused her. It was just a dead head, it would not hurt anyone, it was beyond doing any harm. What did the Pendejo think the head would do? Talk to him? Bite her? She had a hard time figuring the gringo out.

She rode along, wondering what it would be like to be in a traveling show with all the strange people. Joaquin seemed happy; really happy. She did not like the thought of all those gringos touching him and saying bad things about him, but what else could Joaquin do? He could never be paid so well doing anything else, that was certain. It was easy work. He did not have to toil in the fields and he seemed to have picked up a great deal of book learning. He sounded more like Pendejo than how he sounded, or would sound, had he stayed in his village. So, really, the horrible curse that befell him was almost a blessing.

When she arrived at the Indians encampment, the two youngest ones and the women of the village greeted her. She often spent time here with the small group of Indians who herded sheep in the area. They had escaped the white man. They did not have to live on the reservation, as they gave the white man no reason to torment them. The land held no value to the whites, so they did not need to kick them out and onto a reservation. They were good to her and so poor she'd never take their food. She brought the fruits of her labors, so to speak, to these people whenever she could. The money from a stolen watch would go to buy a bag of flour, or the price fetched from a stolen saddle a few chickens.

They ran to see her when they realized the traveler off in the distance and moving their way was the mysterious woman who would periodically come into their lives, adding excitement to an otherwise relentless quest for survival. They were happier to see her than were the traveling show people. She showed off her latest acquisitions: new bangles and necklaces and earrings. She gave the women coffee. She dabbed some of the perfume the Pendejo had given her behind the ears of each little girl.

She lined the children up, by height, and gave the little ones their gifts first. They did not know what to do and Chica urged them to take the toys and candy. In unison, they suddenly understood and ran off to play.

Chica removed Alanza's saddle and hobbled her near the Hogan. She decided she would stay here for a few days. The weather was hot but not unbearable and it would be no better in any town. The women unpacked her bags and washed her clothes. They placed Chica's traps in her own Hogan and laid out her hair brushes, mirror, jewelry, cigars, and extra cartridges near her bed which was freshened and made extra comfortable for their special guest.

This called for a celebration and that evening everyone sang and played and prepared special dishes for the occasion. Chica sang for them and did a little play. They celebrated late into the night. Chica was offered a bottle and declined. She did not want to drink now. She was enjoying the children and glorying in the moment of community. She felt at home here and wondered if her life would ever be this way; to have a real family, to live out her days with a clan of her own.

The next morning she was up early. She felt good. The sun was still a long way from rising. She saddled Alanza and took out her fancy rifle. She counted the bullets for this rifle. She had eighty left. She did not know what she would do when they were gone, but decided that one would be worth using to get something good for the Indios. She and Alanza were ready when the sky began to show the first signs of light. She could survey a wide expanse of desert and she used the telescopic sight to explore the range. She spotted a small herd of elk a quarter mile away and rode around them, setting up from the southeast to avoid having them wind her. She checked again and a warm breeze blew in her face, she should be undetectable to them as she approached.

She hobbled Alanza when she was within a hundred yards leaving her in an arroyo, undetected by the herd. She killed a young cow and the rest ran off a short distance. They looked on as Chica dressed the animal and loaded her hind quarters onto Alanza's back. She would get the clan to come for the rest. She rode Alanza back to the Hogans, proud of her accomplishment and proud that she could provide such a tasty treat for her adopted family.

After the chores were done and the young elk broken down into its most basic elements of usefulness, she taught the older ones Mexican Monte. At least they would have an advantage in this when they got older; maybe the gringos would not be able to cheat them at cards. The old women watched as they worked on the green elk hide. They had already stripped it of its connective tissue and were liberally rubbing its brain into the flesh side of the skin. They would work tirelessly until it was preserved and as supple as the finest tanned calfskin.

To make things interesting, Chica had the

children collect their *money* — shards of broken pottery that had been left by their ancestors over the course of many centuries. The children would run about, digging through the brush, looking straight down at the ground, looking at places they had trampled over all their lives, never before seeing the treasures at their feet. They would run to Chica, showing what they had found. The more beautiful and ornately designed, the higher the value, but Chica would always encourage them. Even the most mundane shard was considered a great discovery.

The younger ones loved to play hide and seek. They waited impatiently for Chica to give them their due. She was not bold and reckless when she was with the children. She reverted to a childlike state, struggling to recreate the childhood she never had and this always made her particularly happy.

Alanza was not a good participant, however, and whenever it came time for Chica to hide, the pony would constantly seek her out and find her before the children could finish counting. They protested and, despite being scolded by all, Alanza would simply shake her head and snort. She liked to play as much as they. Chica led her to a narrow slot which opened to a box canyon. The children sometimes kept goats here when they needed to contain them. They had collected piles of dead graythorn and placed it in the gap. Alanza was irritated, and pawed the ground, calling out to Chica and standing on her hind legs to get a glimpse of her mistress over the newly formed hedge. Finally, Chica tied her to a stout limb. It was either this or remove her saddle altogether, something Chica was loathe to do since she did not like to be unprepared.

Finally, when Alanza was adequately sequestered, they could play in earnest. It was the children's turn to hide and Chica would have to go find them all. It was always this way. The children all got to team up on Chica but she had to find each one individually.

A brother and a sister hid together at the bottom of a canyon. Chica found the others easily, but these two were being tricky. As Chica wandered further away from the others, she detected the unmistakable metallic scent of rain, but there was no sign of a storm. The sky was a cloudless blue. She walked further, and considered going back for Alanza. She did not like to wander far on foot and the two siblings were being especially difficult to find.

Finally, she gave up. A feeling of foreboding inspired her to end the game. She called out to them, telling them they had won, to come in for the great prize. She listened and waited. She continued to call for them as she walked and was drawn to the sound of rushing water.

She could finally make out muffled cries and ran in the direction of the sound. The children had found a good hiding place at the base of a slot canyon and while pre-occupied, became stranded by a flood of brown water. It was running faster and more furious by the minute.

They were trapped on a little island which would soon be under many tons of angry water, full of debris and ready to take them to their deaths. Chica ran back toward the village and repeatedly gave a loud song-like call to Alanza. The pony heard her and began to pace. She pawed at the thorn bushes blocking her path and finally tore free from the limb that had been restraining her. She cantered in circles looking for a way out. Finally, with her ears flattened, she ran at the thorn bushes, jumped, and cleared the barrier before her, running in the direction of her mistress. She galloped up to Chica, snorting and throwing her head.

The two children were frantic. They knew what floods like this could do; they had lost members of their family to them. They clung together at the top of the remaining ground, watching in terror as the earth around them became saturated, then crumbled away into the swirling waters. They called out to Chica.

Chica jumped on Alanza's back in one motion. She rode hard across the rushing water. Alanza quickly became bogged down in the loosened, muddy earth. Chica got close enough to grab the girl. She pulled her onto her lap and turned Alanza around. She made it back to safety.

She wheeled about and rushed toward the boy, but Alanza could not negotiate the water and began to founder. They drifted downstream and crashed into a bank of rocky ground on the other side, which was closer to the boy.

He was crying now. He was holding fast to some brush which was bound to be washed free at any moment. Chica feared the worst. She rode Alanza up the bank and threw a rope around the brush the boy was using to keep from being washed away. She tied the other end to the saddle horn.

Chica dropped to the ground, pulling off her boots and gun belt. She threw her sombrero on top of her traps and waded, barefoot, into the rushing water. She held onto the rope and reached the boy. He clung to her desperately.

His face showed no understanding of what was happening. He was completely overtaken by panic. Chica gained control of the child and tied him to her waist. She waited. She watched the water rise until it was up to her chest and held the boy next to her, which seemed to calm him. This was the first time in her life she was truly afraid. This was not an enemy she could shoot or stab or outrun. The energy of the rushing water was awesome and Chica knew that if it continued to build, or any large debris flowed down over them, they would not survive.

Chica tried to pray but could not remember the fancy prayers the priest had taught her so she just began to call out the names of Jesus, Mary, Joseph, and every saint's name she had ever heard.

She dug her toes into the muddy earth beneath her feet and held onto the rope, which vibrated steadily. She was certain she could feel Alanza's heart beating; the determined animal looked on at Chica, just a few yards away. It was as if the horse knew the danger her mistress was in, and stood, resolute, keeping the rope taut, the lifeline between her and her beloved.

The girl had gone back to the village for help and the family was now waiting helplessly on the bank. There was nothing they could do for the pair. They looked on powerlessly.

The water was now up to Chica's neck. She held the child tightly against her chest, raising him up until he was nearly sitting on her shoulders. Broken sticks and branches had torn Chica's shirt to shreds and scraped her back and neck. She was certain she would not be able to lay down for a week. She thought about the Pendejo. She wondered what he would think if she did not return. She was sorry that she had left him again and resolved to go to him if she were to survive this ordeal. She prayed some more.

And finally, almost as quickly as it came, the waters began to recede.

In another hour, it was down to her waist and after another hour she was able to wade through the receding flood holding onto the rope.

They finally made it back to Alanza. Chica lay down with the boy and held him in her arms. He was shaking from fear and exhaustion.

The sun beating down on them felt good. It felt wonderful to be alive and Chica said another prayer, thanking the Virgin for sparing them. She promised to pay tribute when she saw the priest.

By sundown the torrent was gone, merely a memory. Chica and the boy rode Alanza back across the muddy remains to the family waiting on the other side. They cheered and cried and hugged.

Chica was pleased. She was once again the hero of the Indios. She was proud that she was so heroic and she was proud of Alanza. She had been afraid, but had never lost her nerve. She had behaved with grace and courage. She knew in her heart that if it were not for her, the children would be dead.

They made their way back to the village, and the women pulled Chica's clothes off, bathed her, and tended to her wounds. Like some great, mythical warrior, she was home from battle and the mere mortals were awestruck by this goddess's presence. She was the closest thing to an immortal that they would ever behold and they treated her accordingly. That night, they dined on elk and drank and celebrated the survival of the children. It was more gratifying to Chica than her experience with the traveling show people. She was proud.

She stayed with the Indians for another

week. Her abrasions were healing and she could tolerate her clothes covering them by then. She was able to sleep and rest and dream. She mostly spent time watching the children, enjoying them enjoying the gifts she had brought.

The women never questioned Chica about anything. They did not know why she was so good to them. They never knew when she would appear to them and never gave it a thought to ask her anything about her life. Of course, they remembered nursing her back to health when she had been wounded by the gambler's little gun. This was no small task as Chica was at death's door when she wandered into their lives but Chica had repaid them a long time ago.

They knew that Chica was an outlaw and likely a loose woman, but they could not help but love her. Chica was what every one of them dreamed of being, in a sense. She was fearless and answered to no one. No man, no chief, no boss, not even to any form of society or government that they could see.

She did adhere, loosely, to some form of Christianity, but it seemed to them that Chica even seemed to be master of that realm. As if Jesus Christ himself would have to conform to Chica's world, rather than the other way around.

And now she had defeated death by Mother Nature, the greatest adversary of all. Chica had beaten the flood. She had robbed Death of the two children and she had once again robbed Death of Chica.

CHAPTER XVI:
SUBTERFUGE

The handsome young Texan sat, dried blood pasting flat his curly hair. Two men sat across the table from him. They played cards while they waited. He had been ambushed and they had gotten the best of him. He could do nothing now but wait for what was to come. He asked for a drink of water and the men ignored him. He asked again and one stood up and kicked his chair backward, causing him to strike his head on the floor. He once again lost consciousness.

When he awoke, the man in the mustard ditto suit was sitting at the table. He did not know this man. The little shack was crowded now. He figured he was at an abandoned mine and sitting in one of the outbuildings there. "So, you are one of the Arizona Rangers?" The old man did not look up from his cards.

"I cannot say I know what you are talking about, Mister." He remained polite.

One of the henchmen threw the Ranger star on the table. "We found this on him."

"Oh, so you are not so fond of the star, I see." He put the cards on the table. "By the end of the night, you will wish you had eaten that star, boy." His lips curled into a sneer.

"You can go to hell."

The henchman stood up and approached him. The young Ranger anticipated another beating. He decided that he would do something before they finished him. He stood on his feet and, using the chair, pushed back against the wall and transferred his weight to his trussed arms. He kicked sideways at the man. The heel of his boot smashed the man's jaw, dropping him to the floor. The Texan kicked again, down with the rowel of his big Texas spur and punctured the man's throat. He put all the weight of his body onto the rowel of the spur, and drove it to the man's spine, severing the artery in his neck. The man began gagging on his own blood.

The old man stood up and the young Ranger tried the same trick, this time only gashing the old man's cheek. The third man hit him hard across the face and knocked him back to the floor.

The old man felt the gash on his face. He

looked down at the henchman on the floor, bleeding out. He would not live long. He turned his attention to the Ranger and ordered the second henchmen, "Get him upright."

He grabbed the badge and shoved the star's clasp into the man's cheek, leaving it pinned to his face. The young Texan would not cry out.

"You are tough."

He motioned for the remaining henchman to leave. He took a stick of dynamite from his pocket and began working a fuse into one end. "A half stick'll do." He looked up at the Ranger and smiled. He struck a match.

The Ranger looked up at a sign over the door. It read *No Smoking.* He pulled his tongue free of the pin, and spoke with difficulty. "An open flame's not very safe," he nodded toward the sign and the old man turned to look.

"You have a good sense of humor, lad." He lit the dynamite. He let it burn awhile, smoke began to fill the room. He placed it under the young man's chair. He looked at him. He simply said, "Good bye," and walked out of the little shack.

An ear and the star were recovered and mailed to Dick Welles.

■ ■ ■ ■

Dick Welles paced around the room, waiting for Arvel to finish reading the letter. The box of badges and ears sat on the desk, next to Arvel's coffee.

The letter read:

Honorable Captain Welles:
Enclosed, please find some remains and the badges of two of your Rangers. They died horribly, yet honorably. Please be warned that the contents of this letter should be shared with no one. This is a matter strictly between you and me.
My requirements are as follows. It is necessary that you begin to work with our organization in all matters related to the Arizona territory and its borders. I represent a National organization with powers at the highest levels of this government as well as many governments around the world. Resistance would be futile.
In the event that you choose to ignore this friendly warning, please be advised that you will continue to receive packages containing the badges and ears of

your Rangers. Additionally, you will be interested to note that we are in regular communication with your son, Michael, in San Francisco. As you know, he continues to have a particular problem with laudanum. His bad luck at the various gambling houses, unfortunately, continues to burden him.

I will look for your advertisement in the *Daily Star.* Please enter the following; "Will await instructions." I will send you correspondence when I see you are ready to work with our organization. Please do not tarry, Captain Welles. I will wait until the twenty-fifth of the month, at which time you can expect another package bearing another unpleasant surprise.

Sincerely yours,
A Friend

Arvel beckoned Dick to sit down. "This is a bad business, Dick. But we know something that they don't know."

Dick looked up. "What's that?"

"That we're a team, that you're not corruptible. They think that they can get inside our organization through you. That's good."

"I never thought of it that way."

"But what can we do about Michael?"

Arvel looked Dick in the eye.

"*And* the men. Look, Arvel, you know my problems with Michael. He's been a problem for me for years. But I have all the other men to worry about now, *and* I have an obligation to the territory. I've given this a lot of thought, and that's why I brought you the letter. I've been sending Michael money for years. I've tried to help him, but, he's not gotten any better. I'm afraid this is a hard bed he's made for himself and he's just going to have to lie in it."

"But these boys don't fool around, Dick. If we don't play this right, he might end up dead."

"Then we'll just have to play it right."

"Who else knows about this letter, Dick?"

"No one."

"We'll keep it that way. Meaning, no one, and I mean no one, not my uncle, not your family, not Dan, not any other Rangers. Okay?"

The reality of Rangering hit home for Arvel. Up until this time, to his mind, only his own life was at stake. Certainly the Rangers reporting to him faced the dangers of lawmen, but this was assassination, and now Dick's son was at risk. What next? Could Uncle Bob or the ranch hands, or Pilar be in danger? It was a sobering thought. Who could these people be? An international organization, here, in Arizona? It was difficult to comprehend.

Dick sent his response to the newspaper and received another letter. This time, he was given specific instructions on a planned Wells Fargo coach robbery. The expected take was a forty thousand dollar payroll. The letter detailed exactly what would happen. There was an assurance that no blood would be spilled, providing nothing happened on the part of the Rangers.

Arvel studied the letter.

"What're we going to do now, Arvel? We can't just let them waltz off with forty thousand dollars. That's complicity."

"Well, it's your first test, Dick. You pass this one, and others'll no doubt follow. It's really the only way to keep Michael and the Rangers from being killed." He lit a cigarette and offered one to Dick. He lit it quickly off of Arvel's and paced around nervously, smoking.

"That's not a good enough reason."

"No, but it is also not the only reason, Dick. We've nothing to go on right now. We don't know who these people are or if, in fact, it *is* people. It might just be one person."

"Or an international organization. My

God, I thought we were going to be chasing down some cattle rustlers when I took this job. What have we gotten into, Arvel?"

"Don't know, Dick." He sat back in his chair and rubbed his forehead. It was a bad business, indeed. The villain was into dramatics, that was certain. "Let's see what we've got, Dick. We know that for forty thousand dollars we buy some time, we learn more about this outfit, we save lives in the form of the stagecoach drivers, our Rangers, and Michael."

"Right."

"And the alternative is to go ahead and intervene."

"Right."

"But you know they'll be watching, and if there is so much as a hint of Ranger intervention, they'll just not do the robbery and we'll get nothing except to incur the wrath of whomever is writing these letters. And, we'll lose his confidence in you and we are back to square one and can expect more ears and badges in the post."

"And Michael affected, maybe killed."

"Right." Arvel lit another smoke. "So, the logical thing to do is let the robbery happen."

"We can't do that, Arvel."

"Or maybe we can." He began to grin.

"Dick, you trust me, right?"

"With my life and with the lives of my family."

"And you are willing to do some damage to these hombres?"

"Of course. I'd kill 'em all right now if I could, and sleep well tonight."

Arvel got up and walked Dick to the door. "Let me do some more thinking on it. I'll stop by the office tomorrow and let you know what I've come up with."

On the day of the robbery the two men met at the train station, heading up to Tucson. Arvel had a big article written up in the paper telling about the celebration put on by Governor Murphy to acknowledge the fledgling Ranger organization. Arvel and Dick would be the guests of honor. This would certainly satisfy Dick's pen pal and ensure that Dick was keeping up his end of the bargain. The robbery would take place that evening, south of Tombstone, too far from Tucson for them to be involved in foiling it.

Dick stood nervously on the train platform. He held his hat in his hand. He was wearing his best sack suit and was armed only with a small pocket revolver. He felt vulnerable. The guilt was nearly unbearable.

■ ■ ■ ■

The bandits hit the coach as it lurched up a steep incline. The horses struggled to keep up a steady pace. This was the standard ambush location for stage coach robberies. The driver and his shotgun escort offered no resistance and handed over the strongbox without incident. The robbers galloped off west for a mile or so, then stopped to destroy the lock on the box and remove the contents to their saddlebags. There were three of them, and they had been assured by the boss of the caper that it would be an easy job. Certain they had not been followed, they walked their horses along at a leisurely pace.

Up ahead, they saw a campfire, too large and too bright. It was raging in the middle of the road heading to Tombstone. They approached cautiously and could just make out the form of a man, sitting, back to them, facing the fire. They called out to him and received no reply. One of the bandits became nervous. "I don't like this one bit."

"Settle down, Claude."

"You there, give us the road."

He got no reply. Just as the three bandits prepared to draw their guns, they received an order, high above them on a hill over-looking the road, to put their hands up.

Unable to bolt and too crowded together on the narrow road to turn and run, they were forced to comply. The seated figure stood up and turned. He removed the Indian blanket which had shrouded him from their view. A scarf covered his face. He pointed a shotgun at them and motioned for them to dismount. They stood, dumb-founded, not certain what to do. They heard the hammers on the ten-gauge click into full cock.

They dismounted. The man on the rock above them ordered them to strip. They complied. He came down and collected their horses, guns, and clothes. He, too, wore a scarf. He turned and headed back up the trail. The three bandits stood, slack-jawed, wearing not a stitch. They watched as their horses and traps rode off. They stood for five minutes with their hands in the air. The smartest one finally made a move and they all began walking to Tomb-stone wondering how they were going to explain this to the old man.

"What are we goin' to do now?"

"Shut up, Claude."

The two Rangers rode for a while. Arvel suddenly laughed out loud. "That was some voice disguise, Dick. I thought someone else had joined us."

Dick finally had reason to laugh a little himself. "That was my impersonation of Buffalo Bill."

"Really?"

"Have you seen his show?"

"Never."

"Well, you can believe me when I tell you I sounded just like him."

Arvel rode along for a while. He turned in his saddle. "Why would you go to see Buffalo Bill's Wild West Show?"

"Don't know." He grinned at Arvel.

"That is a lot of foolishness." He lit a cigarette. "Was it any good?"

"Well, I'll tell you. It wasn't like any Wild West I've ever seen."

Arvel shifted in his saddle, "I'll never understand how anyone can ride a horse. Damned most uncomfortable creatures." His big stallion perked his ears and turned them toward Arvel. Arvel patted him on the neck. "Sorry."

"Well, you didn't have to pick the biggest animal you could find. Looks like a shire horse."

"That's what Del Toro rides. I wanted to look like him. He's called Jefe. Do you think I could get the boys to start calling me Jefe?"

Dick looked at him sideways. "I send you on one trip south and you go native." He lit a cigarette as he rode. "What was that silly looking knife you were sporting, anyway?"

Arvel laughed. "They call it a daga."

"Next thing you know, you'll be cavorting with pepper bellies." Arvel felt himself blush, glad that it was not yet daylight.

"I'll just be glad to get back on a mule."

Dick thought about the events of the last few hours. He looked over at Arvel. He was an amazing fellow. "I was sure you were going to let that robbery happen, Arvel. All the way up to the point when we got on the train to see the governor."

"That's called subterfuge." Arvel shifted again in his saddle. "Did it a lot in the war, Dick."

"Well, you pulled the wool over my eyes, that's for certain."

"You know I didn't keep my plans from you out of mistrust, right, Dick?"

"No, no offence taken."

Arvel always prided himself on his scheming abilities during the war. He was ambivalent, at best, about the Rebels. He did not agree with their cause, but he did not hate them. He didn't like to see fine men wasted. Throughout the war, there were many times when he stood by, helpless, as men, thousands of them, would be thrown relentlessly at impenetrable defenses. The slaughter was appalling. He learned early on that he had a gift for various schemes and plots, which often resulted in victories that would avoid senseless loss of life. When he could find leaders smart enough to listen to him, he was often responsible for a decrease in casualties on both sides.

"I always figured I could save lives if I did some good scheming."

Dick laughed out loud.

"What's so funny?"

"You sure have left a pile of corpses behind you since taking up this Ranger business. Not the sort of behavior I would expect from a conscientious objector."

"I'm not a conscientious objector." Arvel smiled and thought of his mother. "I see no inconsistency in my philosophy and my actions." He lit another cigarette and leaned forward in his saddle. The huge girth of his mount was making his legs ache. "Men who fight for a cause don't deserve to die needlessly, Dick. But that bunch, the bandits and those Englishmen, well, they needed to die."

"Oh, so you are judge, jury and executioner, all rolled into one?" Dick was just trying to get his goat, now. Arvel did not take the bait.

"No, no. I'm not saying that. But, you know, Dick, there is no place on earth for those monsters. They just plain needed killing. Why wait and risk an escape, or maybe the chance that they could kill again? A good riddance of bad rubbish."

"That is a nice way of putting it, Arvel. Did you make that up?"

"No, no. It was a minor poet, named Smollett."

"Never heard of him."

"I did say he was a minor poet." He shifted again, lifted one leg up and threw it over his saddle horn and thought of Chica. He wondered what she was up to.

"So, where was I, you've made me lose my train of thought . . . I figured out a long time ago, Dick, that if I was going to formulate a plan, it was best to keep it locked in the old noodle," he pointed to his head. "That way, there are fewer hands and brains in it to get it muddled. I figured you'd understand all this."

He looked over at Dick. He could just start making out his face clearly in the dawning light. "And besides," he smiled. "That look on your face was priceless when we were standing at the train platform. Any spies who were following us would have been convinced that you were doing nothing to stop the robbery. You were guilty as hell. The best actors can't fake that."

Dick looked a little sheepishly. "I guess you were thinking that I didn't trust you then."

"Not at all. There's a lot that goes into all of this. I told you I'd make certain the robbery wouldn't be a success and you believed me. But, I also knew you'd still feel guilty about going up to a dinner, trying to enjoy yourself. I didn't like to make you anxious, but I needed to, at least for a while. I'm just glad you took it so well, Dick. You're a good man and a good friend. I appreciate your trusting me."

Dick felt the weight come off his shoulders. He was tired, he experienced the feeling that only folks who work when everyone else is asleep, can know. The bad man, whomever he was, had been defeated but this was just the first round in a long fight.

The great thing was that Arvel's mind was likely superior to his enemy's. Dick was glad of this. He always had a grudging respect for Arvel's education and social standing. Dick was a working man and never received the advantages of the social class of which Arvel was a member. He always felt that, if given the same advantage, he could be just as good. It was a nagging feeling that haunted him all his life and what drove his ambition. But the stars were never in alignment for Dick Welles. He always came up a little short, was just behind in grasping the next great thing.

Even in this encounter, he was not certain what he would have done, but it would not have likely turned out so well. He recognized this as a limitation. Not a failing, but a limitation. It was good to have Arvel on his side, and he, for once, did not resent the fact that someone other than he had been in charge.

Arvel and Dick got to the ranch around sunup. They locked the Wells Fargo money in Arvel's safe and burned the robbers' traps. They turned the robbers' horses loose in the desert after removing their bridles and saddles, which they threw off a cliff. There was nothing to associate them with the robbery of the robbers and they had an alibi, thanks to the reporter on the Tucson paper. Dick's pen pal could not associate the Rangers with the foiling of the robbery. Dick could not be blamed if the robbers were robbed and, as there is no honor among thieves, the mastermind of the robbery plot would have to conclude that somewhere along the way, his plan was revealed to some other bandits.

Dick was encouraged, but they were no closer to learning about the organization than before. Nothing among the bandit's traps gave them a clue. Their only hope was that Dick had passed the first test and would be given another assignment soon; something that would bring him closer to the mastermind of the plot.

The three failed bandits stood before the old man. Spittle sprayed about them as he shouted profanities. He was out forty thousand dollars. And he was livid. They could tell him nothing. They could not tell him how many men robbed them, they had inflated the number to six but could not be certain. They could not tell what the men looked like. They could tell him nothing.

"Well, there is one thing, sir."

"What?" he stared menacing at the youngest one.

"Well, the man who called out to us, sir."

"Yes, yes?"

"I swear it was Buffalo Bill."

CHAPTER XVII:
INTERLOPER

Arvel nearly clobbered the young deputy with the sack of flour he threw into the wagon. The man was asleep, his breathing so shallow that Arvel initially thought him dead. He tugged at the man who turned slightly to face him and Arvel recognized him. He was shocked at his appearance, though he was a small man he looked even smaller now. He was emaciated. His face was scabby, skin yellow. He had black circles under his eyes. He stunk of vomit and urine.

Arvel shook him by the shoulder to no avail. Finally he resolved to take him back to the ranch. He did not know what else to do with him and still harbored regret at shooting the man's toe. He made a bed of the sacks, then covered them with a heavy blanket so the man would not leak into his foodstuffs.

He rode carefully home with his new ward. He wondered what the man had gotten himself into, to be reduced to such a state. Uncle Bob helped put the young deputy into one of the bunks, away from the hands. He did not want to offend them by putting a derelict into their home.

Arvel went about his work and came back later to check on the man, who by now was sitting at the edge of the bunk, holding his head in his hands.

"Hello."

The man looked up through bleary eyes. He looked back at the floor and grunted hello.

"Here are some clean clothes," he pointed at the foot of the bunk. "Give me yours and I'll have Pilar clean them up for you. I've got a spare razor and some soap and a towel in there. If you want clean water, you can get some at the well. Just ask Pilar if you need anything else."

The young deputy thought on that. Just *ask* a servant? That is what he hated about the man.

Next day, the young man sauntered up to the house and had the good sense to ask for an audience with Arvel. Uncle Bob immediately disliked the man. He told him to wait and after a while returned, escorting him in to Arvel's bedroom, which served additionally as his office.

Arvel sat at his desk and stood up when the young man entered the room.

"Feeling any better?"

"Yeah," he grunted. "I was wanting to know if I could work for you."

Arvel gestured for him to sit down. He looked better today; still pale and scaly, but cleaner, at least. Arvel looked the man over as the lad stared at the floor. He did not trust him to work with the mules or the hands. He knew the man would run his mouth and possibly be killed by the hands, or likely, have his head kicked off by a mule. He didn't want him working around the women, either. He thought for a while.

"Can you read and write?"

"Yeah."

He handed the man a tally sheet and a pencil. "Tell me the sum of these numbers."

Arvel walked out of the room. He sat out on the porch and had a smoke with Uncle Bob.

"What are you planning, son?"

Arvel took a drag on his cigarette. "I know, don't say it, I am too kind."

"Okay, I won't say it." Uncle Bob took a smoke from Arvel's packet.

"That's the boy I shot in the toe."

"I see." He smoked. "You do what you think is best, son." They sat for a while and smoked. Uncle Bob crushed the cigarette out on the sole of his boot. "Just one thing, Arvel. Remember when we first met, and I was teaching you about mules?"

"Certainly, Uncle."

"Can you remember what I said was the most important rule of training a mule?"

"Don't let it kick you in the head?"

Uncle Bob laughed. "No. That's a good one, but that isn't it. I told you to never harm a mule. They will not train to fear, and they will always remember when an unkindness was done to them. They won't forgive and forget."

"Yes, of course I remember that one, Uncle."

"Well, this fellow. You and Dick Welles were a bit unkind to this fellow." He held up his hand, "Not unjustifiably, son, don't get me wrong. The little whelp deserved it. But a man like that, you just don't know how long he'll hold a grudge, or what he might end up doing to you if he gets the opportunity to take revenge."

Arvel finished his cigarette. "I know, Uncle." He looked around to make certain the man was not around. "I just want to give him a chance. I don't know, there's something in him that seems to be alright. He just needs it coaxed out of him."

The young deputy came outside and handed the sheet to Arvel without looking at him. His writing was cryptic and small. The sums were accurate. The man spent the rest of the day sulking around, working at various clerical tasks as Arvel came up with things for him to do.

Arvel set a routine for the young deputy as he felt that some sameness and stability would agree with him. Arvel did not let him wander far, except to let the young man leave the ranch one day a week. He could not say that he liked the young man, but something about him made him think that he had some goodness in him. Arvel believed if he showed him how decent people lived and gave him a square deal, maybe he'd come around.

One evening Arvel was feeling poorly. He was struck by severe cramps and figured he'd eaten something a little off. He lay in bed trying to relieve the pain, and fading in and out of sleep. The young man appeared, standing over him. By the time Arvel could fully awaken and ask the boy what he wanted, he had gone.

Chica finally came. She arrived during daylight this time; uncharacteristic for the girl. She was sober and walked freely into Arvel's room as he tried to eat some breakfast lying in bed. He could not shake the stomach bug.

She looked at the young deputy milling about the room and simply motioned for him to leave with a nod of her head. The young deputy did not wait for Arvel's instructions. He remembered the woman from his days at The Hump. He had hoped he would never see her again but somehow knew that one day he would. He was not surprised to see her connected to Arvel Walsh. It was just his luck that the two people who had been responsible for the most humiliating times of his life should be connected.

Chica did not recognize him. He was just one of many gringos she had seen in her time. To her, one cowpuncher looked pretty much like the next.

She looked Arvel over suspiciously. "Pendejo, you don' look so good." He was pleased to see her.

"Where have you been, Chica?"

"Did you miss me?" She felt his forehead, then looked at his head wound where Billy Livingston had bored the hole. "That black boy did a good job, Pendejo."

"Don't call him black boy." He was irritated with her. "How'd you like it if I called you brown girl?"

She paced around the room. She had only recently recovered from feeling ill herself. She had been terribly nauseated these past weeks and wondered if it was not something they had both picked up in Flagstaff.

"And where's my watch? I've bought three watches since I met you, Chica. I am getting tired of this. I'm going to start buying them by the gross."

"You better start buying better watches, Pendejo. The first one was good gold but the second ones did not fetch a good price."

"I bought you something."

She brightened. "You did?" He directed her to look in the wardrobe.

She liked the dress, and held it under her chin, admiring herself in the mirror.

"I had it wrapped up nice, like a present, but you have been gone so long I didn't want it mussed, so I hung it up. It is supposed to be the latest fashion from New York."

She stripped out of her clothes and put it on, ignoring the undergarments. She was, as he anticipated, radiant in it.

"It is a good fit, Pendejo." She looked at herself and was pleased. She thought about taking the dress off and getting into bed with the Pendejo, but he was too sick. She decided to let him rest.

"How do I look, Pendejo?"

She stopped and looked at Arvel again. "Pendejo, you don' look so good."

Chapter XVIII:
Portent

Chica sat at Dick Welles' desk sipping from a cup of coffee given to her by Dan George. She liked the Indian. He was a pretty man and he treated her well. She liked his nice clothes and could see by the work he was doing that he was smart like the Pendejo. If she were not otherwise occupied, she might have gotten to know him better. She leaned back in the office chair and waited. Dick Welles was late. She was about ready to leave when he finally arrived.

Chica did not like the gringo right away. He talked too quickly and bothered the Indian too much. She waited until he sat behind his desk. He finally acknowledged her, nodding but not speaking to her. Dan intervened.

"The lady has some Ranger business, Dick."

She tried her best to look respectable, but she was not well enough acquainted with

Victorian propriety to pull it off. She had exchanged her vaquero outfit for the dress Arvel bought her in Tombstone while he was recovering from the Indian attack. She wore her sombrero and riding boots. Dick eyed her suspiciously. "I am the friend of your Capitan Walsh."

Dick looked her up and down and Chica felt a pang deep in her gut. She did not understand what she had expected, but thought that Arvel would have at least told Dick Welles *something* about her. She could tell the man had never heard of her.

He was not tolerant of Mexicans, and had specific ideas on how women should dress and behave. Chica met none of the criteria. He began rolling a cigarette as he continued to look her over. She retrieved a cigar from her pocket. She leaned forward to light it from his match. They smoked silently.

Chica finally spoke: "I have heard, from one of the gang that you have been chasing, of a plan to kill you." She inhaled deeply and blew out a cloud of blue smoke.

"And why didn't you tell our friend Arvel Walsh of this plan?"

"He has been sick."

Dick was aware of this, and the girl's story was at least corroborated in that respect.

"When is this assassination to occur?"

"Next Wednesday, at just before sunrise. There will be a full moon. You have been given a tip that some prized horses will be stolen by three men that day, no?"

Dick was impressed. "Perhaps." Dick had been told of the robbery and, interestingly, the owner of the horses had requested that he personally handle the surveillance and arrests.

"They have told you that only three men will be coming to steal these horses. But, there will be a large gang of men, to out-number your Rangers. They will kill you then. They have no interest in horses."

"Why me?" Dick watched her through his plume of smoke.

"I don' know." She shrugged. "You have been doing a lot of damage to the bad men. Maybe they want to get rid of you."

This was interesting to Dick; he had an odd feeling about the tip he received about the horses. He wondered about the girl. What was Arvel doing with this little pepper belly? Arvel was a strange fellow sure enough but one thing was certain about him, he never cavorted with sporting girls. He never figured Arvel for a miscegenist.

"So, you are a friend of Arvel Walsh, you say?"

"Sí."

"In what capacity?"

"Qué?"

"How are you a friend of Arvel Walsh?"

Chica felt her face flush. She was annoyed at this gringo, and she was annoyed that Arvel had told his partner nothing about her. Now he was trying to get at Chica, trying to get her to tell him that she was Arvel's whore.

She blew smoke at Dick's face. She would not give him satisfaction.

"We have business interests. My uncle is Alejandro Del Toro. You and Capitan Walsh have been working with him, no?"

Dick thought about this. It suddenly disappointed him. He was intrigued by the prospect of Arvel cavorting with this young woman. It was just like him to be so squeaky clean that he would not engage in such scandalous behavior.

"Yes, we've been working with Del Toro." He found himself admiring the young woman sitting so near him. She was just a Mexican and he never found them attractive, but Chica was so remarkable that he had difficulty dismissing her.

She could see it in his eyes. The old gringos with the lust in their eyes usually amused her. Dick just made her angry but she could not really understand why. She was angrier at the Pendejo. She crushed her cigar out on a plate sitting at the edge of Dick's desk. She stood up and put her hat on. She nodded to Dick and looked at Dan working diligently at his desk.

She walked over to him and smiled, extending her hand, "Me dio mucho gusto, conocerlo."

Dan quickly stood up, bowed and shook her hand gently, "Encantada, senorita, muy encantada."

She walked out. She did not acknowledge Dick Welles.

Dick walked to a file cabinet behind Dan George. He began to open it. "What do you make of her?"

Dan did not look up from his work. "What do you mean, Dick?"

"I don't know, just what do you make of her?"

"Well, I believe she can be trusted."

"Not that, I mean, I don't know . . ." Dick was becoming tongue-tied.

"Oh, well, I'd like to get into her knickers, if she actually wore any, if that's what you mean."

"What do you think of Arvel and the girl?"

Dan stopped working. He grinned. "Arvel, let's see. Well, God bless'm if he's cavortin' with her. Good old Arvel. I wouldn't be surprised." He was glad now that he hadn't made a play for the girl. He wouldn't want to cut in on Arvel.

"Don't you think that's a little . . . ?"

Dan swiveled in his chair. "That's a little what, Dick? What, you mean because she's so young?" Dan suddenly had an epiphany, "No, that's *not* what you mean at all, is it, Dick?"

Dick felt the blood rush to his cheeks. Dan was making him feel suddenly very foolish. "No, no, let's just drop it, Dan."

"Well, okay, she's a Mexican. I guess at least she isn't an Indian." Dan was tired of it all and he was beginning to unravel on Dick. He caught himself and stopped.

"That's not right, Dan, that's not, oh, God, let's just stop, I'm sorry I said anything."

"Shame on you, Dick." Dick could never get used to Dan's familiar tone. "Shame on you."

"I'm not the one running with a Mexican."

"If that's all you've got to say about it," Dan stood up and put his coat on, "I'm going down to have something to eat." He looked at Dick again, and shook his head. "Shame on you."

He turned back when he'd gotten out the

door and looked in at Dick. "You're a good man, Dick, but sometimes you can be a regular goddamned bone head."

Chapter XIX:
Blind Charity

Arvel's health continued to decline. It had been more than two weeks now, and his condition seemed to be worsening rather than improving. The local sawbones had visited and was certain his recent visit up north was the source of his problem. He was not concerned about him. The young deputy did not leave his side, except for his one day off every week. He was more attentive now that he had become more used to Arvel, and his confidence seemed to improve.

Arvel learned more about the young man and what had happened in his life to form such a weak personality. Arvel's kindness seemed to be having the desired effect; the young fellow would often ask Arvel questions related to character, related to how a man such as Arvel behaved.

He started to address Arvel in a more familiar manner and would even make eye contact now and again. He always called Arvel "Captain" even after Arvel had asked him to address him by his Christian name. He liked to hear about the war. He was infatuated by battle and how Arvel handled himself in conflict.

He also would open up to Arvel about his thoughts on life's general pecking order, which was particularly disturbing to Arvel. Again, he thought back on how his Rangering life had plunged him into this ugly world; yet another poor soul who had been beaten down sufficiently, only to rise up as a monster. Arvel tried every so often to interject his philosophy into the conversations. Perhaps he could make the man hate less.

The young man once commented on his belief that if he could become a real lawman and master control of his emotions, men would respect and fear him. He thought that this would elevate him to a place in society where he would not have to bow down to any man, that he would be higher on the pecking order.

Arvel smiled and thought about an experience in the war. It was probably the single most memorable and constructive advice he'd ever heard, and it was from a grizzled old First Sergeant Arvel met just after enlisting.

"Right after the first battle of Bull Run, all of my schoolmates were ready to go off to war."

He got out of bed and put his robe on and walked over to the desk. He sat down across from the young man who was sorting papers. "We were full of piss and vinegar. I remember my parents having a fit. I was only seventeen. They wanted me to finish my studies. My father had a job lined up for me as a law clerk. But I'd have none of it."

The young man leaned forward, he liked Arvel's stories and, as Arvel never boasted, it was a special treat to hear Arvel talk about himself, particularly as it related to the war. Arvel was enjoying the attention paid by his audience. He did not feel so much the braggart; this might help the young man sort things out in his mind.

"When my parents knew I would not be swayed, they tried to convince me to let them get me a commission, as my father could pull some strings. But no, I was young and invincible and knew best, and I didn't trust my parents. They cared for me so much, still do, and I didn't trust them because of it. They would likely get me assigned as some general's aide, and I had no intention of spending the war out of the fray."

He laughed, looked at the man across the desk from him. "I really thought I knew everything then. Anyway, I decided to sneak off and sign up. I changed my name, so no one would make the connection to my family. I didn't give any qualification. I was a private soldier and in the infantry. I was so proud.

"Well, pretty soon I was under the protection of the single kindest and most fearless man I'd ever known."

"Your commanding officer?" The man put his pen down now and folded his arms on the desk.

"Nope, nope, definitely not." Arvel laughed at the thought. "He was an Irishman, a Catholic, what they call the Green Irish."

He began fiddling with a ring on his right hand. He licked his finger and worked the ring off, handing it to the young man. "He made a ring for every man under him."

The young deputy looked it over. It was made of bone. On top was an American Eagle holding a shield which had on one side the company and the other the regiment. The carving was filled in with red and black paint. "Rebecca always hated that ring. I told her it was made from a Rebel's leg bone. She said it was disgusting. She never did find out it was from a beef."

The deputy handed it back and Arvel slid the ring back on. "Sgt. Mike came to America to escape the British in his home country and had been in the army since he'd arrived at seventeen." Arvel chuckled. "My God he was a funny son-of-a-bitch. He would constantly tease us, call us 'me babbies.' He always knew what we needed, always got it for us. We never went hungry with Sgt. Mike around. He was in the war with Mexico. He'd been shot twice, bayoneted once, and got blown up three times in one day.

"Well, right after I'd been assigned to him, Sgt. Mike gave me advice that I have remembered to this day. I can still remember him saying it, like he was standing in the room here next to me."

"What did he say?"

"Well, we had this young lieutenant, a fellow not much older than me at the time. The kind of fellow I was scared to death that I would have become had my father pulled the strings for me. He was an officious little oaf, what they call a martinet."

Arvel looked at the young man across from him. "Do you know what that is?"

The young deputy squirmed in his chair. He still was not used to showing any weakness. He hated admitting that he didn't know something. "Uh, no, not really," he mumbled.

"A martinet is a person who goes overboard by doing everything by the book, however ridiculous or unnecessary, usually just to make life miserable for the men he commands. Basically, a real pain in the backside."

"I see."

"Anyway, one day, that Lieutenant put us all through the wringer. Sgt. Mike handled him the best he could, but the young officer was relentless. Finally, he let us alone, and we all breathed a sigh of relief.

"I remember Sgt. Mike pulling us all into a group. He looked us all in the eye, every one of us. *'You remember this, me babbies.'* He lit his old pipe and blew smoke into the air. *'Yer man, there'* we all leaned forward, as if the old sergeant was about to tell us the secret to the universe. Sgt Mike was stern-faced. He pointed off in the direction the lieutenant had walked. *'That lieutenant shites out of a meat arsehole, same as you and me.'* "

Arvel threw his head back and laughed and laughed. The young man looked at him, confused.

"That was it?"

Arvel looked back. "Sure. That's it. Don't you see how important that is, son?"

"Not really." He was becoming embarrassed. He did not understand.

"Son, the point Sgt. Mike was making is that nothing — I mean nothing — makes one man any better than another. No amount of money, rank, age, beauty, nothing. That's what Sgt. Mike knew, God rest his soul, and that is what he taught me. It was like someone opened my eyes for the first time. It was . . . you don't see my meaning, son?"

"I, I guess so." He was still not certain. He didn't understand Arvel at all. He couldn't understand how he could be so smart and worldly and well-to-do if none of it made him a better man than his peers. What good was it? He felt like asking, then thought of another question.

"Did your parents ever forgive you?"

"Oh, sure. My mother understood. My father thought me a fool, but he did forgive me, especially when I got a commission. He just pretended my being a private soldier never happened. Dear old dad."

"Captain? What would you do if someone threatened your family? Your mother?"

Arvel smiled. He thought about his mother, looked over at his desk and picked up her photograph. "Here she is. You know that, don't you? My God, son. I don't even know where to begin to answer such a question. What makes you ask it?"

"I don't know. Just wondering."

"I guess I'd just kill 'em. That's about it. I would not hesitate for a moment, son. If any son-of-a-bitch ever suggested they'd harm my mother, I'd gut him. I would squeeze the life out of him if I didn't have a weapon."

He caught himself. Pain seared through his gut and he felt sweat beading up on his forehead. Reminiscing about Sgt. Mike made him forget that he was ill. The thought of his mother being threatened got his blood up. He took a deep breath and smiled at the young deputy. The man became pallid before his eyes.

"I see." His mind raced to think of something to say. "What ever happened to Sgt. Mike, Captain?"

"Oh, he died."

Arvel looked back at the photograph of his mother and put it back in its place, facing the young man. Great tears ran down his cheeks. He didn't try to hide them from the young man. He looked up and smiled.

He wiped the tears from his right cheek, then his left. He sniffed. "He died at Gettysburg, saving that pain in the rump lieutenant."

These kinds of conversations went on, usually in the evenings. Arvel continued to feel worse and he spent most of his days sleeping. He'd take a light meal and his best and most lucid times seemed to be in the evenings. Arvel would hold court, now pretty much confined to his bed, and the young deputy would sit behind the desk. He'd ask Arvel questions about life in general, courage in particular. He wanted desperately to extract out of Arvel the thing that made him the way he was. The young man was convinced that character and nobility could be learned, like a trade.

Arvel was amused by this and he'd indulge the young man. He suggested books for the man to read. The Greek Tragedies, Plato's *Republic,* Virgil's *The Aeneid,* anything that would help get the message across. The young deputy was a good student and he'd often have good, lucid questions about the works.

One day, Arvel called him in and had him sit down. He was feeling especially bad and took the opportunity, out of some morbid predilection that he might not be around much longer; he wanted to get some affairs in order.

"How is everything going?" He motioned him to his bedside.

"Fine." The young deputy looked at the floor. He sat next to Arvel's bed. "You know that we, my uncle and I, offer our top hands the opportunity to homestead on the land."

"Yeah." He did not look up. He sensed that Arvel had something on his mind. The boy suddenly felt sick.

"Well, you've done well, here. I just thought that you'd like to do the same."

He waited for some kind of reaction. The man never showed much of any kind of emotion. He never said please or thank you. This was a plum opportunity, and Arvel expected *something* from the lad, some kind of reaction.

"We give you the land and we'll pay for the materials to build your house. You have to build it and you pay us back for the cost of the materials, interest free. You don't have to pay for the land; it is yours once you pay off the debt. A lot of the folks on the ranch already own their own homes."

The young deputy was unmoved. He thought for a moment. He squirmed a little in his seat and tried to come up with a reply. He finally looked out the window and spoke. "Well, I'm not sure I'll be around these parts that long. I'll have to think about it." He got up and began walking out of the room, then stopped. He looked back at Arvel. "I am glad we met, Captain. I am. I hope you know that."

That night, Arvel experienced a strange incident. It was late and he was feeling particularly low. He slept fitfully, as his stomach was giving him hell. He tossed about, trying to get comfortable. He was just fairly drifting off to sleep when the young deputy was closing up the house. He extinguished the last of the lamps. He stood over Arvel, as he had done before, staring at the man who had given him another chance. This time, he was crying and Arvel was awakened by his presence. He looked up at the man.

"What's the matter, boy?" The young deputy knelt down beside the bed. He grabbed Arvel by the arm and held his hand to his forehead. He was fairly blubbering now.

"I am sorry, I am so sorry."

"Calm yourself, boy." Arvel patted the man's hand. Just as quickly, the young deputy turned and left the room before Arvel could inquire as to what was the source of his anxiety. He thought of following him, but was too weak to move.

Uncle Bob was not so convinced that the young deputy was the faithful servant he seemed. He was sullen and evasive with Uncle Bob and he never interacted with anyone but Arvel. He had the annoying habit of taking over the preparation of Arvel's meals, which particularly disgusted Pilar. She had wanted to help with Arvel's illness, but was continuously stopped by Arvel's self-appointed helpmate.

Ordinarily, this would be the sign of a devoted servant but there was something about the young deputy that made it feel suspicious. Arvel would override all protests, as if he were trying to get the deputy to somehow learn to trust him.

Uncle Bob sat by Arvel's bed and waited for him to awaken. "How's the invalid?"

Arvel looked up and smiled. "Not bad." He lied to the old man.

Uncle Bob looked out through the window. The young deputy was moving some firewood. He looked back at Arvel.

"Uncle, hand me my shaving gear."

Uncle Bob prepared a basin of water, stropped Arvel's razor for him and put a hot towel over his face. He made up a lather in Arvel's shaving cup. "Arvel, we've been worried about you, son. Pilar is beside herself."

Arvel took the towel off his face and, with shaky hands, started to brush the lather on. He fell back on the pillow. Bob took over. He started to shave his nephew.

"We think we ought to get you up to Tucson to be looked at. This has gone on too long to be a bug."

Arvel thought about how miserable a ride to the town would be, even in a wagon. He stayed still and quiet while his uncle shaved under his nose. "And," Bob cleaned the blade on a towel, "we're both full up with that kid." Arvel did not look up. "I just don't like him, Arvel. I don't trust him."

"I know, Uncle. I don't know what having him around has to do with me being poorly, though."

"No, I'm not saying that. But we would like, Pilar and me, and the rest of us on the ranch, we don't feel like we're helping you, Arvel, like we're being kept away from you. I don't understand it, Arvel."

He knew Uncle Bob was concerned. He never called him Arvel unless he was particularly worried about something.

"I know, Uncle. I, I just don't know what to do with him. He's coming around. You know that boy's not cut out for any kind of law work. I'm just trying to get him to come to realize that; trying to instill something in him."

Arvel took the towel from his lap and wiped his face. He felt his beard. "You're a damned good barber, uncle."

Arvel remained unmoved. Uncle Bob worried about him all that day. He rode out to the edge of the ranch, rode back up to Rebecca's place. He liked to ride out around his land when he was particularly worried over something. Being alone helped him think and his horse, Sandy, seemed to know his favorite route.

He came back late and ate supper alone. By late evening he sat on the porch outside of Arvel's room, pondering all these things. He remembered when Rebecca and Kate died. He remembered the telegram and how he and Arvel rushed to San Francisco. How they had been too late. The girls were dead by the time they got there. He didn't want to lose the only family he had left.

It was dark now; only the glow of Uncle Bob's cigarette could be seen, dancing about like a wounded firefly. The young deputy nearly ran into him as he passed by. Uncle Bob stopped him. He was especially annoyed with the young man this evening.

"I don't know what you're playing at," he snuffed his cigarette out on the heel of his boot and glared at the young man.

The young deputy had only just regained his composure from his visit to Arvel the night before. He spent the entire day trying to avoid anyone on the ranch, especially Uncle Bob. Why were old men constantly manhandling him? He looked at Uncle Bob. He was afraid of the man in the plaid suit, but Uncle Bob terrified him. He stood still, said nothing.

"Let me tell you now, boy, if any harm," he swallowed hard, he was so angry that he had difficulty finding his words. He pointed at Arvel's room, "If any harm comes to him," he shook his finger at the boy, "well, son, you remember what happened to that family, the Knudsens?"

"Yes sir, I remember." He would never forget the victims of that slaughter; the headless wife, the defiled little girl and the burning corpse.

"Well, that will look like a church social, boy. That will look like a goddamned church social when I am finished with you."

The young deputy nodded. "Yes, sir."

He did not look up. He waited for his chance and walked quickly out of sight. He did not want to be near Uncle Bob.

Chapter XX:
Artemis

Chica rode aimlessly for a few hours after her meeting with Dick Welles. She felt hollow inside and did not know why. She did not like the gringo Welles. He was typical of the gringos; always looking at her as if she were trash.

She was independent and a free spirit. She drank too much and she was a thief. She knew these things and was unapologetic for them, but she never got over the sting of the revulsion on their faces. The gringos, sometimes, she hated them.

She missed the Pendejo, wondered why he never told his Capitan partner about her; hadn't mentioned that the Mexicana had saved his hide. She wondered if Pendejo cared at all about her. She wondered how he was feeling. She thought he should certainly be better by now and considered riding out to see him, and then, for some reason did not want to.

She did not want to visit him and perhaps see the look of revulsion on his face. Maybe he only used her like a sporting girl. So many of the gringos spent all their time in the whore houses. He might be no different. Perhaps he was ashamed to associate with her.

She rode north, back to her Indios, to the red rocks. She stayed with them for several days. She thought about going further north, to Flagstaff, and getting drunk, perhaps shooting up the town again, but she did not have the energy for it. She put on the dress that Arvel bought her. The old women and children of the village fawned over her and braided her hair sitting on the door of the Hogan.

She thought about the Wild West Show and Ivan Yakovlevich's offer. Perhaps she should go with him and Joaquin. Would she own a house in Bayonne, New Jersey? She heard stories about the world back East. She imagined the great land of Europe would be even worse, more packed with gringos. She would not be able to ride off when she got the urge. She could not carry her pistols and fancy rifle she had stolen from the Colonel. But the people of the show were kind to her, better than any others, excepting Pendejo and Uncle Bob, and the Indian family.

Chica thought about going to see the old priest. He had taught her about Jesus and the Virgin, whom she was named after. She did not come to know about these things until she was nearly eleven, when the priest caught her stealing candle sticks from the alter.

He was a kind old man and treated her well. He was a gringo, too, but spoke Spanish well. He baptized her and asked her to stay in his village, to turn away from the vagabond life of a thief. Chica thought about it. She thought a lot about Jesus and being baptized. She thought about eating the Eucharist. Many things the old priest taught her made no sense. She often stopped at each station of the cross in the church and imagined that, if she were there when Jesus was so terribly mistreated by the gringo Romans, she would kill them all and save Jesus from this terrible fate.

She told this to the priest and he smiled. He said that Jesus *had* to die, so that all our sins would be forgiven. It made no sense to Chica that a good man should die. It made no sense to her that Jesus' dying made all of our sins go away.

It also confused and angered her when the old priest told her that babies who died before baptism could not go to heaven; that they lived in a place between heaven and hell. This was not right to Chica. It was not the fault of the baby that no priest was around, or that the baby was an Indian who had not learned of Jesus.

The Eucharist always just tasted like bread to Chica. She did not think it really turned into the flesh of Jesus.

Most of the time she just went along with the priest. It upset him when she asked too many questions and she did not like to see him sad. He always seemed sad enough to her. He seemed to bear the burden, like Jesus, of all the sins of all the people in the village. He often seemed very unhappy. He told Chica that she would go to heaven one day, when she died, if she lived a life like Jesus and the Virgin. She would have to stop stealing and killing and she must never have relations with a man until she was married. She would go to hell if she did not stop doing these things, and ask for forgiveness for all the things she had done.

This bothered her until one day when she decided that the priest must have gotten this information wrong, as he had with the flesh of Jesus and the babies going to Limbo. He probably forgot what he had learned because he was so old. Chica decided that she really was good, and to kill bad men was not a sin, nor to be with men of her choosing. She could not see how something so fun and that felt so good could be a sin, so Chica formed her own version of Catholicism. It was the Chica version, and she lived by it every day.

She decided not to go see the old priest. It was a long ride and she knew that if she told him about Pendejo and all the Apache bastards she killed that he would be cross with her. She knew he would tell her that stealing and taking too much whiskey and mescal was wrong, too. She just did not have the energy to nod and agree and pretend to be sorry.

She was not sorry and she knew she was going straight to heaven when she died, because she was good. This is why she was never afraid in battle. She was not really afraid to die, yet she was happy to be alive. She wanted to live as long as possible, but she would never be afraid to die. She thought about when she was in the flood and the water was coming up. She was afraid then, but she decided that she wasn't really afraid to die, she was just nervous. She knew that she would have to go to the priest eventually, as she had promised to do so when she survived the flood, but she would not do this now.

The time with the Indians cheered her and she went to the ranch where the ambush of Dick Welles was to take place. She felt renewed purpose and reconsidered how she felt about the Pendejo not mentioning her to his Capitan partner. He probably had his reasons. She thought that maybe Pendejo really loved her so much that he was embarrassed to tell another man about it. Men do not talk of such things, and this was probably the reason why he did not speak of her to Welles. Plus, Welles was more like a servant, she thought, especially after meeting the gringo. He was not nearly as smart as Pendejo. He had a cruel face, and he did not treat her with respect the way Pendejo always had. She thought that probably Pendejo thought the man a fool and a lowly servant. That is why he did not mention her.

She was excited about the ensuing battle. She felt more connected to Arvel and would see the thing through. Her guns were ready, Alanza was rested and well fed, and she was equally well provisioned. She rode back south and planned to be ready well before the attack began.

Dick Welles had planned thoroughly. The Mexican girl was to be trusted after all, according to Uncle Bob, who had given the Ranger captain his full endorsement.

Uncle Bob made it clear to Dick, whom he had known to be pretty rough on Mexicans and loose women, to treat Chica with proper respect, considering her special relationship with Arvel and the fact that she had saved his life. Dick suppressed a grin as he listened to Uncle Bob. He thought that his friend and partner was indeed even more of a complex character than he originally surmised.

The ambush was to occur when Dick and a few of his men were lying in wait in a stable on the ranch property. Dick placed a two-man detail in the stable and the rest of his detail, totaling twenty men, formed a crescent-shaped line on a hilltop surrounding the ranch below. The moon was high and visibility good. They were set up by midnight and rested on their horses, waiting for the assassins to show.

Chica set up further south of Dick's ambush spot. She did not let Dick Welles or his men know she was there. She knew that he would not expect her, but she wanted to be there, nonetheless, to assure everything was as she said it would be. She felt responsible, as if her word was as important to Arvel Walsh's reputation as it was to hers.

She did not want this to go badly.

She situated Alanza on a rise, watching the road that led to the stable. She waited through the night with the strange rifle she had stolen from the rich Colonel. She crouched amidst an outcrop of boulders and peered through her telescopic sight periodically.

She dozed and sometimes dreamed of the Indian children. She always had hard candy for them and she loved the excitement in their eyes when they saw her. She dreamed a little of the Pendejo. And she dreamed of Dick Welles. One day, he would not look at her with that expression.

She thought about the gringo informant. He was an ugly young man. He had beady eyes and his face bore many scars and his one eye looked off in another direction when he spoke to Chica. He was too friendly to Chica. He told her this first tip would be free, but the next time it would cost her, and he looked down at her breasts. She thought about killing the young man on the spot, but decided that he might be useful to the Capitans. The only thing she could do was wait to see if his information was correct.

Finally, just before the eastern sky began to lighten, some riders approached. Chica was surprised at the small number; she counted only four. She began to doubt the informer. She looked at each one through her telescopic sight.

They rode quickly past her, then picked up speed, riding at a gallop toward the stables. She lost sight of them and soon a barrage of rifle fire erupted. Nearly as quickly, one rider was galloping hard back in the direction from which he had come.

More shooting could be heard, sporadic and in clusters, as if small skirmishes were now taking place. It had grown lighter and Chica could make out a solitary rider in full gallop, coming back down the road. He would soon be galloping past her, within forty yards, and traveling at full speed.

She aimed for the horse and dropped him, the rider pitching forward, tumbling several times on the mesa's hard rocky floor. Chica jumped on Alanza and was almost immediately looming over the assassin.

The rider was stunned; he sat up and began brushing off his clothes, as if he had just finished breaking a fresh pony. Chica threw a rope around the man before he could sense the danger he was in. She dragged him at full gallop a hundred feet or so, to take the fight out of him. She tied her rope off, Alanza keeping the rope taut as

Chica walked up on the prone rider. The man looked on in disbelief.

"You little brown bitch, you shot my horse!" He looked at her angrily.

Chica pulled her pistol and shot the man in the thigh; the bullet tore a long trench through his chaps and lodged below his right buttock. He swore and screamed violently.

"Jesus, Lady!" Chica had the man's attention now. She stood over him and placed a foot on the wound in his leg.

"Why are there so few of you, gringo?" She let up on his leg so that he would not scream so loudly.

"I don't know, I don't know. My God, I'm dying."

"You are not dying, gringo, but you are lying." She cocked her piece again, and it barked flame, shattering the femur of his other leg. He screamed again, more loudly this time.

"Oh God, oh God, please don't, please stop." He held up his arms, hands clasped together in prayer.

"Tell me, gringo." She cocked her pistol a third time. "Next will be the cojones, gringo. You speak a Spanish, gringo?"

"No, no, please, no."

"Cojones is your nuts, gringo. You understand?"

"No, please," he was crying more intensely now. He had a hand over each thigh wound, but quickly covered his genitals. "We were supposed to come in and shoot, just shoot, then turn around and ride out. That's all, that's all."

"What about the Capitan Welles, you weren't to kill him?"

"No, no." The man now knew that Chica was aware of the assassination plot. "Welles isn't to be killed. It is the other captain, Walsh, and the governor."

"Keep talking." She ground her foot into his right thigh, then eased up.

"The other Captain, Walsh. They've been poisoning him and he's going to be killed this morning. The rest of our gang is going in to his ranch to kill everyone there and all of his stock, to make it look like an Indian attack.

"Oh, God, my legs hurt *so* bad." He sobbed and began rocking back and forth. "Another group is going up to Tucson and kill the Governor as he travels from his home to his office. I swear, I swear."

"Stop cryin' gringo, soon all your troubles will be over."

She pulled out her knife and walked

around the man, stopping behind him. She knocked the hat from his head and, grabbing a fistful of hair with her left hand, prepared to cut the man's throat.

Dick Welles and his men rode up. Dick stood up in his saddle and tipped his hat to Chica. "Ma'am."

"This son-of-a-bitch gringo said that you were not to be killed, Capitan. They are going to kill Arvel Walsh and the Governor. They told me a bad story to get you and most of your men here, so that they could kill the others without interference."

"God damn it!" Dick Welles shouted orders. The men rode, Dick peeling off toward Tombstone to get a wire to the Governor.

Chica left the wounded man where he lay. She chose not to kill him. She jumped on her horse and rode as quickly as she could to the mule ranch. There might still be time.

Governor Murphy prepared for the day as usual. He was a man of strict routine. He was orderly and precise in every aspect of his life. He arose at six every morning, chopped wood for forty-five minutes, shaved, dressed, and ate a breakfast of one egg, two sausages and one slice of toast. He drank one cup of coffee with one spoonful of sugar and one ounce of cream. He read the most up-to-date *Washington Post,* the *Tucson Daily Citizen* and *The Wall Street Journal* when he could get it.

At precisely seven-thirty, he got into a closed cab and rode for fifteen minutes to his office.

The man in the mustard suit was leaning against a post at seven-forty. He twisted a cigarette and smoked casually. He had a carpet bag at his feet. He looked at his watch, then down the street. He waited.

On this morning, the governor's carriage was delayed by a slow moving wagon pulled by a scruffy looking burro. The wagon was laden with empty beer kegs piled high, well above ten feet. The burro plodded along and the street narrowed; there was no way to pass.

The governor's coachman became terse and called to the man driving the keg wagon to give way. His calls went unanswered. As the coachman's swearing intensified, the keg driver drove even more slowly. The wagon finally stopped in the middle of the street. The driver jumped off and ran through an ally.

The man in the mustard suit lit a fuse poking out of the carpet bag at his feet. He picked the bag up and ran to the Governor's coach. He ran toward the door. It opened and was followed by two violent blasts from the barrels of a shotgun.

The old man fell backward, his derby bouncing on the dusty road, the carpet bag erupting on his chest. It was reported that shreds of mustard brown cloth were recovered from the roof of the *Daily Star.*

Chica neared the ranch before the Rangers, being much lighter and carrying less gear. Alanza was a much faster pony. As she headed toward the ranch, she could make out riders coming from further east. She recognized them as the execution squad. She decided to slow them down a bit and galloped Alanza ahead of them until she could find a good ambush point.

Quickly dismounting, she pulled Alanza onto her side. The pony lay stock-still, as if she was taking a morning siesta. Chica sat behind her, legs crossed, elbows resting on her knees.

Shoot from the bones, she remembered Uncle Alejandro's words. She aimed carefully at the last rider and pressed the trigger. She did not wait to see if she had hit her mark but instead, slid her rifle back into its scabbard and threw a leg onto Alanza, urging her up in one motion.

She galloped Alanza hard, straight at the group of men. She closed the distance quickly and got within a hundred yards before the men finally comprehended that they were under attack. By then, she had her pistols drawn and, at fifty yards fired into the bunch. She hit three of them and the group began to break stride and spread out.

She rode Alanza beyond the gang and hit the last man in the string, knocking him from his horse. She wheeled Alanza and rode up on the next man in line who had finally gotten his bearings. He was putting his Winchester to his shoulder. He fired and missed.

Chica rode hard straight at him and waited until she was within twenty feet before she fired. He dropped to the ground. When she had emptied her pistols, she wheeled again and rode in a wide arc around the confused mob. She had taken five out completely and wounded one who would be able to do little damage at the ranch. She rode so quickly that she was gone before the men could comprehend who had attacked them. They continued on toward Arvel's ranch.

She slid Alanza to a stop at the corral

where Uncle Bob was working with a mule in the early morning light. She shouted to him that he would soon be under attack, and then rode on to the front of Arvel's bedroom; she could see the young deputy standing over Arvel, lying in bed.

She wasted no time and, still mounted, snugged the rifle to her shoulder, put the wire X on the man's breastbone and squeezed the trigger. The morning's silence exploded in a deafening roar.

Arvel was too weak to move and helplessly watched the deputy tumble backward. He could not fathom what was going on.

Chica burst through the door as the distant firing began. The Rangers were engaging the assassins.

"Pendejo. Wha' are you doing?"

He looked at her and finally comprehended. "Hello, Chica." He pulled himself up on an elbow and surveyed the mess in his room. "Did you just shoot my man, Chica?"

"I did, Pendejo." She began pulling on the young deputy's pockets. "You are not sick, Pendejo, you are poisoned." She tossed a bottle of white powder onto the sheet covering Arvel's lap.

"He has been poisoning you a little at a time, Pendejo. Today was to be your last."

Arvel looked out the window, distracted by the shooting. Chica told him of the assassins and the plan to kill him and the governor. "Why did you never tell your Capitan Welles about me, Pendejo?" She sat next to him and hugged him. He brushed the hair from her eyes.

"What?" Arvel was confused. He looked out the window. Uncle Bob was shooting men off horses. Pilar was standing next to him with a shotgun. The hands were clamoring out of the buildings, rifles at the ready. More men on horses arrived. Rangers he recognized. There was shooting in every direction. "What did you say, Chica?"

"I said, why did you never tell Capitan Welles about me, Pendejo?"

Arvel rubbed his head. He thought hard about the question. He was very confused. "Why do you think, Chica?"

"I think you are ashamed of me, Pendejo."

He ducked at shots coming through the window. One shattered a picture on the wall. Chica seemed not to notice.

"Is it the right time to discuss this, Chica?" He ducked behind his pillow, as if the goose feathers would afford some protection.

"I don' know, Pendejo. It look like Capitan Welles din' know nothing about me." She watched Pilar shoot an assassin in the face, his corpse dragging from his terrified horse.

"Good shot, Pilar," she spoke under her breath.

Arvel regained his composure. The fighting was moving further away from the house. The shooting began to slow. The assassins were riding off and the Rangers were after them. He looked at Chica again.

"So you want to discuss why I have not told Dick Welles about you?"

"Well, if you are not going to tell about me, then it mus' be because you don' like me, Pendejo."

"Oh, so, it could not be that it would just sound very strange for me to say to a Captain of Rangers: 'Oh, by the way, Dick, I have an outlaw half woman, half wild cat coming to visit me every now and again, who steals my watches and money, then runs off, God knows where, and does not show up again until she starts shadowing me from a mile away and then shoots a bunch of Apaches and saves my life, then takes me to a Negro with blue eyes who bores a hole through my skull and replaces the hole with a gold coin and dumps me in Tombstone with a bunch of dead Indians' traps, and again steals my watch and doesn't come around again for God knows how long, and then takes me to a traveling show where we meet a young man covered in hair like an ape, and we find a severed head in a bottle, which the young woman knew of and was responsible for?' "

"Do not say Dios name in vain, Pendejo."

She loved him. She laughed and looked down at him. "Well, I guess you cannot say all these things, Pendejo."

He felt awful and his stomach was killing him more now that he knew he was poisoned. He thought that he might die at any moment. He looked into her eyes. He became annoyed with her.

"*Ashamed of you!* What kind of damned foolishness is that? *Ashamed of you?* I *should* be ashamed of you. You speak nonsense. Why would I be ashamed of you?"

"Because I am Mexicana, and a bad woman."

"And when did I ever give you an idea that I was not happy with the way you were?"

"I don' know, Pendejo."

She stepped over the deputy lying on the floor and found a wash basin of water. She grabbed a fresh cloth from the washstand, wet it and wrung it out. She wiped Arvel's brow. He looked bad, but she was hopeful that now he would get better, as the one poisoning him was out of commission.

Arvel had begun to drift off when the man on the floor groaned. Arvel opened his eyes and looked down.

"Chica, look. He's still alive." Arvel forced himself out of bed, and leaned over the man. The young deputy opened his eyes, looking at Arvel and then at Chica who was busy lighting a cigar.

"Captain."

"Yes, take it easy, boy. You'll be all right."

"I can't feel my legs, Captain." Chica blew a cloud of smoke and looked on, indifferently.

"We'll get a doctor for you. Just try to take it easy." The man was dying and Arvel knew it. He could not help himself. Even the man who was poisoning him deserved to die with as little pain as possible.

"I'm sorry, Captain. I didn't want to poison you. The old man made me do it. He said he'd kill my mother and I was too afraid to do what you said you'd do if anyone ever threatened your mother. I'm sorry, Captain. I'm a coward. I wanted to stop, you've been good to me. Better than I deserve. Captain . . ." He was fading.

"Take it easy, son. It's okay." He looked up at Chica who was beginning to tire of all of it. She should have aimed higher and taken a head shot. She was beginning to regret that she had not.

The young deputy became lucid again. "Please tell my mother what happened. Tell her everything. I want her to know. And please help a girl in the laundry in Tucson. She's a Chinee girl, name Ging Wa. She's a good girl, Captain, she saved my life."

He began coughing up ropes of clotted blood. Arvel struggled to lift him enough so that he wouldn't choke. He breathed more easily. "I have a bit of money saved in my room, Captain. Please split it between Ging Wa and my mother. Please, Captain. I know you don't need to do any of this but I am asking, please."

He reached up, felt the air, and touched Arvel's face. "Captain, I wrote everything down about the gang. I got it in my room. Use what you can." He breathed hard again, suddenly overcome with terror. "Oh, God, I'm scared. I'm . . . I don't wanna die."

He convulsed and coughed hard, a gout of blood poured from his mouth and nose. He breathed in deeply and his throat rattled. "Oh, I'm, I'm scared."

He was dead.

Arvel looked up at Chica, *"Why'd you have to shoot him?"*

Chica was unfazed. She ignored the

Pendejo's question and his anger. He was tired. He was not thinking clearly. Of course the man needed to die. She waited a moment, then nudged the man's head with the toe of her boot. When she was certain he was dead, she moved to get Arvel back into bed, as if the deputy had never stirred.

She threw a blanket over the corpse and put her cigar out. Arvel lay back on the pillow and began to lose consciousness again.

"Pendejo, I have to tell you something." She shook his shoulder. "Wake up."

"Yes, Chica, what is it?"

"I have a swollen belly, Pendejo." She had already decided she was happy to have a child, regardless of what his reaction might be.

"That's nice, Chica. I am sure Uncle Alejandro will be pleased." He rolled onto his side. She slapped his backside.

"Pendejo, that is a mean thing to say about your baby."

"How do you know it is my baby, Chica? The baby could come out brown as a bean for all I know; we'll just have to wait and see."

"I know, Pendejo."

"How?"

"Because you are the only one I have been with, Pendejo."

"*Really?* What of Uncle Alejandro?"

"Pendejo, you are muy estúpido. Uncle Alenjandro really *is* my uncle. I never had anything to do with him." She thought for a moment. "It is really kind of a terrible thought, Pendejo. What do you think I am? He is, so, so, obeso, and his breath *stink.*"

"You little brat." He turned back to face her. "All this time I thought you were with that old man. You just told me a story to get at me."

"I am sorry, Pendejo." She kissed him. "I just wanted to see how much you cared for me. You din' seem to mind my story about Uncle Alejandro too much. I was very unhappy when you did not say to stop being with him."

"Which you were not all along, anyway, so I don't see what difference it makes." He rubbed his head. "Oh, you give me a headache, Chica."

"But you din' know, Pendejo. At the time, you thought I was with the old man. And you never said no. Don' do that. You hurt me, Pendejo."

"Chica, what *do* you want? You come and go, you steal, you lie, you run about like a reckless child. What am I to do with you?" He was certain now that he loved her. She made him feel less pain, just being with her.

377

"How do you know I don' want you to tell me to stop doing these things?"

"Okay, stop doing these things."

"And why should I?"

"Because I said so."

"And what am I to do?"

He pulled her into bed and wrapped his arms around her. "I will show you." He kissed her forehead and felt her belly; felt the beginning of a baby. He fell asleep.

ABOUT THE AUTHOR

John Horst, (1962–) was born in Baltimore, Maryland, and studied philosophy at Loyola College. Among his interests are the history and anthropology of the Old West.

The employees of Thorndike Press hope you have enjoyed this Large Print book. All our Thorndike, Wheeler, and Kennebec Large Print titles are designed for easy reading, and all our books are made to last. Other Thorndike Press Large Print books are available at your library, through selected bookstores, or directly from us.

For information about titles, please call:
    (800) 223-1244

or visit our Web site at:
    http://gale.cengage.com/thorndike

To share your comments, please write:
    Publisher
    Thorndike Press
    10 Water St., Suite 310
    Waterville, ME 04901